A JONATHAN MUNRO ADVENTURE

THE ELIXIR OF LIFE

MICHAEL J. SCOTT

Ellechor
PUBLISHING HOUSE

www.ellechorpublishinghouse.com

For Terry Silence: the best Bible teacher I've ever known and the man who taught me the meaning of God's grace.

PROLOGUE

A MEATY PAW GRIPPED Joseph's forearm and star-tled the old man into dropping the spoon into the pasta fagioli. Joseph stared across the buffet table at the six foot, dark-suited behemoth looming over him. With a linebacker's build, the bald man stood apart from every other man in the drab dining hall of the New York rescue mission. His bright blue eyes bore a cunning intelligence without a hint of compassion, and none of the dull resignation or furtive maneuvering that characterized so many of the mission's clientele.

"Who are you? What do you want?" Joseph demanded, tugging in vain to get his arm back. The brute smiled and said nothing. He forced Joseph's wrist over and yanked his sleeve up, revealing a six-digit number tattooed on his forearm.

"What's going on?" Wearing a greasy apron over a rum-pled NYU sweatshirt, Nicky appeared at Joseph's side. He planted his legs as if fully intending to take this gorilla on. "What are you doing to Joe?"

Another man, easily as large as the first, stepped into view and thrust Nicky back, holding up a shiny badge. "Is not your problem, *non?*" the new man said in a thick, French accent.

"And who are you?"

"This is William, and I am his partner." As if that settled the matter. Joseph shook his head.

"Oh yeah?" said Nicky. "Well, I'm Joe's partner. You gotta problem with Joe, you gotta problem with me."

The newcomer grinned.

Nicky picked up a large spoon and a pot and banged them for attention. Heads in the dining hall looked his way. "Hey," he called. "Who's with me, eh? We stand strong together. There's only two of them."

Joseph frowned. Most of the homeless men ducked their heads and eyes, already too beaten by life to risk themselves for another's troubles. Nicky seemed undaunted.

"Come on, boys. You guys gonna let 'em do this to Joe?" With no further response from the others, he turned and faced the heavies.

The bald brute named William turned to his partner. "Andre, quit screwing around. The numbers match. It's him."

Andre nodded. "Then put him in the car."

"Mr. Lake," said the bald man. "Will you come with us, please?"

It wasn't a request, and Joseph knew it. He said anyway, "My name isn't Lake."

"Sure. Whatever." He tugged Joseph forward, as if intending to pull him over the serving counter.

"Hey, hey!" Nicky dropped the spoon and picked up a carving knife. "Don't make me hurt you." He held the knife low, ready to slash. Despite Andre's size, Joseph could see Nicky meant it.

"*Incroyable!* He thinks he's is going to cut me."

"Side of beef like you, who could blame him?" William returned.

Andre smirked and moved aside the front of his jacket. Joseph glimpsed the butt of a pistol in a shoulder holster.

"Back off, little boy, or I will bring you in, too."

A filament of doubt flickered in Nicky's eyes. "What are you, cops?"

"You saw the badge, no?"

"Seen a lot of badges. That don't look like no cop's badge to me, and I don't know no cops in New York speak with that accent."

Andre showed a toothy smile. "*Trés* clever," he murmured. His hand moved toward his gun. "People, they get hurt that way."

"Wait." Joseph tore his forearm free from William, glaring at him. Turning to the younger man, he said, "Nicky, put the knife away." Joseph removed his apron and smoothed out his shirt.

"Joe—"

"This is not the way." He put his hands on Nicky's shoulders. "Remember what I taught you."

Nicky opened his mouth to argue. Joseph shook his head. "Everything will be all right." He turned and faced them. "I will go with you. Leave these men unharmed."

"You see? He can be *raisonnable*."

Joseph vented a long breath. "I have faced worse

monsters than you in my time. Men like you are all the same. All destined for the same place: the ash heap of history."

Andre smirked. *"Allons-y."*

Outside, Joseph paused on the sidewalk. The two men pressed up behind him, flanking him. In front of him, a limousine waited at the curb. The driver opened the door and stood ready beside it.

"Get in," William growled.

Joseph ran a shaky hand through the white tufts of hair still clinging to his head and shuffled forward, peering into the limousine before climbing inside across from a well-dressed woman smoking a cigarette. She was a striking beauty, somewhere between twenty and thirty years old, he guessed, with flame red hair, green eyes, a thin build and bare, slender legs poking beneath a dark skirt.

"Mr. Lake?" she asked with a smile. "Thank you for joining us."

"That is not my name," he said. "You have me mistaken for someone—"

"I think not. The numbers on your arm tell us, quite definitively, who you are, Isaac. May I call you 'Isaac'?"

"That is not my name!"

"Yes, I know." Her eyes flickered impatiently. "That is not your name. Right now. But we both know who you are. We know you have worn many names through the years. Were it not for that unfortunate war, we might never have found you. You are a master of hiding in plain sight, Mr. Lake."

She signaled the driver and the limo pulled away from the curb. Joseph glanced outside as the two heavies disappeared into a dark SUV behind them.

"Do you mind if I ask you a question?" she said.

"What do you want with me?"

"You have such a gift." She enunciated the word "gift" carefully. "You could be anything you wanted to be. Wealthy beyond the dreams of avarice. Why do you waste it here, among the indigent?"

Joseph narrowed his eyes. "You think you know so much. You understand nothing at all."

The woman settled back into her seat and ordered the driver to take them to the airport, then smiled demurely at him. "We shall see."

ONE

D R. JONATHAN MUNRO choked on his champagne. His eyes widened, and he ducked his head, trying desperately to breathe. Within the garish ballroom, surrounded by men in tuxedos and women in evening gowns, a few heads glanced his way. The loud buzz of conversations and music from the string quartet across the room covered the sound of his wheezing.

"Jonathan? Are you okay?"

A heavy blow thudded through his back. Someone was clapping him hard, trying to assist. He tried to wave off the help, smiling weakly at the concerned faces grouped around him. "I'm okay," he gasped. "Just—wrong pipe."

Dr. Harold Bryce stopped slapping him long enough to apologize to the students and their friends, effectively dismissing them while he assisted his friend. Jon blinked his eyes, grateful for the excuse of choking, if only Bryce would stop hitting him. He peered around his coworker's girth. Bryce leaned toward him, helping him back to his feet, but also blocking his view of the face that couldn't have been on the other side of the room.

Not that that was a bad thing. Bryce was effectively hiding him as well. Unless... A surge of panic grabbed his stomach and compressed it to the size of a golf ball. He peeked around his friend.

"Jonathan? Are you all right? You look pale."

He hadn't been seen. At least, he didn't think so. "I need to get out of here."

Bryce frowned. "All right. Come."

"No. This way." Jon tugged his friend, pulling him along toward the kitchen area. Behind him, servers slipped through the swinging doors, carrying trays of hors d'oeuvres and glasses of champagne to the assembled guests in the Founders room of the University of Michigan's Alumni Center.

"Jonathan, what is going on? You act like you've seen a ghost."

He steered Bryce through the swinging doors, glancing once through the tiny window before pressing his body against the wall. "Call campus security. Better yet, the police."

"What? Whatever is the matter?"

"Wait." He jerked his thumb toward the window in the door. Bryce pushed his round glasses up and stepped to the door peering through the window.

Jon said, "Look for a blond man with a square jaw, blue eyes, about six feet tall or so, thin, and very athletic. See him? Is he coming this way?"

Bryce frowned, wrinkling his mustache against his nose. He studied the crowd mingling in small groups across the floor of the room, with wait staff in white coats and black trousers expertly weaving among them holding aloft trays of champagne and hors d'oeuvres beneath the glowing chandeliers. After a moment he said, "I don't see anyone. What was he wearing?"

"Dark," Jon replied. "A dark suit, I think."

Bryce looked again, but after a moment shook his head and gave up. "I don't see anyone like that. Who is he?"

Jon caught his breath. "I must be seeing things. For a moment I thought I saw Sean MacNeil."

"Who?"

"As many times as you've made me tell the story..."

Bryce's eyes bulged. "The Irish mercenary? The terrorist from your adventure in Turkey?"

"And one of the last people I ever want to see again."

"What would he be doing here?"

"I can't even begin to imagine. I don't *want* to know."

"You're sure you saw him?"

"I think so. It was only a moment. A passing glance." Jon ran his hand over his forehead, surprised at the sweat. "He's not the sort of man you'd forget easily, as much as you might want to."

He stared at the stainless steel counters in the kitchen. Any moment now, the wait staff would send for the maitre d' to escort them out. This was supposed to be a simple affair. Just another end-of-the-year dinner party to thank the University's supporters and alumni and remind them to keep giving.

But if that really was Sean MacNeil, then he hadn't come alone, and this simple dinner was about to become unbearably complex. Dangerously so.

Bryce shifted his weight impatiently. "What do you want to do?"

Jon swallowed. "I don't—I don't know."

"There you are!"

They turned toward the musical voice belonging to a young woman who'd just stepped through the door. She wore a forest green evening gown with matching emeralds. She'd woven her long, apricot tresses in a thick coil over one shoulder, and her smile glistened in the stark light of the kitchen.

Bryce opened and closed his mouth. "I-uh-who… sorry, have we met?"

"You're Dr. Harold Bryce, professor of archaeology and a renowned specialist in the Middle Ages."

"Ah, well, that's very flattering."

"And you must be the famous Dr. Jonathan Munro."

"And you are?" Jon eyed her warily.

"Evelyn Rothman." She extended her hand. Bryce took it, kissing it gently. "Oh, charmed," she said. Then she cocked her head. "Why are you two hiding in the kitchen?" She studied their faces, then covered her mouth with a surprised, "Oh, I'm so sorry. How rude of me. You must be tired of all the publicity and the—fame—and here I am gushing over you like a school girl when all you want is a moment to breathe—and…" She grinned. "This isn't how I pictured this."

"What is it you want, Ms. Rothman?" Jon asked.

"I only wanted a moment of your time—that is, Dr. Bryce's time. I have an artifact I wanted to show you. It's something I think you'll find very interesting. You could come, too, Dr. Munro."

"I don't know," said Bryce. "This might not be a good time." He glanced at Jon, his eyes searching.

"I think that's a splendid idea." Jon turned with Bryce and muttered into his ear, "The quicker we get out of here, the better I'll feel."

They followed the woman back into the ballroom as she wove her way through the crowded guests. Before they reached the exit, Jon felt a hand touch his elbow. "Dr. Munro, a word please?"

He turned to see the gnarled face of the dean waiting expectantly by his side. Bryce paused, clearly concerned.

"This isn't a good time, sir," Jon protested.

The dean took him by the elbow and drew him across the floor. "As the new director of Antiquities, you have an obligation to our donors. I don't care if you have to meet every one of them. Someone in here may be the one who donated ten million dollars to your department. The least you can do is shake his hand—even if you have to talk with every last one of the guests to discover who he is."

Jon's eyes darted around the room. Harry and Ms. Rothman were already gone. He had to get out of here!

"It is part of your responsibility, Dr. Munro. One you have been ducking far too long. Now, do be gracious, and try smiling for once. You look sickly."

Jon swallowed his fear and tried to compose himself. It was possible he'd imagined seeing the mercenary. He'd been on edge ever since the money came into the department. True, the donor was anonymous, but Jon had his suspicions. It felt too much like Turkey all over again, especially after his Blackberry was stolen and mysteriously reappeared. His colleagues blamed it on his chronic absent-mindedness, but he knew for certain he'd left it recharging in his car. It disappeared that morning and reappeared in the exact same spot that evening. Somebody had taken it. He just couldn't prove who, let alone why.

The dean brought Jon to face a couple at least as old and frail as the dean himself. "George, Pauline? I wanted to introduce you to one of our rising stars: Dr. Jon Munro, professor of ancient literature and, uh—"

"Paleography."

"Paleography, and our new director of Antiquities. Jon, this is George and Pauline Greyson, some of our oldest alumni and very generous benefactors." He pressed his aged lips into a thin line, clearly waiting for Jon to say something.

"Well, surely not *that* old." Jon said with forced charm as he kissed Mrs. Greyson's hand. She tittered apprecia-tively. The dean nodded, satisfied, and moved on alone. Jon gritted his teeth and smiled. "Old is, after all, a rela-tive term."

"Yes," returned George. "It's a term you only use for relatives."

Jon pasted on a smile, pretending George was funny, and tried to find a way out. "Well put, sir."

He didn't really want to be the director of Antiquities. He'd only taken the job because it felt right at the time—his way of striking back at the board for sending him on the Turkey assignment in the first place. For years he'd been content to live quietly, squirreled away in his corner office with his beloved books and histories, begrudgingly coming out to teach his classes before disappearing down his hole again. Then his whole world upended when he was sent to validate a find by a dubious relic hunter who happened to be a former friend, as well as the brother of his ex-fiancée. Within hours of arriving he'd been held at gunpoint, shot at, nearly blown up, and chased down a tree, not to mention kidnapped twice and forced to flee the country. He'd been turned into a border-jumping, international fugitive, now permanently banned from Turkey and still wanted by Syria—all for the sake of finding the lost autograph scrolls of the New Testament. Still, he couldn't quite shake the feeling that just finding those documents—holding them in his hand however briefly—made it all worthwhile.

He scanned the room, his heart thudding. What if Sean were here? It wouldn't take the mercenary long to spot him standing out in the open like this. For that matter, he might have already.

"Tell me, Dr. Munro," Mrs. Greyson asked, "is it true that you found some of the oldest manuscripts of the New Testament in existence?"

"Hmm? Oh, well, nothing has been confirmed."

"That's right. They were stolen again, almost immediately. Is that correct?" said George.

"Sadly, yes. Before we could validate the find." He

stopped looking long enough to smile at the Greysons. How long before he could ditch them and make his escape?

"It must have been quite an experience to hold something that old in your hands."

Jon bit his tongue and nodded. There were too many ways this conversation could go wrong. He glanced in the direction of the door where Bryce had followed the young Ms. Rothman out and didn't see either one of them standing there. What if Sean had done something to Bryce?

Mrs. Greyson was saying something else about cuneiform tablets when Jon interrupted her. "I'm terribly sorry, Mr. and Mrs. Greyson. It was lovely to meet you both, but I have a pressing engagement I must attend to."

"Oh dear, I hope we haven't kept you."

"Not at all. Please excuse me."

He offered a polite bow and edged toward the door, trying hard not to run. Pushing through to the outside, he felt a blast of warm, night air envelope him. At the bottom of the stairs, Harry Bryce waited.

Swallowing his relief, Jon skipped down the steps to his waiting friend.

"I was getting worried," said Bryce.

"Had to ditch the Greysons," he explained. "Dean Richards wanted to show me off. I'm not sure it worked in his favor."

"Mm. Mine either. I told her I had a prior engagement. You owe me one."

"What's that?"

"Oh, the lovely Ms. Rothman was quite eager for my company this evening. Told me so."

"Did she? Just think of the ethics charge I've kept you from. You'll thank me later."

"Yes. You're a true friend."

"Feeling's mutual. Let's get out of here." They turned to go, but Jon stopped short as a lithe figure pushed into the streetlight's halo, hands shoved into his pockets and a sly grin on his face.

"Leaving so soon?" Sean MacNeil asked. "I was hoping we might have a wee chat."

TWO

B RYCE, CALL CAMPUS security," Jon whispered. Bryce nodded stiffly, but didn't move.

Sean held out his hands. "If I'd wanted to kill ya, Dr. Munro, you'd have never made it out of the party. I come peaceful-like. I'm not here to hurt you."

"Why do I find that hard to believe?"

"Well as I said, if I'd wanted to, I would've." He nodded at Bryce. "Tell your friend there to relax a wee bit. He looks like my nephew when he's about to have an accident and wet himself."

"Y-you're the man Jon saw at the party," Bryce stuttered. Sean nodded. Bryce waggled a nervous finger at him. "You're a cold-blooded killer."

"Mercenary," Sean objected. "Or I was. I'm not free-lancing these days. I provide security now for a wealthy benefactor."

"How nice for you," Jon growled.

Sean grinned. "Glad to see you've still got a bit o' spark. I should thank you for it. You being the man what saved my life and all. I'm not the sort who lets a debt like that go unpaid, if you catch my meaning."

"I'm afraid not."

"I owe you my life. I'll not be harming yours. If anything, I'll be there to protect it."

"Protect it from what?"

"Och. That remains to be seen. As it is, I didn't come here on me own accord, and as much as I'd like to settle up with ya, there's someone else who wants a talk. I've a car waiting, if you're willing to come."

Jon stood his ground. "Why would I want to go anywhere with you?"

Sean threw his head back and gazed at the streetlight. "Aye. She said you'd say that. My employer is your benefactor. She has already given your department a cash donation—the sum of ten million dollars—to be used in whatever way you see fit. All she wants in exchange is a moment or so of your time."

Jon and Bryce exchanged glances.

"No thanks. Bryce, call security now."

Bryce patted his pocket. "I've forgotten my phone!"

Jon stared at him, and with a nod of his head, sent him scrambling back toward the ballroom.

"Jon, what are you doing?" Sean's voice sounded eerily calm.

"I'm turning you down."

"Why would you do a thing like that?"

"Because I don't trust you. And I don't know who your employer is, but anybody who'd hire you isn't someone I particularly want to meet."

"Come, Doctor. Be reasonable."

"I am being reasonable. Last time I was with you, you

were trying to kill me. Now you show up here at a private party, and I'm just supposed to willingly go wherever you want to take me? Thanks, but no thanks."

"You're really narrowing me options."

"Yeah? Well, security will be here any minute."

Sean reached behind his coat and pulled out something that looked like a short, stubby gun. "Then we'd best be going."

Jon heard a sudden pop and felt a sharp pain in his chest, followed a split second later by an electric jolt that knocked him to the ground. He lay there stunned as Sean rushed forward.

"So sorry it had to come to this, but you left me no choice."

Rough hands picked Jon up as he slipped into unconsciousness.

Harry's lungs burned as he rushed along the sidewalk. He could feel his heart thudding in his chest. He reached the steps to the ballroom, staring up at the gaily-lit windows and the party still reveling within. Twenty concrete steps led to the landing. He knew, because he'd counted them when he'd first arrived earlier, before his lungs burned and his legs felt ready to fall off. He swallowed gulps of air, cursing his luck, and started to ascend the steps.

"Dr. Bryce?"

"Oh!" he startled. Evelyn Rothman rushed down the steps to take his arm in hers. "Ms. Rothman."

"I thought you had a commitment," she said.

"Uh, change of plans. Bit of an emergency, actually. You wouldn't happen to have a phone?" he panted.

"As a matter of fact," she began. A dark minivan pulled up to the sidewalk. "I believe these gentlemen can help us." She tugged him off the steps toward the curb.

"What's that? What are you—?"

"Very sorry, Doctor," she said.

A sudden sting pierced Harry's neck. He cried out and fell backward into the waiting arms behind him. Even so, he slipped toward the ground.

"Help me," Evelyn grunted, pushing him backward toward the van. Harry felt his limbs go limp, losing all ability to control his body. He stared up at the face of the young woman who grimaced as she tried to heft him into the van.

"*Mon Dieu*, he is big!" a voice muttered.

"Andre!" she chastened. "Next time don't stick him till he's in the van."

"*Oui, cheri.*"

A moment later, Harry saw the ceiling of the vehicle and the chiseled faces of two men hovering above him.

"Get us out of here," Evelyn demanded.

They slammed the door shut and pulled onto the street. Harry stared through the window at the trees flashing past, taking him farther and farther from the life he once

knew, and the friend he was trying to help. Then all faded
to black.

Jon groaned and turned over, knocking his head into
the window glass. The jolt jarred him to full conscious-
ness. He rubbed his forehead, staring through the tinted
window of the BMW X3 at the landscape that flashed
passed.

He turned around. Sean MacNeil glanced his way and
kept driving, a slight smile playing across his lips.

"What did you do to me?" Jon slurred.

"Taser. Generally harmless, but packs a helluva wallop,
wouldn't you say?"

Jon frowned, letting this information register. "You kidnapped me?"

Sean nodded. "More or less."

Jon shook his head. It was all happening again. Only
this time, he had an idea who was behind it. "Thought
you'd reformed," he muttered.

"Och, I wouldn't go that far. Maybe just a smidge of
good in me now, but not so much I can't do me job, yeah?"
He chuckled lightly. Jon wondered what was so funny.

"So right now your job is taking me to this benefactor,
huh?"

"That's the long and short of it."

"Don't suppose there's much point in arguing."

"No, not really."

Again, Jon shook his head. No surprise there. He returned to the window, mentally marking the journey so he could tell the cops later where Sean had taken him. They drove that way for thirty minutes, taking Interstate 94 east to Yipsilanti. Sean turned on South Harris Road, bringing them to the northern shore of Ford Lake. Here he took a left and then right, drawing them past scores of middle class homes clustered against the edge of the lake, all vying for a tiny slice of the good life. He turned yet again down a long, semi-private drive through a grove of maple trees until he came to a stop in front of a large, iron gate. Sean rolled down the window and punched in a code on a keypad mounted on the wall, and the gate swung open. Jon glanced through the rear window once they cleared the gate, watching it swing shut again.

He studied the three-story house that rose before them, frowning. Even at three thousand square feet, the house seemed to be worth far less than what Jon would have expected, considering the owner had made a ten million dollar donation. Tall columns supported a front porch, the roof of which jutted out from the second story, beneath a round window where a chandelier hung down in the foyer below. Lattice windows peered out from peaked dormers in the roof—ten of them on the front of the house alone. A circular sitting room sat on one corner, farthest away from the detached garage. Behind it, Jon glimpsed an in-ground swimming pool and deck overlooking the lake. On either side of the property, tall privacy fences obscured the view from inquisitive neighbors.

Sean pulled the car around to the front of the circular driveway and parked. He faced Jon. "Go right inside. She's expecting you."

Jon considered making some sort of biting reply, but nothing sufficiently compelling came to mind. Sighing, he climbed out and crossed the concrete and brick steps leading to the front door. He hesitated at the knob for a moment, then opened the door and walked in.

Inside, the foyer was warm and brightly lit. Light from the chandelier cascaded down through edged crystals, scattering tiny rainbows across the polished wood floor. Mirrors on either side made the room look bigger than it was. He glanced in one of them, straightened the tie on his tuxedo, feeling for a moment like James Bond, then walked through the only open door on the left, where soft piano music filtered out.

A fire crackled in the fireplace, and bookshelves lined the walls. In one corner, near the floor-to-ceiling latticed windows, sat a baby grand piano. A table with an archaic document sealed by a glass pane lying atop it stood in the center of the room. Jon approached the table and peered at the document. It was quite old, probably dating from the early Middle Ages, and written entirely in Latin in a long, flowing script.

"Twelfth century," said a voice behind him.

Jon recognized the voice instantly. He braced himself on the table, and without turning around said, "Hello, Izzy."

Across the street, a man dressed in dark fatigues lowered his binoculars and spoke into the headset mic extending from the transmitter by his ear.

"Now they've both gone inside."

His earpiece crackled briefly, then, "Proceed with caution."

"Sir," he replied curtly. He motioned with a raised hand, and a team of five men rose silently from their hiding places, bringing their Mac-10s up to hip level. Furtively, they crept across the wide expanse of lawn, approaching the house from the side.

THREE

D R. PHILIP ROTHMAN pushed his glasses further up his nose and stared at the computer screen. A chart with thin blue lines against a white background showed deep peaks and valleys like jagged teeth. He frowned and clicked on the number next to the highest peak, showing a 95 percent concentration in the sample. The screen flickered and opened a new window, providing the raw data table. He scrolled through the list, shaking his head.

Those incompetent fools! The sample must be contaminated. No other explanation could reconcile such a discrepancy. If only the company had given him the researchers he'd asked for, rather than these corporate favorites. He leaned back in his chair and glanced around, searching for answers in the reclusive shadows. Pale light from a single desk lamp and the glare of the screen did little to illuminate the room. The black steel and wire of the desk, cabinets, and office furnishings absorbed the light and almost disappeared into the shadows themselves.

Through the expansive windows of his sixth floor office, he could see the twin head and taillights of the cars rushing endlessly on the streets below, pursuing unknown destinations in their meanderings through the city of Detroit. The traffic reminded him of the ant farm he'd had as a child—the one his father made him get rid of. Collectively, the ants functioned as one, but individually, their steps and choices seemed random and chaotic. Given the hard hits on the economy, the efforts of the cars seemed as futile as those of the ants he had to destroy. Flooding the farm turned their random chaos into panic, lending a discernable purpose to their steps, but only for a moment. He sometimes thought, if he were far enough above, he'd be able to discern the pattern in the chaos below, but it always eluded him. Barring a disaster, their patterns would never make sense. Like the solution to this sample.

He made a notation on his spiral pad with his pencil. A sharp rap at the door shattered his concentration, and he snapped the pencil lead. He pursed his lips, then slammed the pencil down on the desk and marched to the door. Flinging it open, he stuck his finger in the apologetic face of his secretary.

"Susan, I gave very explicit instructions: I am not to be disturbed. What is so hard to understand about that?"

Susan shrank before him, clutching her notes to her chest. "Sorry, Doctor, but you insisted—"

"I insisted on quiet!"

"It's the 595, sir. The number."

He cocked his head. What was she blathering about?

"They're on hold right now."

Realization dawned. "Why didn't you say so?" He thrust

passed her into his outer office, grabbed the phone, and waved her brusquely out of the office. "Rothman here."

"Peter is gone."

Peter? He nearly dropped the handset. "I-I'm sorry?"

"He's off the reservation."

"Oh!" He breathed relief. "I thought you meant he was dead."

A moment's hesitation, then, "He will be."

Peter Schaumberg's face dodged into mind. Dead? He and Peter had been friends since grad school—if that's what their relationship could be called. They used to be roommates, back in the day, sharing late night lattes and theoretical discussions that led nowhere but fostered a sense of camaraderie. Then they were coworkers—fellow scientists in pursuit of the noble truth, or what Peter liked to call, "the Nobel Truth." Even when Philip transferred to Detroit, they'd kept in touch.

Which, he realized with sudden dread, was why they were calling him now.

It couldn't be. They wouldn't make him do that, would they? They couldn't! "I-I don't understand."

"Yes, you do."

The voice on the other end was calm. Way too calm for what he was asking. Philip tried to picture what sort of man owned the voice. He'd never met him in person—or any of them, for that matter. The voice had no face and no name. Only a number, one Philip had committed to memory but never called.

"Implement the protocols," the voice said. "We'll be waiting."

Philip hung up, staring a long time at the phone, wondering whether or not he should call them back, tell them no. His shoulders drooped. He had no choice but to obey. To refuse meant sharing Peter's fate, and no friendship was worth that. Not to him, anyway.

Besides, Triprimacon had been good to him. More than fair, even. This was the price of participating—the levy due for all the benefits the company provided him. He was not so naïve as to think the car, the house, the phone, the computer, the vacations in Aspen, and the bonuses were all just compensation for his work. They were simply the retainer paid him for a service he'd hoped he would never have to render. In fact, he'd almost bet his life against it.

Why, Peter? He furrowed his brow, unable to conjure a reason the doctor would defect. Peter was meticulous and thorough, and above all things, pragmatically deliberate. Would he really have gone rogue without reason, or without an awareness of the consequences—not the least of which was the bind he put Philip in?

He snorted. It wasn't true. Couldn't be. Peter would not have done something so unalterable, so indelible, unless he felt he had no other choice. And if that were the case, which it surely must be, then whatever consequence might affect his former roommate and one-time friend would be slight in comparison to the consequences he'd have to face for not doing it.

But if Peter foresaw this, then he would necessarily have

foreseen Philip's actions as well. For that matter, he might even be counting on it.

Regardless, Philip had orders, and if he delayed much longer...

He strode to the door and flung it open, summoning the timid secretary back in with a curl of his finger. She gathered her notebook and pen and hustled back into the office beneath his baleful glare.

"Get me the Cleaners," he said.

Her mouth opened and closed a moment, and then she furrowed her brow, as if completely misunderstanding the nature of the question.

"The cleaners?" she stuttered. "Don't they come in automatically?"

He grimaced in disgust. "The number's in your Rolodex. Just call them."

He retreated into his office, slamming the door behind him. He slumped into his desk chair and picked up his pencil, returning his eyes to the tabulated data on the screen. He stared at the numbers, uncomprehending, then seized his notepad and flung it across the desk.

"It's done," said Casper Williams, hanging up the phone. He bent forward to the marble chess set on the table between them and moved his pawn forward one pace, leaving room for his bishop to slide out and oppose the black knight.

Frederick Lee leaned against the doorpost, studied the man, and concluded he was fat. Casper, the CEO of Triprimacon, had been his sponsor, mentor, confidant, and closest thing he'd had to a friend ever since the man had hand-picked Frederick at St. George's Academy in Rhode Island. Casper had invited him to come on board as a summer intern twenty years ago, provided him with a generous scholarship to Harvard, and secured him a position within the company after he graduated. For his part, Frederick Lee had not disappointed. He graduated summa cum laude from the prestigious law school and passed the Massachusetts bar exam on the first try. Frederick was brilliant, good-looking, athletic, and impatient. He'd been named the youngest vice president in the company's storied history. That was five years ago. Now pushing forty, he felt the glow of youth slipping away, and there were things he wanted to accomplish before it was gone. All that stood in his way rose up before him now in a gray Armani suit with gold cufflinks and an Italian silk tie.

Not just fat, Frederick thought as Casper patted his belly, but soft as well. He moved his knight forward and one space to the left, challenging the bishop if he came out.

Casper grunted at the move and left it unanswered. "We should grab some dinner," he said instead.

"Your man will come through?"

"Of course he will. We own him. He knows this."

"They have a friendship."

Casper snorted. "Don't be maudlin."

"I'm not."

"Then what's the problem?"

"It's just that— " Understanding dawned. "You're testing his loyalties. Deliberately."

The old man grinned. "Naturally."

"Do you plan to promote him?"

"Always groom your talent. You need to know who's with you, who you can rely on," Casper narrowed his eyes, "and who you need to cut loose."

"That's not fair."

"Schaumberg was your man. Your recruit."

"I stand by my decision. He's done immeasurable work."

"No one disputes that. But if he's not stopped now, he'll do irreparable harm. Loyalty, Frederick, is more precious than talent." When Frederick didn't reply, Casper grinned and moved to the door. "Come. You can buy me dinner at *Chateau La Lune* to make up for it. I have a hankering for some red meat." He laughed and left the room. Frederick picked up his coat, draped it over his arm, and followed. As he did so, he pulled out his iPhone and sent a quick text message, and then deleted the record.

Schaumberg was performing exactly as he'd anticipated. He wondered what the old man would think about that.

FOUR

TWO HOURS AFTER his secretary left for the evening, Philip stayed at his desk, staring at the text message on his phone. His computer program had long ago logged him out, saving his research on the server and sending the computer into sleep mode. Now only a flashing light at the bottom of the monitor showed any power going to the machine at all.

The traffic on the street outside had diminished in the evening hours, the ants and their drivers finding their destinations at last.

In the darkness, he finally became aware of how utterly still the building was at night. No janitorial staff muddled through the office corridors collecting trash or sweeping the floors. That wouldn't happen until Wednesday. No guards shuffled through the halls shining flashlights on the office doors or kept watch on the grounds. An off-site firm managed building security through cameras and motion sensors. The whole ten floors of office space were cold and silent—deathlike. It reminded him now of the time he had to go to the city morgue to identify his father's body. He'd stood in that room next to a ghoul of a man in a white lab coat, one not at all different from his own, and waited.

The cold, sterile drawers containing the lifeless remains of human aspirations had filled him with a leaden dread. *This is it*, he'd thought. *Everything my father once was has been reduced to this.* And when the ghoul opened the cabinet and drew out the shrouded form, Philip felt like an empty hole had opened up beneath him, threatening to engulf him in its dark abyss—a cold womb from which nothing would be born.

He remembered he'd thrown up on the floor. The ghoul had said nothing at first, not even offering him a handkerchief, but then mumbled, "I'll get a mop." It was the closest thing to human decency Philip had seen in a long time.

Six years and thousands of dollars worth of therapy helped him crawl out from that hole, to find anything meaningful or passionate in his existence again. And now, with one phone call, he found himself right back where he'd started.

The Cleaning Crew was a cold-hearted machine. They didn't let Philip talk. Didn't let him explain. He'd wanted to tell them to try to reason with Peter, draw him back to the safe embrace of Triprimacon—and if not, then to be gentle and swift, in consideration of all the work Peter had done over the years.

But they never gave him the chance. They'd asked only one question, "Name and address?"

"Uh, Peter Schaumberg. I have no address. Listen, I know this is against protocol, but I was wondering if you couldn't... Hello?" He was talking to a dial tone.

He felt like he could throw up all over again.

He'd done his best to put it out of his mind, but thirty minutes ago, a text message came through from an unlisted phone number. Just four words. *You can save him.*

With that he plunged into the abyss. He sat in the darkness now, feeling the hole of death surrounding him, as though he'd been shoved into a steel drawer and forgotten, like his father. Peter wasn't much of a friend, but he was the only friend Philip had. And if he wouldn't do this for his only friend, then just what sort of man was he?

On the other hand, the consequences for crossing that line were clear. There'd be no forgiveness for disloyalty. Any doubts he'd ever entertained on that matter had been settled by the Cleaning Crew. If he acted now, they'd come for him. If he failed to act... either way, his life was at stake.

A scripture he'd memorized long ago snuck unbidden into his mind, from a Vacation Bible School program he'd attended once as a child. *What does it profit a man to gain the whole world and lose his soul?*

He frowned, uncertain what to make of it. He'd never given any credence to faith. Thoughts of God were long ago banished to the same place where, as a child, he'd once held beliefs in the Tooth Fairy, Santa Claus, the Easter Bunny, and the Devil. Still, the words spoke to the heart of his dilemma.

The cars outside his window ran to destinations that seemed random and meaningless. The same could be said for his life. What difference did it make how long he lived or how many problems he solved, if he lived without purpose?

Like one of the ants in his ant farm watching the flooding waters come rushing at him, he could let the flood engulf him or he could scramble for the surface, risking death for the chance at life.

Yes, he could do this. He could try. Maybe he couldn't save himself, but he just might save someone else. And with that realization, he was no longer afraid.

He picked up the phone and dialed.

Frederick felt no remorse at all for pushing Philip over the edge. He stabbed at a piece of steak, lifted it to his lips, and chewed thoughtfully. The dim lights at *Chateau La Lune* cast a pallid glow over the table, ensconcing the room in pale shadows. The lights were filtered to provide the exact pallor and luminosity of a full moon. With a cool breeze wafting across the room from carefully concealed air conditioners and a starlight ceiling with fiber optic "stars" twinkling in an azure dome, one had the impression of dining outside. Pale candles flickered on the table, providing the only real light to see what he was eating.

Casper's man Philip was a sad sack of humanity. He had no parents, no family, no friends—nothing but his job and his routine. His psychographic profile suggested he was susceptible. It only took a little effort to nudge him right where Frederick wanted him to go.

Frederick reached for his glass of wine, catching sight of his mentor gleefully carving yet another slice of prime rib.

He took a sip of the blood-red merlot, letting it wash the smoked mushroom flavor down his throat.

Casper would be furious if he found out about Philip— scratch that—*when* he found out, but Frederick could just as easily throw his words back in his face. It was, after all, a loyalty test. And if Casper really had overlooked such a glaring weakness in the man's character, whose fault was that?

In fact, it was entirely possible that Casper was testing Frederick as well. More than likely, even. The man was nothing if not manipulative. He could've taught Machiavelli. Frederick studied his mentor. In the silver light he looked spectral and bloodless. It suited him well.

Casper was fully prepared to sacrifice Philip. The man was just a pawn—nothing compared to Schaumberg, Frederick's queen. It would be insulting not to take Casper up on his gambit and use Philip for his own ends.

The whole point in unleashing Schaumberg was to speed Casper's retirement, to demonstrate to the board what new blood capable of decisive action could do. Only this would break them free of the centuries-old stalemate that hobbled the company for so long.

In the beginning of their relationship at least, Casper had seemed to understand this. He'd expressed the same sort of frustrations that Frederick felt—the irritation with tradition, annoyance at old men content with the status quo. He'd often spoken of bringing them to the apex, of fitting the final pieces in place so they could all realize their destiny. What else did Triprimacon exist for, if not this golden dream?

Only now, in his later years, Casper had fallen prey to inertia. His momentum spent, he had no energy left to break free of the gravity of their continual failure. Hence, he should go. In fact, he should take the board with him. They were too bloated, too bogged down in bureaucracy, letting apathy and petty infighting keep them from grasping the brass ring. Allowing Schaumberg's desperation to drag them exactly where they wanted to go only made sense.

Frederick frowned and put down his glass. If Casper had anticipated Frederick's text message to Philip, then he was aware of how Frederick might be using Schaumberg. It was little more than a chess game to Casper anyway, one he played with relish, anticipating Frederick's actions five to six moves ahead and imperceptibly forcing him to go right where he wanted him to.

And if Casper knew, then he had an end-game Frederick had not anticipated. He smiled inwardly. Casper wasn't the only one capable of making sacrifices. It was time Frederick called out his dark knight, the one not even Casper knew about.

He dropped his napkin on the table and pushed back his chair. "You must excuse me," he said. "Nature calls."

Casper snorted and waved him off with his fork. He rose and left the table behind, heading for the men's room. Once out of sight, he pulled out his cell phone. He counted on the probability Casper had cloned his phone and knew everything he said or did. That's why he deleted the messages sent from his company phone. What better way to deceive your opponent than to lull him into a false confidence and feed him misinformation, all the while letting him think he was getting the drop on you? The phone Frederick held now was his other cell phone, not his company-paid iPhone. It was just a cheap, disposable model he'd paid cash for only two days before, but it would get the job done. He typed in a simple text message and pressed send.

FİVE

BRYCE STIRRED, GROANED, and rolled over. The throbbing pain that coursed through his skull made him wish he hadn't. He took several deep breaths, waiting for the head rush to abate. Somewhere in the past hour, they'd given him more of the drug; at least he thought they did. He couldn't remember. He ran a hand over his face and opened his eyes, wincing as firelight dazzled his retinas and spiked his headache. Gradually, the pain subsided and the light felt less intense. But things were still blurry. His impressions of the past few hours were hazy, disconnected. Images that ought to have made sense assailed him, incoherent and nebulous. Trying to comprehend them was like grasping fog. He stared up at the ceiling, not recognizing it at all.

As his vision improved, he discerned the shape of the room he occupied. Rough-hewn timbers supported the vaulted ceiling, from which four sets of wrought iron lanterns hung suspended over the floor. The lights were out now, but an orange flicker moved the shadows across the plaster. He smelled smoke, and for a brief moment, he was transported back to the fire that engulfed his family's home when he was six. *Maybe the room is on fire now.*

He started and bolted upright and a fresh surge of pain screamed through his skull. With a moan he rolled off the couch and thudded to the floor. *Stay low, where the good air is,* he thought. His head throbbed. He scrambled to the door and reached for the latch. Locked. He banged his fist against it. The sound of his fist on the wood made it feel like he'd struck his own head with a sledge hammer. Heedless, he struck it again.

The fire did not consume him, but the pounding in his skull made him want to retch. He collapsed against the door and covered his eyes, waiting for the ache to dissipate. A moment later, he dropped his hand, and saw a blazing fire in a brick fireplace. A wooden beam, thicker than a railroad tie, served as the mantel.

So that was the fire. His initial panic subsiding, he stood and took in the rest of the room. The couch he'd woken up on faced the fireplace, with two other loveseats arranged on either side to face the flames diagonally. Before the fireplace sprawled a large, bearskin rug, its lifeless snarl growling at no one. On the other side of the couch, tall windows overlooked a body of water shrouded in darkness, just past the copse of trees outside. Moonlight flickered off the surface of the water, broken and refracted into tiny rivulets of silver, barely illumining the ground.

He was in a cabin or lodge of some sorts, lost in the woods, with no recollection of how he got there. He padded around the room. The door he'd already tried appeared to be the only way out. Not that he could leave with it locked from the outside. The windows had neither locks nor hinges, nor any visible way to open them. He supposed he could always shatter them, maybe use one of the couches as a battering ram, assuming he could lift it. The ground waited several feet below, strewn with sharp-edged rocks. Past the rocks the ground tumbled away through a maze of thorn bushes to the edge of the water. Beyond the water lay the silhouettes of mountains brooding beneath the cloudless sky. He shuddered. There was no way out.

There was little else in the room save for a long table set against the wall behind the couch. This held a decanter of brandy and a set of crystal glasses. He opened the brandy and poured himself a shot but hesitated. *What if it's poisoned?* Then it dawned on him that if whoever took him wanted to poison him, they could have done so already. He downed the liquor, letting it warm his throat and settle comfortably in his gullet.

Liquid courage. That's what they called it. It didn't work, at least as far as he remembered. The last time he'd relied on alcohol for courage he'd been in college, trying to win over Francine Viera—his gorgeous study partner. She'd been dating the quarterback of the football team, who immediately challenged Harry to a fistfight once he learned of Harry's ambitions. Despite the warnings of his peers that he could die, or at least be seriously injured, Harry downed a couple of shots of Wild Turkey and went out to the fight. A matter of honor, he told himself. A matter that was settled rather quickly, too.

One punch had dropped him, and for the rest of the semester, that was his moniker: One Punch Harry. He never did go out with Francine. Alcohol hadn't helped him then—except maybe to dull his pain when he came to. Ever since, he made a point not to need liquid courage, mostly by avoiding conflict as much as possible. Always choosing the safe route. That was Harry.

Now he was in over his head.

As he raised the bottle to pour a second glass, the door opened. He turned, startled. A young woman stepped in. He frowned. It took him a moment to recognize her from the party. She'd asked him to go home with her before Jon intervened, and then something about a van. What was her name? Evelyn. She'd changed out of her evening gown into a gray blazer and skirt, and she'd pulled her hair back into a ponytail. She entered alone and closed the door behind her. What had they done with Jon?

Harry set the decanter down, feeling a little guilty. He didn't know whether to apologize for taking a drink or demand an explanation, and the fact that both thoughts occurred to him at once left him at a loss. He stood there and did nothing.

"Dr. Bryce," said Evelyn. "Please accept my apologies. My grandfather has long been an admirer of your work."

"My work?"

"Yes. It's why we wanted you to come with us. We don't normally abduct people in the middle of the night."

"You prefer the day?" He felt the false courage loosening his tongue. Maybe it worked after all.

"I suppose I deserve that. What I meant to say is we are not kidnappers."

"I beg to differ."

"Extraordinary circumstances require extraordinary measures. I'd like you to think of yourself as our guest."

"Your guest?"

"Yes."

"May I leave?"

She smiled sweetly. "Not just yet."

"Then, madam, in no sense am I your guest."

"You may yet change your mind—"

"Doubtful."

"—but I've been asked to bring you downstairs when you have recovered from the Diazepam we gave you earlier. Side effects include headaches and short-term memory loss."

"I see." He glanced at the now empty brandy glass, grateful he hadn't drunk more of it, and set it down on the table. "Then I suppose I'm ready."

She pointed toward the door. "This way."

He followed her into the hall, taking a short flight of stairs down to a landing below. To his left was a door, beyond which he observed a white and red helicopter standing idle on its pad. *So that's how they got me here.*

He'd always wanted to ride in a helicopter. It irked him that he spent his first ride unconscious.

"You won't get away with this, you know," he said.

She glanced back, frowning. He stopped and thrust his hands in his pockets, unwilling to move. For once in his life, it was time he took a stand.

"I want to know where Jonathan is," he demanded.

"Dr. Munro?"

"What have you done with him?"

"I-I'm sorry, I don't know what you're talking about."

"So it's like that, huh? Well, then, you won't find me nearly so cooperative now. Nor the easy target, I think." He raised his hands in what he hoped approximated a karate stance. A wry grin passed her face, and he realized he wasn't that convincing. He frowned, looking as fierce as he could manage.

"Dr. Bryce, we don't have your colleague," she insisted.

A flicker of doubt crossed his eyes. "No. I know that's not true. I saw him with Sean, that *mercenary* you've hired. I know he works for you."

"Who?"

"Sean *MacNeil*," he sneered.

"I really don't know who you're talking about. If you'll come with me, I'm sure all your questions will be answered."

He clenched his teeth and dropped his arms. This was pointless. He was no hero, and what's worse, she seemed to know it.

"All right, then," he said. "I'll play your game." She turned to lead him again. "For now," he muttered, and followed.

Down a second flight of stairs, she opened a pair of double doors, revealing a spacious room with a roaring fire. Standing beside it, an elderly man with thinning white hair bowed toward him.

"Good evening, Dr. Bryce," he said in a raspy voice. "Thank you for joining us."

Harry realized the man couldn't straighten. He was

bent from age, not courtesy. Harry cleared his throat. "It's not like I had much choice."

"Yes. I am sorry for that. Normally, we would have taken a more courteous approach, but exigent circumstances preclude civility, I'm afraid."

"So I've been told."

"Thank you for understanding."

Harry smirked at his presumption.

"Come," the man said, waving him forward. "There is much to explain."

Harry remained rooted to the floor. He shoved his hands in his pockets and straightened himself up as best he could. "Who are you?"

The man smiled. "All in good time."

"You won't tell me who you are, but you want me to trust you."

"Very much," he replied.

"And why is that?"

"Because we need your help."

SIX

SURPRISED?" ISABEL KAUFMAN came up beside Jon and leaned against the table. She wore an elegant white cocktail dress in stark contrast to the darker tones of her skin and her raven black hair. He detected the faint aroma of perfume—the same brand he'd bought her on their one-month anniversary so many years ago. Strange he hadn't forgotten it after all this time.

In spite of himself, he smiled. "Not really."

"Oh, please tell me Sean didn't spoil it."

"Not a word, boss, I swear," said Sean, coming into the room.

Jon glanced between the two of them, unsure how to reconcile their relationship. In Turkey, Sean had held them both at gunpoint, threatening to kill them, and now he worked for Izzy? "So what's this all about?"

She smiled and tapped the table. "You're looking at it."

"And you had to kidnap me for this?"

"Well, you don't return my calls."

"There's a reason for that." He met her eyes evenly, waiting for the apology he deserved. Somehow, he didn't think he'd be getting it any time soon. Just when he had found the single greatest archaeological discovery of all time—manuscripts so old they might well have been the original autographs of the New Testament collected and preserved by the Apostle Paul himself—Izzy stole them out from under his nose and left him to answer to the Turkish authorities. And to think he once hoped to marry her.

"Now you're just being sore," she said.

Sore? The woman was unbelievable. "You're a thief, Izzy. And a liar. And Sean here is a murderer."

"Mercenary," said Sean. "Please."

"You say 'to-may-to,' I say 'to-mah-to.'"

"Weren't you the one who said, 'We're all bad guys, but God loves us anyway'?" she reprimanded. "Or does that only count for the self-righteous?"

He shook his head. "You presume upon the mercy of God, Izzy. He does love us, but He also demands repentance."

She rolled her eyes and turned to the table. "Whatever. I didn't bring you here to discuss theology. I need you to do something for me."

"No." He pulled away from the table and folded his arms. There was no way he was falling for this again.

"Excuse me?" She seemed genuinely startled. Catching her off-guard actually felt pretty good.

"No to that, too. I won't excuse you, and I won't do anything for you. Now will you drive me back to campus, or do I have to call a cab?"

She bit her lip and traced a finger along the edge of the glass case housing the manuscript. When she turned back to him, there was a hard edge to her eyes he'd never seen before. His euphoria dissipated. "This is important,

Jonnie. More important than you or me, or anything that's passed between us. I am not exaggerating when I say the world hangs in the balance. Now, you've come this far. You might as well help us while you're here."

"Oh, I'm sorry. Am I being uncooperative?" Jon let the sarcasm drip from his tongue. "Maybe you should've thought of that before you sent your goon out to Taser me." He glanced back at Sean. "No offense."

"None taken." Sean smirked.

"Taser?" Izzy glared at Sean. "We talked about this! You were supposed to convince him to come."

"I did. In a manner of speaking." He shrugged. "Sorry, luv. Never been much in the diplomacy department."

She gritted her teeth, nostrils flaring. She turned back to Jon and opened her mouth.

"No," Jon refused.

"Jonnie, please! Just look at this and tell me if it's real. I'll give you anything you want. You want access to the autographs? I'll arrange it. No restrictions. I'll even donate the remaining scrolls to the university."

"You've already offered this to me. I've already refused it. The autographs need to go back to Turkey, where you stole them from."

"Done," she said.

"All of them. Even the ones you sold, which I presume have paid for all this."

"That and more," mumbled Sean.

"I will dedicate my life to recovering them. Please, just tell me, is this real?"

"And I want my name cleared. I've been banned from the country. Do you know how difficult that makes my job? I can't even arrange a field trip!"

"I'll get my lawyers working on it first thing."

"Now."

An invective tumbled off her lips. She whipped out her iPhone and tapped out a quick message before turning the phone to him. "There. Satisfied?"

He stared at the text message. It appeared to direct her lawyer to open a case with the Turkish government on his behalf. He sighed and closed his eyes. "Can't believe I'm doing this," he muttered. "All right, what is this? What am I looking at?"

She tried to embrace him, but he put a hand up, pushing her back. "No. We're not going there again. Just tell me about the book."

"Okay." She shrank back to her own side of the table. "We obtained this through a private auction at Christie's four weeks ago."

"An investment?"

"No. At least, not in the way you're thinking." She handed him a pair of latex gloves and slipped on a pair of her own. After drawing out a slender key from a chain around her neck, she opened the case and withdrew the manuscript. Jon took it from her and moved it to the back of the piano, where he laid it out on the flat surface. He slipped on his glasses and peered at the ancient text. Sean moved closer and stood beside him.

"Just the one page?" Jon asked, trying not to notice the mercenary standing so near to him.

"It's from the *Flores Historiarum*," she answered. "Composed by Roger of Wendover in the early thirteenth century. It's a Latin chronicle of English history, said to be based on the compilation of John de Cella, Abbot of St. Albans. Over the years, numerous chroniclers expanded on the history, including Matthew Paris and Robert of Reading. There were only twenty known manuscripts in existence, until about six months ago. This," she tapped the piano top, "is from the twenty-first. Not only is this manuscript reputed to be older, but it also contains a variant account of an ancient legend."

"Okay," he said cautiously, studying the page. At first glance it certainly appeared that old, but then, so did clever forgeries. Had she realized just how easily she might have been taken in? Even serious experts could be fooled by a clever and diligent forger, let alone an amateur collector like Isabel Kaufman. In the world of antiquities, plenty of money could be made by the unscrupulous.

"Have you ever heard the story of the Wandering Jew?" she asked.

"I've heard of it. I'm no expert."

"The Wandering Jew was said to be a first century shoemaker who taunted Jesus on the way to the cross, whereupon Jesus cursed him to wander the earth until the second coming."

"Yeah. I knew that much. That's one reason why we know it's just a myth. Jesus wouldn't have done that."

"Stay with me. In the account of Roger of Wendover—told

in the *Flores Historiarum*—around the year 1228, an Armenian bishop came to visit England. The monks at St. Albans asked him about Joseph of Arimathea, said to still be alive twelve hundred years after Christ. Wendover records that the bishop corrected the monks by telling them the man's name was Cartaphilus, who was the shoemaker we've heard about."

"All right, wait a minute." He waved dismissively. "Let's just stop right here. For one thing, you're talking about Middle Age myths. I am not a mythologist. I teach paleography. Ancient writings and literature. Think seventh century and older."

She furrowed her brow.

"This isn't my field," he explained. "You need Bryce for this. He's the expert in the Middle Ages."

"Bryce?"

"Dr. Harry Bryce. He teaches at the University." He nodded to Sean. "You've met him. He was with me on the sidewalk."

"Big guy. Glasses. Wears a tux like you?"

"Yeah, that's him."

Sean glanced at Izzy, who shrugged. "I'll make the call," he said. He turned on his heel and left, inserting a blue tooth headset into his ear.

"You could've just asked," Jon said to Izzy. "Saved us a lot of trouble." He lifted the manuscript and brought it back over to the glass table, gently returning it to the safety of the display case.

"I tried." She followed him. "You didn't return my calls, my emails. What's a girl supposed to do?"

He closed the cabinet and pulled off his gloves. "I suppose you could've cornered me in my office."

"Couldn't happen." She leaned against the cabinet and shook her head. "I have to keep a low profile these days."

"Imagine that."

"Speaking of which," said Sean, striding into the room. "We need to move. Now."

"What is it?" she asked.

Sean tossed her a plastic document tube. She returned a worried glance and pushed Jon out of the way to reach for the manuscript.

"What's going on?" Jon stared, appalled at the way Izzy grabbed the manuscript and hastily rolled it up, recklessly stuffing it inside the tube.

"We've got company." Sean grabbed Jon's elbow and followed Izzy to the bookshelves across the room. He pulled out a book from the shelf, revealing a red button mounted on a switch plate behind it. When he depressed it a portion of the bookshelf nearest to them swung loose, making no sound on the thick pile carpet. Sean replaced the book and pulled on the swinging shelf, now exposing a door behind it.

"You have a panic room?" Jon asked incredulously.

"You'll see why in a moment," Sean replied.

SEVEᴨ

ᴀɴᴅ ᴡʜʏ ᴅᴏ you need my help?" Harry fumed.
The old man motioned him forward again,
smiling disarmingly. After a moment's hesitation,
Harry came around to the man's side of the room.

"We require your professional opinion," the man said,
offering him a seat nearby. Harry sank into the couch, trying
to relax. "There is a particular artifact we wish you to validate. One based solely on a legend. One not even we believed
existed until very recently."

Harry grimaced. "You abducted me for this? You could've
just asked, you know. You could have simply dropped it off
at the University in the morning. I'd have been more than
happy to take a look at it."

The old man chuckled and took another sip of his
brandy. He turned to Evelyn and said, "Evie, be a dear and
fetch our artifact, would you?"

"Are you sure?" She gave Harry a cautious look. He
frowned, uncertain what to make of it.

"I'm sure it will be fine, dear," the man said. He glanced
at Harry and smiled. "I have the good doctor's curiosity
piqued. I suspect he wishes to know just what sort of artifact would send us through all this trouble."

She opened her mouth to object, but he raised a finger, giving her a hard look. "Now."

Evelyn turned on her heel and stalked out, closing the door behind her. The old man swirled his drink, watching her leave. Harry heard the distinctive click of the lock. Despite appearances to the contrary, they were taking no chances with him. He was still their prisoner.

"Do you have children, doctor?"

"No," Bryce answered, wiping his brow. "None that I'm aware of, at any rate."

The old man cracked a grin and sighed thoughtfully. "Aah. They are a wonderment and a burden."

"Evelyn is your daughter?"

"Granddaughter, from my first marriage. And a tad overprotective, I think." He shook his head. "Regardless. I would like your opinion, if I may, on a related matter. Of all the legends from the Middle Ages, which is your favorite?"

"Well, I suppose there are several I'd take a fancy to. The Arthurian legends, for example, and their association with the Holy Grail, or the myth of the Fisher King. Or more remotely, that of Prestor John. I did my dissertation on the relationship between—" He caught himself. Why was he speaking so freely to this man? He might inadvertently give them the information they wanted, and then what would they do with him? "Uh, never mind."

"Saints and Somniacs."

"How did you know—?"

The man smiled. "I have a copy. There are not too many

who have researched the ancient legends quite like you have, Dr. Bryce. Examining the stories of the seven sleepers of Ephesus; the various kings under the mountain, such as Frederic Barbarossa and his six knights; Arthur biding his time in Avalon, 'till he shall return at England's greatest need. Or the enduring tale of the Wandering Jew. A somewhat dubious connection, but one you made nonetheless. Very impressive work, I might add."

"You have a copy of my dissertation?" Harry marveled.

The man smiled, his gray eyes glinting in the firelight. "I know a great many things about you, Dr. Bryce. I know you never married, have had few close relationships. I know you sparred with the previous director at your college, and were often at odds with the man—a situation you found most uncomfortable, given your psychological profile. You see, Doctor, like you, I am a man who does his homework." He poured a second glass of brandy and offered it to Harry, who took it and lifted it to his lips. His hand shook, and he hoped the man didn't notice.

The man continued, "What I especially appreciate about your work is the seriousness you give to men like the Brothers Grimm. Most see them and treat them as simply the authors of a fairy tale."

"They were chroniclers," Harry couldn't help adding. He took a long swallow from the liquid, hoping it would calm his nerves. It burned his throat instead. He cleared his throat and said, "They attempted to wring history from folklore. Their methods were flawed, but not their premise. They simply lacked the tools to separate fact from fiction."

"Indeed. Unlike today."

"The trouble we have today is distance coupled with disbelief. We are so far removed in time from the events we can barely understand the worldview in which these myths were recorded, much less differentiate between the fanciful elements and the truth."

"And what, in your opinion, would be the truth of something like, say, the Holy Grail?"

Harry forced a smile. If the man had a copy of his dissertation, he knew quite well what Harry's thoughts were on the matter. But he decided to play along, warming to the discussion. After all, it was one of his favorites. Doubtless, the man knew this as well.

"The Sangreal myth is quite old," Harry explained. "The versions we know today are almost exclusively a blend of Christian and pagan traditions. The basis of the Grail legend is in the myth of Pheredur, found in the Red Book of Hergest. You can read it for yourself in the Jesus College at Oxford. There is nothing remotely Christian about Pheredur, except that his exploits mirror the Grail adventures of Perceval, and is undoubtedly one source of the Arthurian legends. In another myth, Bran the Blessed receives a sacred vessel from a mystic lake, which can heal all wounds, even raise the dead. That's your Grail legend right there."

"Do you say it's a cup or a person?" The old man sipped his drink.

"Oh, don't be ridiculous! It's a cup, or more likely, a bowl. To suggest otherwise is etymologically embarrassing, the stuff of Gnostic pop fiction. The original word is Sancgreall, from 'sanc' meaning 'holy' and 'greall,' a type of container."

"Indeed. So, does the cup have no basis in fact?"

"Do you mean as the cup of Christ? There's nothing in the accepted canon of scripture to suggest that Peter kept the cup from the Last Supper, or that Joseph of Arimathea was involved in any manner other than as a kind-hearted follower who lent his tomb to Jesus. In fact, we don't even hear about the Grail for another twelve hundred years. That's quite a long time, I think you'll agree. The first recorded instance of the Sangreal is in the account of Helinandus, thirteenth century. He writes that an angel visited a hermit in AD 720. The hermit had a vision of the paropsis Christ used in the Last Supper with the disciples. Of course, how Helinandus knew this some five hundred years later isn't explained. But he called it the Graal, after the French term *gradal*, which is, essentially, a large gravy boat. They'd use it for dipping meats in the sauce."

"So the Holy Grail is a gravy boat."

Harry chuckled. "Similar, at least according to Helinandus."

"But you haven't answered the essential question. Is the Grail real? Do these myths have a basis in fact?"

Harry took off his glasses and polished them in the firelight, letting his guard down. "We are talking about the Middle Ages. It was a time ripe for myths. Ideas were halfheard, half-remembered, passed down orally from generation to generation, and largely forgotten before being picked up and embellished upon by some monk eager to prove his pet doctrine, or else distinguish himself significantly enough to advance his career and enhance his comforts."

He put his glasses back on before continuing. "The Grimm brothers were right in their thinking that folklore has a basis in history. But who knows how many perfectly normal and completely explainable life experiences were transformed into the supernatural and spectacular by bards eager for an audience, encouraged as they were by audiences equally eager for stories? And so we have the written remains of fish tales. The larger and more elaborate they are, the more likely their foundations are merely benign and boring facts."

"Hmm. Perhaps you ought not to be so condescending to the bards and monks of old. 'There are more things in heaven and on earth, Horatio, than are dreamt of in your philosophy.'"

Harry stared at the old man's stooped back, befuddled. "Hamlet. Act one. Scene five," he referenced. "What are you getting at?"

The doors behind them opened, and Harry turned. Evelyn entered, pushing an elderly man in a wheelchair. A blanket had been thrown over his lap, but Harry caught sight of a pair of cuffs binding his hands to the chair.

"Ah," said the man behind Harry. "Our artifact has arrived."

"What?" Harry turned to stare at him. "What is the meaning of this?"

"Bring him into the light, dear."

Evelyn wheeled the man closer to the fire. Orange light glinted off the chrome chair and the handcuffs that held him to it.

"Who is this man?" Harry demanded. "What are you doing with him? Why is he handcuffed?"

"As for why he is bound, that answer should be obvious. To prevent his escape. As to who he is, well, perhaps you'd better take a look."

"This is your artifact?" Harry gaped.

"Indeed."

"He is a man! A human being. I insist you let him go this instant. I'll not be part of this."

Evelyn's grandfather nodded at her. "Show him," he said. She reached down and pulled open the captive's shirt, revealing an intricate tattoo stained over his left breast. Reluctantly, Harry leaned in close, adjusting his glasses to get a better look. What he saw took his breath away.

Harry stared into the captive's eyes. "It can't be," he whispered. "It's impossible."

"Nothing shall be impossible with God," said Evelyn's grandfather.

The captive's eyes flickered toward the voice. He looked back at Harry and his gaze softened. Harry felt as though the man were looking right through him.

"Who are you?" Harry whispered.

EIGHT✝

S EAN PUSHED MUNRO forward into the room then grabbed the handle on the back end of the book-shelf and swung it closed behind them, feeling it latch securely. Four deadbolts sprang into place with the whirl of a dial in the center.

The room was now as secure as any bank vault, but could only be unlocked from the inside. Built of bullet-resistant fiberglass and reinforced steel, the safe room was the primary reason Sean picked the house. He'd come here a month ago while Isabel was at the Christie's auction. It took him a full week to find a suitable location. Most of the wealthy homes the realtors showed him were designed to prevent penetration by the average burglar. Not what he needed. He had to look for something suitable for a foreign diplomat to find the right level of security and risk protection. And though Isabel insisted on spacious bedrooms with walk-in closets and a hot tub in the master bath, a safe room was the only essential element he'd looked for. Sometimes he wondered if she really understood the nature of the game she was playing.

This particular room came equipped with a full security desk and a month's supply of food and water, with fold-out beds and toilet facilities for a prolonged siege. A separate ventilation system pumped in air through an underground shaft that led to an intake manifold in the boathouse. Buried T-1 lines ran in opposite directions from either side of the house, providing redundant communications and instantaneous contact with emergency responders. But its best feature was a little something Sean cooked up all by himself.

"Send the all-clear," Isabel ordered.

Sean grinned in admiration. The woman was always a step ahead. If police converged to rescue them now, there'd be too many questions to answer. They had to handle this on their own. He sat down at the computer and logged in, then tapped in the code that instructed the security company to report a false alarm.

He and Isabel had been working together now for the better part of two years. Shortly after Dr. Munro had cinched a tourniquet on his leg after he was wounded in a gun battle at the Cave Church of St. Peter's in Antakya, Turkey, Isabel Kaufman had come inching past him with nothing more than a pen light and her arms full of the very scrolls he'd been sent to recover by a private investor. She'd hesitated when she saw him lying there wounded and actually moved past him several yards before doubling back and asking, "Can you walk?"

"Not well," he'd confessed. He'd been momentarily distracted by the thought that he should shoot her and take possession of the scrolls right then, but three realizations struck him at once. First, the gunshot would draw the rest

of the authorities to his location. He could already hear
them arresting Dr. Munro in the front of the church. Two,
he wouldn't be able to make it out of there without some
kind of help. And three, he was effectively out of the game
unless he threw in with her.

"I don't know how to get out of here, except through the
front," she'd said.

"Which is blocked up with gendarmerie."

She'd nodded.

"But you're also afraid I'll kill you first chance I get."

"The thought has crossed my mind."

"Mine too." He'd pulled out his gun and set it on his
lap. He'd heard her sudden intake of breath and knew he'd
made his point. "Thing is," he'd added, "first chance has
come and gone, yeah? I don't know how you did it, but the
two o' you beat me fair and square. I'll trade you this gun
for that torch, and maybe you and I can help each other
out."

She'd handed him the pen light and taken his weapon,
and together, they navigated through the labyrinthine catacombs to come out on the other side of the mountain.

They'd been together ever since.

He switched on the monitor now and brought up the
external cameras, studying the approach of the men from
different vantage points. The split-screen held six different feeds, providing him a complete view of the outside. Motion detectors had gone off ninety seconds ago,
warning him of their approach. The men came at the
house from five angles: two men from the northwest and

southwest, two more from the northeast and southeast. One more came directly from the north, approaching the front door.

He shook his head. This was not good. Professionals. He could tell from the way they ducked and ran—weapons held at the waist for quick fire response. Ex-military, probably American. He depressed a button engaging the magnetic locks on all the doors and flipped on the floodlights on the lawn, bathing the men in light. They reacted as he'd imagined they would, firing their guns at the locks and breaking through the doors. He didn't know how much ammunition they carried, but the less they had left by the time they reached the library, the better.

"I count five men," he said aloud. Isabel and Munro stayed well back, out of his way.

"What have you gotten mixed up in?" demanded Munro. Sean shook his head. There'd be time for that later. How Munro managed to best him in Turkey continued to elude him.

"It's DuChamp," said Isabel.

"No doubt," Sean muttered. "Told you we shouldn't have come here."

"That's not why and you know it."

"Aye."

"Who's DuChamp?"

Sean switched feeds to the interior cameras. Images of the men flashed into view. They were sweeping the house, drawing nearer to the library. One of them looked directly at the camera. He lifted his wrist to his mouth, and a moment later fired at the camera. One of the six screens instantly went blank, showing snow.

"They've spotted the cameras."

"Can you take them out?"

Quickly two, then four more screens went blank. The remaining camera, mounted above the mantel in the library's fireplace, stayed on, showing no one.

A moment later, the power went out. Sean swore, muttering, "That was fast." The back-up power kicked in automatically. "They've cut power and outside communications. Trying to isolate us."

"Who's DuChamp?" Munro persisted.

"Pierre DuChamp," said Isabel.

"What does he want?"

"Something he can't have. Sean?"

Sean shook his head, looking away from the useless screen. "There's too many of them. I can't take them out without pulling a Samson."

"A Samson?" Munro asked.

"Are you sure?" Isabel ignored Jon's question.

Sean's smile faded. "There's not many options, luv. We can't go out there. They'll mow us down. Those Mac-10s just spray bullets. Safest place to be is behind 'em."

"What's a Samson?" Munro asked.

He smiled wryly. "And here I thought you went to Sunday School."

"Samson, judge of Israel," said Munro. "Killed the Philistines with a jawbone."

"Keep going. Get to the end. You'll understand."

"At the end of his life he killed the Philistines by bringing down the temple of Dagon—oh, you can't be serious!"

"Can't I? Whole house is wired with Semtex. Lady here gives the word, we'll be the only ones left standing. And good riddance to it all, I might add."

"Let's not," Isabel said to him. "Your personal feelings notwithstanding, it's better they find nothing. I don't want to give DuChamp the satisfaction of knowing how close he came. Get us out of here."

"You might want to think about that, luv." He turned and faced her. Doubt etched her eyes. "We leave without taking them out first, they'll keep coming after us. DuChamp's a smug one, and that's no mistake. Bloodying his nose might make more of an impression."

She turned away from him, pinching her lip. Munro shook his head, bewildered. "I can't believe you're considering this."

"You got a better idea, yeah?" Sean shot back.

"No. 'Course, I didn't wake up this morning expecting this, either."

"Do it," Isabel ordered.

Sean smiled grimly and left the desk, heading for a panel on the wall.

"Wait a second," said Munro. "What happens when the explosives go off?"

"Don't worry yourself, none. We won't be here."

"Samson went down in the temple of Dagon."

"Aye, world's first suicide bomber, after a fashion. But we're doing this Irish style, and that means one thing."

"What's that?"

Sean grinned. "We all walk away." He opened the wall panel, revealing a set of switches resembling circuit breakers and a digital clock hidden behind the main wires. He flipped two switches simultaneously and the clock blinked on, flashing four red zeros at him. He set the timer for five minutes. The lights stopped flashing and began counting down. Last, he flipped one of the switches off again, engaging the circuit.

"Time to go." He brushed past them toward the back. He picked up a pry bar from the wall rack and yanked back the rug from under the shelf of food, revealing a steel circle the size of a manhole cover. He lifted the ring in the center of the circle and turned it, depressing the spring-loaded release. Steel bolts holding the cover in place instantly retracted from the hole.

"Gimme a hand with this, eh?" he said. The professor leaned down and helped Sean pry the cover loose. He set it down just under the fold of the carpet and looked at Munro.

"Okay. You first."

Munro stared into the hole. "Where does this go?"

"Down," Sean answered, pushing on the top of Munro's head. Munro ducked and climbed down the ladder. A moment later, Isabel followed. Sean waited until she was clear, then slipped into the tunnel himself.

"Ain't gonna miss this house," he muttered. He stepped onto the ladder and braced his feet on both ends of the rung. Pulling the rug over the top of the hole, he then drew the steel cover back into place, released the spring holding the deadbolts, and rushed down the ladder.

ΠIΠE

WHEN THE MAN in the wheelchair didn't answer, Harry glanced back at his host, who pursed his lips and nodded toward him. Harry turned back and tried again.

"I'm not with them," he whispered. "My name is Harry Bryce."

The captive stared past him at the old man by the fire, who calmly sipped his brandy, and then looked back into Harry's eyes.

"My name is Joseph," the man replied softly. His voice was like dry leaves blown by an autumn wind. He instantly dropped his eyes as soon as he'd spoken, as if staring into a grave.

"Do you know what they want from us?" Harry asked intently.

After a moment, Joseph shook his head. "They think I am someone else. They do not know who I am."

"Who are you?"

"No one."

Harry smiled thinly. "I'm going to try to get us out of here."

Joseph turned up the corner of his mouth and shrugged. Harry straightened and faced Evelyn and her grandfather.

"I think this has gone far enough."

"Indeed. And what do you think of our artifact?" asked the man by the fire, who still remained nameless to Harry.

"You have an old man handcuffed to a wheelchair. What am I supposed to think?" Harry retorted.

"You must think we are mad, naturally. To have drawn you here under these circumstances. To have handcuffed someone to a wheelchair. We must be insane, right? Tell me, good doctor, how old would you say this gentleman is?"

Harry glanced back only briefly. "In his mid-sixties."

"Why don't you tell him, Isaac?" urged Evelyn. "Go on, tell him how old you are."

Isaac? Harry wondered. *He said his name was Joseph.*

Joseph said nothing.

"Tell him!" the old man bellowed.

"I am eighty-seven," Joseph mumbled.

"Eighty-seven," the old man repeated. "Would you have believed that?" Harry shook his head. The old man smiled. "Now look at his arm. What do you see?"

Puzzled, Harry turned around and examined Joseph's arm. He did a double-take when he saw the tattoos. "Are these real?"

"From Dachau," Evelyn answered. She handed a manila folder to Harry, who opened it and took a look at a photograph of a very gaunt, young-looking Joseph. Beneath it, the same number that was stenciled on Joseph's arm. Harry read the numbers twice. They still matched.

"You were in Dachau? You'd have been—"

"I was eighteen years old when they liberated the camps."

"You survived the Holocaust."

"Oh, he has survived much more than that, haven't you Isaac?" asked Evelyn's grandfather.

Harry looked between Joseph and their captor. *Why did he keep calling him "Isaac?"*

"A genuine Holocaust survivor," intoned the old man. "Not too many of them left in the world, wouldn't you say? And yet here we have one, and he looks to be in incredibly good shape, so much so that you assign him an age twenty years his junior, by his own account. In fact, if you give him long enough, by the time he reaches a hundred, he'll look like he's in his twenties all over again. Dr. Bryce, this man is far older than a scant eighty-seven years."

He came forward, leaning over the wheelchair, muttering excitedly, "No, the concentration camps didn't frighten you, did they? You knew they wouldn't kill you. No one can."

"What? What is this?" Harry sputtered.

Evelyn's grandfather traced the scars on the man's wrists. Two long slits on each wrist. He let his fingers brush the numbers stenciled on his arm. "He is immortal. Isn't that so? Cursed by the Son of God to wander the world until the end of time."

Joseph pulled vainly against the handcuffs.

"You've had many names, haven't you? Cartaphilus, Ahasuerus, Josephus, Isaac Lakedion. Isaac Lake. And recently, just plain ol' Joe."

Harry shrank away from the two of them. "Are you mad?"

The grandfather shrugged.

"You're seriously trying to pass this man off as the Wandering Jew?"

"Is that so hard to believe?"

"It's preposterous! The Wandering Jew is a myth. A clever invention of the St. Albans monks."

Evelyn's hand flashed to her ear, where a Bluetooth headset lit up.

"You need proof, don't you?" their captor inquired. "I can respect that. You are, after all, a man of science, as I am. There's no such thing as magic. Therefore, when we encounter the miraculous, we can either refuse to believe it." He took the photograph from Harry and held it up. "Or we can find the science in operation behind it."

Evelyn swore and spoke directly to her grandfather. "We're out of time. They're coming."

The old man straightened, "Are you sure?"

"Your old friend Philip just sent us a message."

The old man's eyes flicked briefly to Harry. "Who'd have thought it," he said. A moment later, Harry felt a familiar sting on his neck.

"Not again," he exclaimed, falling back into blackness.

Joseph watched as Andre and William entered the room, wheeling a second chair. He studied them sadly.

Hired guns. Men who knew nothing better than pushing people around and doing as they were told. Their only redeeming quality was loyalty. Together they hefted the stout professor into the chair.

"Put them in the chopper," Evelyn's grandfather ordered. Evelyn nodded at his directions and left with the two body guards.

"You never change, do you Simon?"

The old man turned, startled. "What did you call me?"

"Simon Magus." Joseph replied. "Always trying to buy the gift of God with money."

He laughed. "Money? Who said anything about money?" He came around to stand in front of Joseph. His usual hunch had vanished, and he stood fully upright. "If I thought money mattered to you, we'd have made you very wealthy indeed. Money doesn't interest you, though, does it? If it did, we would not have found you in such a state, living in a homeless shelter. No, you'd have been a king."

"Do you really think you'll succeed? You are no different from the pagan priests of old, trying to compel God to bless, when they simply ought to have asked." Joseph felt his lip tremble.

"'From the days of John the Baptist until now, the kingdom of heaven suffereth violence, and the violent take it by force.' What we cannot buy, we will take," the old man asserted.

Joseph raised his voice. "You have no idea what you are up against, or Who you are opposing! Empires have broken upon His anvil."

"Jacob wrestled the angel, and the angel was overcome," the man replied. The door behind them opened, and Evelyn returned. She released the brake on the wheelchair and started moving Joseph toward the door.

Futilely, Joseph hollered, "I am not what you think I am. I am not who you think I am!"

Neither listened as they wheeled him out.

Outside, the wind whipped a frenzy of leaves around their heads. The harsh, *whup, whup, whup* of a helicopter thudded through Joseph's chest. Evelyn wheeled him straight toward it, up the ramp, and over to the hydraulic lift that raised his wheel chair to the height of the helicopter's cabin, then swung him inside. Andre rolled him off the lift and secured him and the chair with straps to the back of the cabin beside an unconscious Harry Bryce, then undid Joseph's handcuffs.

A moment later, Evelyn and her grandfather climbed aboard. Joseph listened as the whine of the motor increased, and the helicopter shifted off the pad. A *pop!* splintered the glass in the cockpit, and something warm and moist spattered Joseph's face.

Evelyn swore, grabbing for the controls as the helicopter lurched in the air.

Joseph wiped his face, startled to see blood on his hands.

The helicopter spun wildly in the air. It felt like a carnival ride. Both Evelyn and her grandfather shouted to each other. Andre and William fired their guns blindly through the open door.

Just off the side of the craft, several men darted toward the helicopter, firing automatic weapons. More popping sounds pierced the air, and the side window of the helicopter splintered, sending fragments of glass into the cockpit

After a sudden shout, Andre tumbled from the cabin, his hands grasping at nothing as he disappeared from the helicopter.

"Get us out of here!" yelled the old man.

Evelyn thrust open the door and shoved the pilot's body out, then took the pilot's seat. Two more bullets pinged off the aluminum frame of the aircraft.

"Evie, now!"

"I'm trying!" she screamed back. Pulling hard on the stick, the helicopter veered backwards, then soared up and away from the gunfire below. William tumbled back, tilting toward the open door.

Joseph grabbed his shirt, and for a moment William hung suspended over the open air before the craft righted and he fell to the floor. Speechless, William stared up at Joseph, who could only nod in reply. Far below, the woods and cabin dropped away into a mottled, indigo blur.

The pursuers stared after the departing helicopter. The leader turned to study the two bodies lying tangled on the helipad. One was the pilot, clearly dead. Their first shot

had blown the side of the man's head off. The other lay semi-conscious on the pavement. Blood leaked from his ears and nose, and he was coughing shallowly. The leader pursed his lips and brought his cell phone to his ear.

He wasn't supposed to make direct contact with the company. They insisted that he use an intermediary, but in this case, they'd have to make an exception.

Dialing the front desk, he left a simple message, "Someone warned them," and hung up.

He stepped over the body of the guard, bent down and looked him in the eye. The bodyguard stared back from his broken body, his expression pained and fearful.

"We need to talk."

TEN

A T THE BOTTOM of the ladder, Munro and Isabel waited in the shadows. Sean dropped down to join them, pointing the way through the shaft. The tunnel was dry and narrow, forcing them to move through it single file. "Keep your head down, yeah?" he said, crouching in the low corridor.

He led them down the length of the tunnel, following a line that drew them away from the house at a forty-five degree angle. At the far end of the shaft stood a ladder near the water's edge. He glanced at his watch and frowned.

"What's wrong?" Isabel asked.

"It's been five minutes."

"Nothing's happened," Munro observed.

Sean swore, making Munro wince. "You are a brilliant one, aren't you?"

Isabel touched his arm. "Sean?"

He shook his head. "When they cut the power, they must've short-circuited the fuses. Either that or there's not enough juice in the back-up generators to kick 'em off."

"You're kidding." Munro smirked.

"Well it's not like you can bloody test 'em now, can you?" he shot back. He glanced down the tunnel they'd just left.

"They figure out we're gone, they'll be after us in a lickety." He paused for a moment, forming an idea. "Wait here," he instructed, and climbed the ladder. At the top, he removed the lid and swung it down into the tunnel. He was in what appeared to be a covered well at the southeast portion of the property. A rope and bucket dangled overhead.

Digging into his pocket, Sean pulled out a small pair of binoculars and studied the house. One of the men stood on the back patio, scanning the perimeter. Sean pressed his lips into a thin line. Peering back into the tunnel, he caught Isabel's eyes and motioned to the left with his hand. She nodded, grabbed Munro's hand, and disappeared from view.

Sean glanced out the faux well again. The boathouse was a scant hundred feet away. He looked back to the guard on the patio. As soon as the man's gaze panned to the other side of the property, Sean vaulted over the ledge of the well and dashed for the boathouse. He ducked around the side and flattened himself against the wall. Motionless, he waited for the guard to look away again before slipping into the water.

The cold soaked through his clothes and skin, and he sucked in a deep breath before ducking beneath the water's surface. He swam straight down, under the boathouse wall and resurfaced inside the safety of the boathouse. Once inside, Sean pushed himself up onto the deck that ran around the interior of the boathouse, next to the 247 Islander speedboat docked inside. He grabbed a bungee cord from off the wall and dropped it on the captain's chair and retrieved the keys from a panel in the side, inserting them in the ignition. From a hatch in the stern, he withdrew a belt of grenades and carried them to the bow, where he placed them beside a pair of half-filled gas tanks. He pulled the pin on a single grenade and wedged it between the tanks. With a furtive glance through the window at the main estate, he unlocked the bay door and rolled it up. The sound may have carried. He scrambled around the boat, tearing the lines off the bow and stern before leaping onto the boat's deck. He tethered the steering wheel to the frame with the bungee, and with a turn of the key, the 375 horsepower MerCruiser 496 Magnum engine growled to life. Sean swung out of the wheelhouse to squat on the running board alongside the wheel and thrust the throttle forward halfway.

A throaty roar gurgled from the stern. The boat surged forward, frothing and bubbling the water in its wake. As soon as the boat cleared the bay doors, Sean leaped to the side, landing in the lake with a splash. He bobbed to the surface as the boat tore away toward the horizon. He sucked in a deep breath, and disappeared under the water again as shouts from the house echoed across the lawn.

Bearing right, he swam underwater, hugging the coast-line. The cold soaked his skin, making even his bones feel wet. He pushed his protesting muscles against the current, demanding that his aging body give more than it wished. He came up for air twice, twisting in the water to bring his mouth to the surface just long enough to grasp a lungful of air before disappearing under the water again. After a hundred yards, he moved to the rocks and scrambled onto shore. He paused to catch his breath, annoyed to be so winded, then ducked into the weeds and clambered over the rocks to come to a parking lot at an apartment complex, due west of the house. Several people lounged in easy chairs on the balconies of their apartments, and a half dozen young lads tossed a basketball half-heartedly around a dimly lit court, but none seemed to mark his passing there.

A small, Volkswagen Beetle stood parked in the carport to his right. He opened the hood and pulled out a lug wrench to pry up the manhole cover in front of the car. Seconds later, Isabel stuck her head out. Sean took her hand and helped her to her feet, then retrieved Munro and dropped the cover back into place.

From across the water, an explosion pounded the horizon, sending a fireball arcing into the night air and briefly turning the carport a brilliant orange. The basketball players and people on the apartment balconies turned as one to stare at the fire.

"What was that?" Munro asked.

"My boat?" Isabel eyed Sean.

"Aye, luv. Needed a diversion."

At that moment, a second, much more massive explosion rocked the shoreline, turning everything as bright as day and knocking them to the ground. People screamed as they fell. Windows in cars and in the buildings next-door shattered. Sean swore and covered his head as splinters of wood, broken glass, shards of metal and ceramic rained down on the parking lot.

"What the hell was that?!" Munro bellowed. Sean

scrambled over the Volkswagen to the top of the carport and peered over the lawn to where Isabel's house had once stood.

He grinned down at Isabel and Munro. "Samson came through after all," he said, and jumped down.

Isabel rolled her eyes and climbed into the Volkswagen, letting Munro have the front seat. Sean sat in the driver's seat, watching as a crowd gathered to squawk about the explosion. *That'll slow them down,* he thought. He fired up the Beetle, shifted into first and drove away.

Jon studied Sean and Izzy. "Do you mind if I ask you something? Why a Beetle?"

Both grinned. Sean looked at him. "Not what you'd expect, is it?"

"No, not at all."

"Precisely."

After a moment, he nodded. "We can slip right past them and they'd never see us."

"The rich always drive limos, don't they?"

"I suppose not."

Izzy reached forward and touched his shoulder. "Do you think you can get a hold of Dr. Bryce?"

"Excuse me?"

"You said we needed his help."

"Well, yeah. This is his field of expertise, but—I don't think—that is, I—"

"He doesn't want to get him mixed up in this," said Sean.

"Right," he nodded. "You just had a bunch of armed men break into your house, which you then blew up on top of them. This isn't exactly Harry's speed. Know what I mean?"

"This isn't anybody's speed, mate. Guys who get into this 'cause they like excitement are the ones what get themselves and others killed, yeah?"

Jon frowned. The thought hadn't occurred to him before.

"Bottom line is," Sean continued, "we got a job what needs doing, and your man Bryce is the only one to help us. Soon as DuChamp back there figures out what happened to his men, he'll be coming for us. I wouldn't be a bit surprised to see them go after Bryce themselves. Or you."

He shook his head. "That doesn't make any sense. Why would they go after Bryce? You've got the manuscript. You're holding all the cards."

"Jonnie," said Izzy, "this isn't about the manuscript. The *Flores Historiarum* is just piece of the puzzle. We're all after something much bigger."

He looked in the back seat, trying to read her expression. Izzy was a masterful liar. He'd learned that the hard way in Turkey. Now she was asking him to trust her.

"Please," she said. "We don't have much time."

How could he expose Bryce to this? The poor man broke a sweat crossing the room. The thought of him running around with Izzy and Sean while people shot at them was preposterous, at best. Of course, he realized, the same could be said for himself.

On the other hand, if Bryce found out that Jon denied him the chance to examine a manuscript as old as Izzy claimed this one was, he'd never let Jon hear the end of it. Besides, they weren't really trying to get Bryce involved. They just wanted his opinion. What could it hurt?

"All right," he said, pulling out his cell phone. He dialed Bryce's number and waited. After five rings, the phone went to voicemail. He frowned and tried his office number. After two rings, someone picked up.

"Dr. Harry Bryce's office, Julie Newsom speaking."

"Julie? This is Dr. Munro. I was trying to reach Harry. What are you doing there this late?"

"Oh, Dr. Munro. Thanks for calling. Have you heard from Harry?"

"N-no, Julie, that's why I was calling you."

"I haven't heard from him. Nobody has. He was supposed to check in after the party, but nobody remembers him leaving, and no one has seen him—"

"Julie—"

"—He asked me to bring him his insulin, but he wasn't at the party when I got there, and somebody said they saw him leaving with you, and then when he didn't come back I went looking for him. His car was still in the parking lot, so he couldn't have gone home. So I came to his office, but he hasn't been here, either, and he's due for his shot, and if he doesn't get it—"

"Julie, listen to me! Calm down. Call the police. Tell them everything you just told me, okay?"

There was sniffling on the other end. "Julie?"

"All right, Doctor."

"Okay. Don't worry. We'll find him." He hung up and turned back to Izzy and Sean.

"Bryce is missing."

ELEVEN

VASILY IVANOVICH SLIPPED on his cybergloves and flipped a tiny switch affixed to the back of the right glove. The switch activated a micro-computer and transmitter on his belt. Sitting in the darkened café in downtown Seattle, he could just as easily have logged in via the café's Wi-Fi. But not this time. Right now, he required a secure connection, nothing that would leave a trace of what he was doing. He leaned back and closed his right eye.

The left eye remained open, seeing not the wall nor the customers chatting amicably at round tables sipping their lattes and mocha chais, but rather a computer readout visible to no one else. His eye was the absolute latest technological development, not available on the open market, nor, in all probability, to anyone else—a fact which brought Vasily no end of amusement. The artificial eye beamed images directly onto his optic nerve, enabling him to see, and with a little tinkering of his own, to receive data.

He typed on nothing with his gloves. The cybergloves themselves were a breakthrough technology just waiting for this sort of application. With a little programmatic improvement, he interfaced them with the computer on his belt. His eye registered the movements as keystrokes, and supplied the requisite images. He probably could have used a Blackberry or an I-phone with less trouble, but each of these systems required him to interface with an ISP. Again, such activity was traceable. He preferred a direct link to the Internet.

Two years ago, the loss of his eye meant the end of his career. Of what use was a one-eyed operative to anyone? Too easy to blindside, literally. He didn't have the vanity to replace his eye with a glass prosthetic, and wearing a patch would make him too easily identifiable. For a time he was tempted to surrender to the vodka, like so many had before, but Fate had other plans.

He remembered the meeting like it was yesterday. The impeccably groomed businessman from America had sat down next to him in a bar in St. Petersburg, like the many obnoxious Westerners now infesting his country, and tried to strike up a conversation about nothing relevant. But when the man had spoken to him and had called him *"Zayka,"* he'd turned, ready to send this obnoxious capitalist back to America in a box.

"Zayka?" It meant "bunny," and was not a compliment for a man like Vasily. "Is this what you call me?"

"No, comrade," whispered the American, "it is what your grandmother called you."

His grandmother hadn't crossed his mind in years. She'd raised him after his parents were killed in a car accident when he was two. But no one could've known what she called him. Not even his comrades in the service knew that tidbit. He sank back down on the stool, his senses fully alert. The man was a professional. Someone to be reckoned with. "What do you want?"

"From time to time, I find myself in need of someone with your particular skill set—a dark knight, if you will. I offer you a quid pro quo. I will help you, and in return, you will offer your services to me when I need them."

"Go on," Vasily'd said, unsure where this was headed.

"I work for a company which holds the patents on some rather unique technologies." Here he reached into his jacket pocket, withdrew a printed sheet of specifications, and slid it over to him. "Including this one."

Vasily scanned the document. "A bionic eye?" He noticed the logo on the bottom of the page. Triprimacon. Undoubtedly some clever American technology company. He'd never heard of it.

The man was talking. "It's not exactly Steve Austin stuff— oh, you probably never watched the Six Million Dollar Man..."

Vasily shook his head, doubtful.

"An American TV show, from the 1970s. Science fiction. Now becoming science fact." He tapped the page. "I can fit you with one of these. Restore your sight. Give you some... advantages."

"And what is it you want in return?"

The man smiled convivially. "As I said, your services. On retainer. I know all about you, Vasily Ivanovich. I know you were meant for more—" he clicked his thumb against Vasily's shot of vodka— "than this. The number is on the back. Call if you are interested. Oh, and uh, the specifications there aren't complete—nor entirely accurate. Should you try to sell them or," he laughed, "produce them yourself, they would be utterly worthless. But the offer is good. *Dosvadanya*."

It was tempting. How could he refuse? Still, he'd spent the rest of the day studying the specifications. The American had been right. The specs were neither complete nor accurate. Had they been, he probably could have made the eye himself—though he'd have had to find a surgeon to install it—and finding one with sufficient skill in either St. Petersburg or even Moscow was a dubious effort at best. He'd called the number the following day. Within a week he could see again. Within a month he'd asked for, and received, the special gloves and computer, and set about retrofitting the eye to improve its efficiency and uses.

The eye turned out to be a most useful tool. It came with both infrared and night vision capabilities, and when networked into his computer, could provide real time GPS for anywhere on earth. He'd even figured out how to task a satellite to give him an overlay of his immediate position. In short, he could see everything around him, leaving him practically invulnerable to surprise attack. Like a god, he thought. For a time, he actually considered having his remaining eye removed, the technology worked so well. But the nameless man in Triprimacon advised against it. An accident with a live electrical wire confirmed his wisdom. He'd been left partially blind until the system rebooted. Further experience revealed additional limitations, such as the static he received near cell towers and strong electromagnetic fields. As much as the technological American wizards could do, they were still unable to replace nature.

He wondered what his former comrades in the *Sluzhba Vneshney Razvedki,* the Russian Foreign Intelligence Service, would think of his current activities. Despite the demolition of the Soviet Union by Gorbachev and the dismantling of the service by General Vadim Bakatin, most of his comrades were still KGB. The *Cheka,* now and always: the Sword and Shield of the Great Russian Empire. Undoubtedly they would upbraid him for serving the Capitalists, for assisting them in their efforts to oppress the proletariat. And they would be right. He could justify it as serving a larger purpose all he liked, but in the end, he was only serving himself.

Unless, of course, he could get back in the game. And now, with the superior ability foolishly given him by the Capitalists themselves, he could do so—a more formidable adversary than they'd ever faced before. The *Cheka* might not approve his working with the Capitalists, but they would recognize and approve of his stealing their technology only to use it against them later. All he had to do now was get away with it.

He opened the file on Peter Schaumberg, using a Perl script to find easy access into Schaumberg's home computer, and quickly copied the contents of the hard drive to his own. Before logging out, he uploaded a rootkit virus of his own design – one that would allow him instant access to every keystroke Schaumberg made on the machine without revealing his presence. Satisfied, he sipped his coffee and began scanning the files now on his own computer, searching for the most recent documents and examining the browser log.

He remained expressionless while he searched the documents, maintaining a visage of bored detachment that was due in part to his training—emotions could get you killed—but also due to the weary cynicism born out of years on the job, which was ripped out from under him without warning. Now that he'd been called on to fulfill his debt to the man who gave him back his sight, he could soon return to Mother Russia—a changed and improved operative they'd be fools not to embrace.

Two coffees later, he found what he was looking for—a cookie received from an airplane hangar rental in Muskegon, Michigan.

He smiled through his mustache and said in Russian, "Yes, why do you now go to Michigan, my good doctor?"

He pulled up his web browser and hacked into the airport's mainframe. The firewalls and security protocols on the hangar rentals were substandard, and down within seconds. He sorted through the rental agreements by date, scanning for the most recent changes until he found what he was looking for.

Interesting, he thought. *Why would the name "Rothman" be on the rental agreement?* He opened the PDF and looked at the signature. Evelyn Rothman. He smirked. A coincidence? Unlikely. The hangar was only rented for a week, set to expire today.

He also found a flight manifest for a private jet heading to Belgium. With a little additional homework he could confirm everything, but he already knew what he needed. He finished the coffee and left the shop, heading for the airport. On the way, he booked the earliest flight to Belgium and secured a rental car.

With any luck, he'd finish this assignment quickly and be back in Seattle before the week was out. And then...

Then he could finally tell the pigs at Triprimacon that his contract with them was finished and go home to Russia.

†WELVE

HARRY SHOOK HIMSELF awake, feeling an odd vibration in his feet, legs, and back. A loud thrumming sound filled his ears. He blinked his eyes and then looked out the window...

To the ground rushing by several thousand feet below.

He was flying.

He blanched. They'd strapped him into a wheelchair and put him aboard the helicopter again. What did they want with him? Where were they taking him?

A rank, coppery odor filled his nostrils. He looked down and saw blood staining the floor, dripping from a dark splotch on the cabin wall. "What happened?"

No one answered, nor even acknowledged his presence. After a moment, he realized why. They were all wearing headphones. A final pair dangled just above his head. He put them on and tried again. "Excuse me, uh, what happened?"

In the front, Evelyn and her grandfather exchanged glances. The old man turned and regarded Harry with eyes marked with weary frustration and cold calculation. Finally, he said, "Nothing you need concern yourself with."

A hand patted Harry's knee. Joseph, strapped into a wheelchair like himself, gave him a weak smile. "We were attacked," he explained, pointing at the bullet holes. Grandfather glared at him.

"Attacked? By whom?"

"A cleaning crew," Evelyn replied. Grandfather turned his glare to her. She shrugged.

"A what?"

Evelyn opened her mouth to answer, but her grandfather cut her off. "Cleaners are a special ops team that my company employs. They clean up messes."

"By shooting people?"

"Whatever works."

Harry struggled fruitlessly against his bonds, swearing epithets. The chair jerked a bit, but remained in place. His heart raced, and he felt a little light-headed. *Uh-oh.* He needed his insulin. He'd already missed his shot by several hours. He glared at his captors. "Who are you people?"

Grandfather sighed and came back to the cabin, sending William to the front and taking his seat.

"I am Dr. Peter Schaumberg, a geneticist by training. My former employers have been researching the secret of longevity, looking into the past for clues to the future. They are very anxious to get their hands on this technology. I intend to get there first. To that end, I've become a problem for them. Hence…" he waved his hand at the bullet holes.

Harry blinked, not at all sure he understood. Even less that he wanted to. Curiosity got the better of him. "So what do you want with me?" He felt thirsty.

"We need your help. You are an expert in the Middle

Ages, especially the sleeper myths. We think one of them holds the key to what we seek. My former employers believe the clues lie in the past—in a great secret that has been lost or kept hidden from generations that might otherwise have reaped its benefits. I say it is time to take what has been whispered in the inner rooms and shout it from the house-tops. This is what led me to you, my ancient friend," he said, tapping Joseph's knee.

To Bryce, he said, "Doctor, look at this man, and tell me what you see. An old man? A Holocaust survivor, even, but that's all. There is much more to him than that." He looked at Joseph. "It's ironic that you are calling yourself Joseph, isn't it? That was your name in the beginning. Dr. Bryce, I would like you to meet Yosep of Ramathaim, a man you know as Cartaphilus, Isaac Lake, sometimes Lakedion, and at least one time called Ahasuerus, isn't that right?"

"I've already told you," said Joseph, "I am not who you think I am."

"Ah, but the evidence says otherwise."

"Evidence?" Harry ran a hand across his brow, feeling feverish. He wanted to object further, but his throat was too dry.

"Yes, Doctor. Evidence. Surely you did not think we would reach such a conclusion out of thin air. Dr. Bryce, I work for a company that has been following the exploits of this man for several hundred years. In fact, we obtained an interview with him in London, during the early 1850s. There has been much written about him. Most of it false. We have allowed this misinformation to prevail, both to protect the public and defend our interests. Until recently, we were content to live and let live. But now, well, things have changed."

"Why?" Harry panted.

"In time. What you must understand now, Dr. Bryce, is that this man does not die. He was in his thirties when he became infected, and though he is aged now, his youthful demeanor returns when he reaches a hundred. This has happened perhaps twenty times now, with no sign of it stopping soon. I'm sure you can see why this interests me."

Harry put two fingers on his pulse, feeling it throb beneath his skin. He licked his lips. He'd missed his insulin injection by several hours, and if he didn't get help soon, he'd be in real trouble. "Do you have any... water?"

"If we could find the secret to his immortality, it would change everything. Think of the lives that could be saved. Is that not worth a small sacrifice on your part?"

"Sacrifices must be given willingly," Joseph retorted, "or they mean nothing."

"Semantics."

"On the contrary. What you have done is unconscionable. You lust and do not have. You murder and covet and cannot obtain. You fight and war. Yet you do not have because you do not ask. You ask and do not receive, because you ask amiss, that you may spend it on your pleasures."

"Pleasures? What pleasures of mine do you think I desire? I seek only to help others—a noble cause you should willingly support."

"Sugar..." gasped Harry. Peter and Joseph kept talking,

but he no longer heard them. Their words were lost, jumbled together, making no sense. The helicopter's cabin spun, then all turned red.

Philip drove his Aston-Martin at seventy-five miles an hour, downshifting and whipping around turns even as he glanced in his rearview mirror for the telltale signs of pursuit. Two hours had passed since he'd placed the phone call to Schaumberg and left the office, heading home. But as he slipped into the flow of ant-traffic weaving through the maze of interstates, he found himself looking in the rearview mirror at every pair of headlights that appeared. Before long he recognized the lump growing in the pit of his stomach as a warning of what was to come.

He'd called the Cleaners out on Schaumberg, and then warned him they were coming. That kind of duplicity could only get him killed. Would get him killed, in fact. If Triprimacon had a man like Philip willing to call in the Cleaners on Schaumberg, could he doubt they also had someone similar out there with his name on file, ready to implement the protocols should he go rogue? It only made sense.

He glanced in the rearview mirror again. Not only did it make sense, but it was likely happening right now.

The twin headlights in the mirror were those of the same SUV that had been following him ever since leaving his office that evening. He was sure of it. One of the lamps burned a little dimmer than the other one, and the parking lights on either side were the same.

Was it the Cleaners? Someone else?

Whoever it was, he had little choice but to try to outrun him. He depressed the accelerator, watching his speedometer needle climb past eighty to eighty-five miles an hour. The next turn came quickly.

He veered into the left lane, hearing the tires squeal as he took the corner. An air horn blast added to the noise as he rounded the bend and caught the glare of an oncoming semi bearing down on him. He spun the wheel to the right, feeling the car fishtail onto the side of the road and spew gravel before righting itself. The truck blasted past him, brakes screeching. It started to jackknife.

He laughed as it disappeared behind him. Let the Cleaners deal with that! Accelerating to ninety, he shot down the narrow decline and entered another turn to the right. As he did so, he glanced back, stunned to see the SUV swinging wide around the jackknifed eighteen-wheeler. They kept coming. He swore and punched it, realizing too late that he was entering another turn to the left.

He slammed on the brakes as the car spun toward the guardrail. Sparks flew as the car collided with the metal, shifting to the left as he struggled to bring it to a stop. With a sickening *ping!* the railing shore free of its weld, clanging down the side of the embankment. The Aston-Martin lurched to the left, slipped off the road, and started to corkscrew down the side of the hill. Philip screamed, but the sound was cut off as the car landed upside down, caving in the roof, crushing him beneath its weight.

Five minutes later, the Cleaner scrambled down the slope, edging his way closer to the overturned vehicle. He gritted his teeth as he neared it, surveying the wreckage. *No way anyone survived that*, he thought. But he had to check anyway. It was protocol. Every death had to be inspected and verified.

He slipped as he reached the downed vehicle, and he grabbed it for support. The car grated on stone, threatening to slide farther down the hill. Gingerly stepping around to the driver's door, he bent forward and peered inside.

He shook his head. No question about it. Shame, too. If Rothman had only let him do it, it would've been far less painful. He at least could've had an open casket. He pulled out his phone and made the call.

"Rothman's dead. Looks accidental, just like you wanted."

He snapped the phone shut. So what if Rothman actually had died in an accident? That was no reason he shouldn't get his bonus.

THIRTEEN

"THEY GOT TO him," said Izzy. The Volkswagen continued to fly down the expressway, going five miles over the speed limit, but no faster despite their hurry. Jon found the pace aggravating, made more so by how little he understood what was going on.

"DuChamp?" he asked, trying to keep up.

"No." She shook her head. "DuChamp's a bit player. A collector with an overstuffed ego and equally stuffed pockets—enough to fund a small army so he can steal what he can't get any other way. Still, he has no more idea of what's really going on than you do."

"Nice. Glad I have you to fill me in on all this."

"Didn't mean that personally."

"What's happened to Bryce?" He had an edge in his voice. But Bryce's health—if not his life—was on the line. Civility could fly out the window for all he cared.

"As I said, they got to him."

"Who's *they?!*" He felt like reaching over the seat and slapping her.

"Hey now," Sean growled, touching his shoulder. "Don't make me pull this car over."

"Sorry, *Dad*." He steadied his voice. "Who's *they*?"

"Have you ever heard of Triprimacon?" she asked.

"No." He furrowed his brow. "Should I have?"

"Probably not. Until a year ago, neither had I. They're a privately owned company with offices all over the world. Headquartered in Europe. They have three primary concerns: nuclear physics, genetic engineering, and pharmaceuticals."

"I get it: Tri-prima-con. What about them?"

"They're vigorously collecting artifacts from the Middle Ages. And when I say vigorous, I mean violent. Collectors are scared of them. Just the mention of their name is enough to close out the bidding—even at highly reputable auctions. Rumor has it a few buyers who opposed them have disappeared."

"Yeah, the market's cutthroat. I've learned that first-hand. What about it?"

She ignored the jibe and ticked off on her fingers: "Nuclear physics, genetic engineering, pharmaceuticals, and middle age antiquities?"

"Okay, it's odd. So what?"

"I thought it was odd, too. I stumbled across them at Sotheby's in New York. They were aggressively outbidding anyone in the room. Including representatives of some of the wealthiest men in the world. I thought, 'who are these guys that they can take on people like Soros, Gates, Murdoch, or Turner? And why all this interest in the Middle Ages?'"

"A lot of people have hobbies. Maybe the CEO is into reenactments and stuff."

"If only it were that simple. I did some checking. Triprimacon is one of the oldest firms in existence.

Leadership is all good old boys, country club, blue-blood types. I'm talking like, *beyond* exclusive. Ironically, you don't find them in the corridors of power. They explicitly avoid political entanglements of every kind. This company is so under the radar, it's as if they don't even exist.

"And yet, Triprimacon has resources we can't even begin to imagine, all owned through their subsidiaries. They're invested in South African diamonds; real estate markets in Monte Carlo, Moscow, London and Tokyo; energy stocks, green power, domain name investing, Saudi oil, you name it. If there's money to be made, they're in it. In a big way. All of this has one purpose: to raise for them an unending supply of large amounts of cash."

"Yeah, but so what?" he protested. *What did this have to do with Bryce?* "They're a privately owned company. They're allowed to earn a buck."

"This goes way beyond earning a buck, Jon. This may be the single most powerful company in the world."

"Again, so what?"

"So why, if they're invested through their subsidiaries in all these other fields, would they risk exposure by investing themselves directly in the antiquities market?" She looked at him as if expecting his understanding. He shook his head.

"Still nothing all that spooky here, Iz."

"I'm getting to that. Be patient. So this company is really old. It's been changing hands from one generation to the next for at least five hundred years. Maybe longer, but the records don't go back that far. I found mention of them as early as the fifteenth century."

"There's a lot of companies that old, Izzy. Some of these places have been around for hundreds of years. One of my seniors did a term paper on it. It was quite informative. There are eight companies in Japan that are over a thousand years old."

"True, but most of them are just mom and pop operations. Family businesses passed on from one generation to the next. Not like this. Not with these interests."

"Wait a minute. What were they?"

"I'm sorry?"

"What were they before they became this Triprimacon group? I mean, they couldn't have been interested in genetics, nuclear engineering, or pharmaceuticals five hundred years ago. So what were they then?"

"That's just it, Jonnie. There never was anything else. They were *always* interested in these things. Probably from the beginning."

"You must've misread something."

She shook her head.

"That's impossible."

"Is it?"

"Not to rain on your picnic," said Sean, "but we need to make a decision here. Your man Bryce is missing. We couldn't get to him in time. DuChamp delayed us at the house." He slammed an open palm on the steering wheel. "I shoulda seen that."

"You really think he's a step ahead of us?" asked Izzy.

"Wouldn't be the first time."

"Bryce needs his insulin," said Jon. "He could be in real

trouble if he doesn't get it." After a moment, he added. "We should go to the police."

Sean smirked. "Not gonna happen."

"Oh, right. Sorry." *The burden of being an international fugitive*, he thought. "What do you want to do?"

"We should regroup," Sean suggested.

"Highland." Izzy said.

Jon looked her way. "What's highland?"

"I was hoping for something outta state," said Sean. He flipped on his signal and took a right off the interstate.

"Wait a minute, aren't we going back to the university?"

"No can do. We're going to Highland."

"What's highland?"

"We have a safe house there, Jonnie. It'll be all right."

"A safe house?" he stared at Izzy. "Like the last house was safe?"

"Think of this as a backup," Sean explained.

"No one knows about this one."

"Why can't we go back to the university?"

"Because it's the obvious move. DuChamp's men are looking for us, and they're not asking questions first. We go there, they'll find us." He waggled his finger at Jon. "Besides, you want to find your friend, yeah? We've got to figure out the best way to do that. Highland's the best option we got. It'll give us a chance to think."

Frustrated, Jon leaned back in his seat and vented breath. Taking a right on South Huron Street, Sean drove them past the commercial district into a residential neighborhood. The houses and small businesses gave way to another commercial district, this one with two, three, and four-story brick buildings housing sidewalk shops and apartments on their upper levels. Here, Sean turned right and drove them across the river, then north again on a less populated road with numerous small houses poking their driveways out into the street. After a mile, Jon saw a cemetery on his left with a chain-link fence roping off the sundry headstones from the road. A minute later, he saw the sign.

"Highland Cemetery?"

"That's the ticket, lad." Sean turned into a driveway before a nondescript house across the street, parked, and led them up to the front door. Jon stared at the house, the neighborhood, and the cemetery. Not so long ago he'd been at a party trying to dodge the dean. He shook his head, and went inside.

Nicky Sarris put the last pot onto the drying rack, wiped down the counter, and turned off the lights. He offered a sigh to the darkened kitchen of the Rescue Mission. All was set, ready for the morning, just like Joe had taught him. He sank against the counter, his mind once again fleeing unbidden to the last time he'd seen his mentor and friend. Those two men pretending to be cops. The redhead in the limousine he'd seen after following them downstairs.

The police had been no help at all. He'd given them the license plate number from the limousine as soon as they'd shown up. More than a week went by before they finally returned his phone call—and only then did they grudgingly tell him the limo was rented in the name of a private company—something called Triprimacon. He'd only found a corporate phone number after hours of scouring the web. The secretary on the phone curtly told him that Triprimacon *owns* their limousines, and would never stoop to *renting* them. He asked for the fleet manager, and after an icy silence, the secretary put him through. But this man asked if Nicky was a cop, and when he said no, he was pointedly told they didn't give out that kind of information. He was at a dead end.

Silently now, he bowed his head, mouthing the prayer Joe had made him memorize—trying to mean it in his heart, because that's what Joe said was important.

He did mean it, of course, but it was hard to trust in God when He'd allowed his only friend to be ripped from his life. Then again, Joe had told him about tests of faith, too. And for whatever reason, God had seen fit to test Nicky's faith.

I'm probably failing.

He pushed away from the counter and left the kitchen behind, climbing the stairs to his one-room apartment, next to Joe's. He paused by the door, his fingers tracing the wood. It was so strange, knowing no one was home.

For four years now, Joe had been the only father Nicky had ever known. His real dad left before he was born, leaving him with a single mother more intent on finding a new man than on raising her son. Naturally, he got into trouble.

Through sheer talent, innate intelligence, and an uncanny ability to say exactly what people wanted to hear, Nicky garnered himself a full-ride scholarship to NYU, only to squander it by selling drugs—something he'd never admitted even to Joe, though he suspected the man knew anyway. Joe was the one person Nicky couldn't lie to—someone who saw through his pretense and presumption with a clarity that was truly frightening, and a compassion that scared him even more. Nicky had met Joe during a particularly dark point in his life, when he'd crossed the line and begun using his own product—something even his supplier had warned him against. He'd turned to thieving to support his habit, but it only furthered his fall.

Joe found him strung out in jail, and with the judge's approval, had taken him under his wing. He cleaned him up and set him on the straight and narrow. And over time, Joe introduced him to the spiritual rules for his order, an ancient brotherhood predating even those of Saint Macarius, with his desert ascetics in Egypt. Nicky hadn't taken vows yet. He wasn't sure why he was waiting, but Joseph assured him he'd know when the time was right. But without Joe around to tell him, how could he possibly ever know if he was ready?

He shook his head, pushing away from the door. It creaked open. *Joe*, he shook his head at the unlocked room. *That's so like you.* He reached for the handle and was about to shut it when he stopped. Something nagged at the back of his mind—a fragment of a memory.

If anything ever happens to me, I want you to have this.

It was something Joe had said, showing Nicky a locked, miniature trunk he'd kept under his bed. He hadn't known what to make of it at the time—it wasn't like Joe was ever in any real danger.

But that was before.

Nicky pushed his way into the apartment. Maybe Joe had known all along someone was after him. Maybe he even knew who. Entering the bedroom, he reached under the bed, drawing out the wooden chest. He set it on his lap and began fiddling with the lock, feeling like the answers he sought were just minutes away.

FOURTEEN

"So, ROTHMAN IS dead," said Frederick.

Casper grunted and said nothing. Together they walked through the parking lot toward their car. Dinner had been fabulous, Frederick thought, especially after they'd received word of Philip's defection. It came just in time for dessert. They'd driven across town to a special place Frederick had discovered, a tiny nook of a restaurant off the beaten path. Casper had wrinkled his nose at the thought of eating anything in such a dive, but Frederick pointed out that the restaurant had recently won a five-star review, and it was worth a look. Naturally, he was right. He ordered for them both. The waitress, a buxom brunette with full lips and legs that didn't quit, brought out their order just as the news came. Frederick savored his: a turtle cheesecake with rum topping, washed down with an Irish coffee. Frederick had ordered his made with espresso, contemplating the odd combination of alcohol and caffeine. But after hanging up the phone, Casper had taken two bites of his dessert and pushed it to one side, his appetite apparently gone with the news about Philip. Frederick couldn't help but smile. He'd gotten to the Old Man. It wasn't so much that Casper cared for his pawn. Far from it.

He simply hated losing.

Cones of light cascaded from street lamps over the asphalt surface, glinting dully off the chrome surface of the Cadillac Escalade that waited for them in the lot. For all the trappings of wealth available to him, Casper still chose to drive his own vehicle. Preferably something big. It was one of his more endearing traits, Frederick thought. He liked to be in control. He liked to win. Driving with Casper was always something of an adventure. Invariably it involved weaving in and out of traffic, vying for position with the other vehicles that occupied the road. Sometimes he'd swerve into the oncoming lane to get around a recalcitrant slowpoke who didn't quite grasp Casper's need for speed. Frederick had learned to take it in stride.

They'd only crashed twice.

When they reached the vehicle Casper put his hand on the handle, and then stopped, turning to face Frederick. "Don't think for a moment that I don't know you had a hand in this," he growled.

Frederick feigned innocence. "What are you talking about?"

"Rothman, of course!"

"Oh that. A trifle. You're not sorry for him, are you?" His tone was delicate. Solicitous. It would only infuriate the man.

Casper made an exasperated noise in his throat and opened the door. Frederick wandered around to the other side and climbed in, trying hard not to smile. He strapped on his seat belt and looked through the windshield. Casper glared, staring straight ahead, his jaw muscles chewing on nothing.

"I was surprised, actually," Frederick said after a moment, "by how little it took. Four simple words. Just the slightest lie."

The old man fixed him with a baleful eye. "He wasn't yours."

"Evidently, he wasn't yours, either. You yourself said it was a loyalty test."

Casper grunted. "What was it you said to him, anyway?"

"I told him he could save Peter."

Casper stared at him, but then a sly grin broke out over his face. He chuckled at first, but then laughed uproariously, slapping the steering wheel. Starting the car, he said, "Well played, Frederick. Well played." He shifted into gear and turned down the road. "Save him," he snorted. "He deserved what he got."

Frederick reveled in the compliment. "My thoughts exactly."

A faint hum droned in his ears. Harry felt it in his feet, his legs, his loins, his belly, chest, and hands. It was different from the heavy vibration of the helicopter ride. He pried open his eyes, glimpsing a golden light beaming down on him. A faint breeze blew steadily on his face.

He blinked and opened his eyes fully, expecting to be in a hospital. Instead, he saw rows of seats standing in front of and behind him. Above him, the ceiling curved downward toward the wall, with a raised seam running down its length, disappearing behind the headrests. To one side floated an IV bag, with a tube that entered his arm. On the other side, a round window with a sliding shutter. He frowned.

What am I doing on a plane?

He sat up, and immediately his head began to swim. He groaned and lay back down. A hand reached over, touching his forehead.

"Huh?" He looked over, somewhat relieved to see the concerned eyes of Joseph watching him.

"You're awake. Are you better, now?" Joseph asked.

Slowly, he sat up, studying the needle in his arm. "Much," he said. "What happened? Last I remember we were on a helicopter."

"You passed out. Must've been all the excitement."

He shook his head and sank back against the hull. "Insulin shock. So where are we going?"

"Europe."

"*Europe*? This has gone far enough. Really." He looked around, frustrated, seeing no one to blame.

"Schaumberg do this?"

Joseph nodded. "They are determined to secure our help."

"What do they want from us?"

"Secrets to the universe, I think."

He rolled his eyes. "And they think we have the answers."

"Yes." He chuckled. "We just don't know it."

"Wonderful. So no matter what we say—"

"They will not believe us."

Harry nodded. He reached up and studied the IV bag. "What were they putting into me?"

"Electrolytes. And insulin. Something like that. You are diabetic?"

He nodded. "Yes. I neglected to bring my insulin to the party. My assistant was to bring it to me."

"It gave them quite a scare. They were very worried for you."

"Touching."

Joseph waved it off. "Not really. If you die, they won't have your help anymore."

Harry found that thought slightly less comforting than intended. He disconnected the IV and pulled the needle from his arm, patching the pinhole with a piece of the gauze and tape from the line. He stopped. A new thought occurred to him, one he hadn't taken seriously before. "Do you really think they'll try to hurt us?"

Joseph shrugged. "I don't know. Not really. Dr. Schaumberg is not a killer, but he is very determined. They might try to hurt us, if pushed. They are willing to kidnap us. Make us do things for them. Take us to Europe."

Harry half-laughed. "All-expense-paid. Always wanted to go to Europe."

Joseph grimaced. "Not me. I didn't have such a good experience last time I was there."

Harry's shoulders relaxed. "That's right. You were in Dachau."

"It was a terrible time to be a Jew. Terrible time to be anyone. I've never wanted to go back."

"Did you lose your family there?"

Joseph's gaze grew distant. "No. Not there. My family died a long time ago. 'Woe to those who are pregnant and to those who are nursing babies in those days. For then there will be great tribulation, such as has not been since the beginning of the world until this time, no, nor ever shall be.'"

Harry cocked his head. "That's from the Bible, right?"

"Matthew twenty-four."

"Huh. That's surprising."

"What is?"

"Well, it's just that you said you were Jewish, but you're quoting Jesus."

"Jesus was a Jew."

"Yeah, you're right. Guess I never thought of that."

He pulled the tape off his arm and checked the needle mark, then turned around and opened the window shade. In the darkness outside, he could see nothing but the faint outline of clouds hovering below them.

"I wonder how much longer till we land," he muttered.

"Hard to say."

He grimaced. "You seem awful calm."

"Getting upset only wastes energy." Joseph smiled. "There's nothing we can do until we land anyway."

"Do you think we'll be able to get away?"

Joseph raised a finger to his lips and pointed up. Harry followed his finger until he saw an intercom indicator lit up on the panel above.

He came over and sat next to Joseph. "Can they hear us?" he whispered.

"I think so."

"What do they hope to gain?"

"They hope we'll talk. Give away clues." He raised his eyebrows and grinned conspiratorially.

"Clues to what?"

"Secrets."

Harry rolled his eyes, and Joseph continued. "One thing I have learned about Peter Schaumberg: he doesn't do anything without a reason."

"But what does he want?"

"He wants a cure for his son's illness. He thinks we have it. Or rather, I have it. You, I gather, are supposed to help me find it."

"What illness?"

"Progeria," said a voice behind them. Joseph and Harry turned, startled to see Peter Schaumberg looming in the aisle.

"You!" Harry rose to his feet, standing fully erect and puffing out his chest. He was suddenly aware of just how much bigger he stood than the frail geneticist.

Schaumberg smiled. "Sit down, Doctor."

"I will do no such thing. Turn this plane around this instant!"

"No."

"You have kidnapped me, and you are taking me against my will to a—a foreign country! Y-you are an international criminal. I demand you turn this plane around!"

Schaumberg drummed his fingers on the back of the chair. "Dr. Bryce, even if I wanted to turn around, which I don't, I could not. We are more than halfway to our destination. We don't have enough fuel to make a return. Besides, I want you to come to Europe. And you yourself have always wanted to see it, just as you've said. Think of this as an accidental vacation. All-expense-paid, right?"

Harry fumed. "Why are you doing this?"

"Doctor, I am sure you can appreciate there are some things so important, so vast, they are worth breaking any law to achieve." Schaumberg took a seat beside them, suddenly looking far older and tired than he had at first. "I won't bore you with apologies you will not believe. I probably wouldn't mean them, anyway. But I meant what I said. I need your help. I suppose if I am to receive any of it willingly, you are at least entitled to an explanation. And I am now prepared to give it to you."

FIFTEEN

A T THE HIGHLAND safe house, Jon studied his surroundings, which were not much different from his own home, though a little smaller. A loveseat and couch were set at right angles to each other, facing a fireplace in the wall across from the door. A bookshelf in the corner held some nondescript knick-knacks, and the wall hangings looked like nothing more than department store prints. The décor reminded him of a model home—designed to look lived in, but artificial nonetheless. He sat down on the couch, exhausted, and checked his watch. It'd be morning soon. He smirked. No wonder he was tired.

Izzy lit the fire in the gas fireplace and pulled over a coffee table, setting the document tube on it. He ran a hand over his face.

"You all right?" she asked.

"Little tired."

She called into the hallway. "Sean, could you make us some coffee?"

He came out from the hall carrying three sets of sheets and blankets. "You sure about that, luv? We'll be needing a rest at some point."

"We're staying the night?" Jon asked, eyeing the bedding Sean carried.

Izzy shook her head. "We've got miles to go before we sleep."

"Coffee it is."

He set the bedding on the sofa nearest him and disappeared into the kitchen. A moment later, Jon heard him rattling around and running the water.

"All right," she said, sitting next to him. "Let's talk about Triprimacon. What is the purpose of genetic engineering?"

"Research, I suppose."

"No, I mean, what's the goal—the money maker?"

He squinted his eyes against the fog in his brain. Why did she have to do this now? "Well," he said, "there've been breakthroughs in cancer treatments and disease. Most of it's in like, biotech or something, isn't it?"

"Increasing crop yields," she offered.

"Sure, okay. Protecting plants from diseases. Making the crops grow bigger, better...genetically engineered animals...that sort of thing." He yawned.

"In the Middle Ages they searched for something called alkahest, the universal solvent. It would enable them to extract the essence of anything, to dramatically increase crop yields."

"Isn't water the universal solvent?"

"It is, but that's not what they meant by solvent, I don't think. Anyway, water isn't alkahest. It doesn't reveal the essence of something, or enable them to increase crop yields the way alkahest should. But that *is* what genetics is all about."

"Part of it, anyway. Okay."

"Nuclear physics." She moved down the list. "What's that about?"

"Splitting atoms."

"Or fusion. Fission or fusion, releasing tons of energy by transmuting one substance into another."

"Transmuting—wait a minute, you're talking about alchemy."

"Exactly. Transmutation of lead into gold. Quest for the universal solvent. Genetics and Nuclear Physics are the modern-day equivalents. Triprimacon has been doing this stuff for hundreds of years. They've been pursuing the Philosopher's Stone and the Universal Solvent for centuries. Now, aided by modern science, they are achieving two of the three objectives of the alchemists. The Philosopher's Stone would enable them to transmute metals—one substance into another—lead into gold. The universal solvent would make plants grow, ensuring a harvest."

"You mentioned three objectives."

"The Elixir of Life," she replied. "That's the third thing the alchemists wanted. The Elixir is a substance that would enable them to cure any disease, even allow them to live forever."

"Forever."

"If you believe the legend, anyway."

"Right. So everybody's wealthy, healthy, and well-fed. These aren't exactly diabolical motives."

"They are if you restrict access," said Sean, coming back into the room. He carried a tray bearing three steaming cups of coffee, a dish of sugar, and a pitcher of cream. Jon took his black, letting the bitter liquid wash hot over his tongue.

"Well, that's just capitalism. If they solve the problem, they shouldn't be required to just give it away. They ought to recoup their investment and turn a profit."

Izzy shook her head. "We're not talking about turning a profit. They've got more money than you can shake a stick at. We're talking about control. I said they eschew political involvement. That doesn't mean they don't have aspirations. Think for a moment what these men would be if they got what they were after. They would never be hungry. They would never be sick. They would be wealthy beyond imagining."

"God-like. Total control," said Jon. "Okay. I sorta see where you're going with all this. So besides the obvious connection—I mean, they came out of the Middle Ages, but why are they still looking for answers there? It seems like they're finding all their solutions in the modern era. Not the past."

"Because the answer has eluded them for far too long, and they've grown impatient. The world is changing too rapidly. The irony is this: Paracelsus believed he was nearer to finding the Elixir of Life than locating the other two substances."

"So what happened to it?"

"Paracelsus never possessed it. But he knew, or at least suspected, what it was. Unfortunately for the alchemists, the secret died with him. All their searching since his time has not provided them the answer. But that doesn't mean the answer isn't already known. In fact, I believe it's been staring us in the face this whole time. It's all a matter of putting the pieces together. And in a certain configuration, it all makes sense."

Now she uncapped the document tube and pulled out the fragile page, unrolling it on the table. She set her mug on one end to hold the paper down.

"Careful." Jon moved her mug off the page. He still couldn't believe she just rolled it up like that, but putting a cup of coffee on it? It bordered on sacrilege.

"It's in Latin," she said.

He nodded.

"Before we get too far into this, we need to know for certain this is the real deal."

Jon laughed. "Sorry. W<u>here</u> exactly is that boundary?"

She furrowed her brow. "What do you mean?"

"Too far? Really? How far is too far, anyway? I mean, I'd really love to know your limits."

Izzy pressed her lips into a thin line and ran a hand through her hair. "Could we not do this now?"

"Do what?"

"Fight. I mean, I'm sure you're owed one, but right now we need to focus."

Jon bit back what he imagined might have been a suitably terse reply and instead said, "Okay. Validating the document. You think it might be a forgery?"

She shrugged. "It's possible. We have found red herrings

all over the place. Some of them quite old. I think Paracelsus tried to throw people off his tracks. But it doesn't make sense for this to be a forgery."

She got up and started pacing through the room. "I think the other documents—the other twenty documents—those are the red herrings. Designed to make us believe they are the real deal, all the while obscuring the truth."

"Izzy, that's a lot to swallow. I mean, those documents have been well-known and circulated for hundreds of years. You're asking me to believe a conspiracy to silence the truth has been in operation for hundreds of years?"

"Why not? The company's been around that long. And they certainly have motive—to keep anyone else from learning their secrets."

"I don't know."

"Just read it."

With just a slight turn of his wrist, the lock popped open. Quickly, Nicky undid the latches and grasped the lid. Then he stopped.

If he went any further, he'd be violating Joe's trust.

He pulled his hands away from the tiny chest, flexing his fingers. *If anything happens to me, I want you to have this.*

That's what Joe had said. And something *had* happened to him. So Joe *wanted* him to do this. He *wanted* him to break the lock and open the chest.

So why wasn't he convinced?

He pushed away from the bed and crossed to the window, peering through the curtains at the street below. A few pedestrians mingled along the sidewalk, huddled in private conversations or conducting illicit deals under the cover of darkness. Cars slid by, their headlights probing the street. But nothing and no one looked out of place.

He was just being paranoid. "My conscience is clear," he muttered, "but if I'm wrong, it's an honest mistake, and I pray fer your forgiveness, Father."

With that, he returned to the bed and snapped open the lid on the box.

He should've left well-enough alone.

Inside, a set of five passports sat neatly bound together with a rubber band, along with three stacks of different currencies from countries whose names he didn't recognize, a ring with an odd fish emblazoned on the sides, a compass-like medallion on a gold chain, and an envelope with his name on it. He flipped through the passports, recognizing Joe's face, but none of the names—except one: Isaac Lake. That's what those men had called him. *So,* he thought, *they were telling the truth.*

He dropped the passports on the bed and stared at the shadows on the wall. The whole room felt less familiar—more foreign—than it had just minutes ago. Why would Joe lie to him? Why wouldn't he tell him who he really was?

It didn't make sense. But then, so little of this did. He picked up the letter, hoping for answers, not entirely sure he wanted them, and began to read.

Half an hour later, he looped the medallion over his

neck, slipped the ring on his finger, stuffed the cash and passports in his pocket, and left the room behind. The chest, empty now, lay open and discarded on the bed. The rest of the stuff in the apartment was even less important than that, the trappings of an old life no longer needed. In a way, he felt the same, like his chrysalis had burst, and he'd just been opened up to a wider, far more dangerous world than he'd ever thought possible. His old life was over now, and he could no more return to it than he could his mother's womb. His new life waited.

And he had a plane to catch.

SIXTEEN

*I*N THIS YEAR, *a certain archbishop of Armenia Major came on a pilgrimage to England to see the relics of the saints, and visit the sacred places in this kingdom. As he had done in others; he also produced letters of recommendation from his holiness the pope to the religious men and prelates of the churches, in which they were enjoined to receive and entertain him with due reverence and honor.*

Jon rubbed his scratchy eyes and continued translating.

On his arrival, he went to St. Albans, where he was received with all respect by the abbot and monks. At this place, being fatigued with his journey, he remained some days to rest himself and his followers, and a conversation was commenced between him and the inhabitants of the convent by means of their interpreters, during which he made many inquiries concerning the religion and religious observances of this country, and related many strange things concerning eastern countries.

In the course of conversation, he was asked whether he had ever seen or heard anything of Joseph, a man of whom there was much talk in the world, who, when our

Lord suffered, was present and spoke to him, and who is still alive in evidence of the Christian faith.

In reply to which a knight in his retinue, who was his interpreter, answered, speaking in French, "My lord well knows that man, and a little before he took his way to the western countries the said Joseph ate at the table of my lord the archbishop in Armenia, and he had often seen and held converse with him."

He was then asked about what had passed between Christ and the same Joseph, to which he replied, "At the time of the suffering of our Lord Jesus Christ, Joseph was a follower, but in secret only. When the Lord was crucified, this Joseph made bold request of Pilate the governor, that he might take and wash the body of our Lord, and receive Him into his own tomb. Pilate, wishing to dispense with the matter of His body, quickly gave consent, whereupon Joseph came unto the soldiers who had crucified Him and repeated this selfsame request.

Having received the body of our Lord, Joseph brought a basin and washed the body of the Lord. Loathe to pour out that precious blood, he preserved a portion thereof within a cruet, which he later conducted to Glastonbury on his travels as a tin merchant, whence he would also teach the heathen the gospel which he had received after the resurrection of our Lord, performing miracles of healing with the blood, and enjoining the heathen to believe.

Having taken the blood of our Lord upon His flesh, this self-same Joseph has received the same fate as that of Longinus, the centurion who pierced the flesh of the

Lord with his spear, and was sprinkled with the blood, and now abides perpetually, awaiting the return of our Lord in fear, lest he be justly condemned by the One he had pierced.

This Joseph is still awaiting His return; at the time of our Lord's suffering he was thirty years old, and when he attains the age of a hundred years, he always returns to the same age as he was when our Lord suffered.

He often dwells in both divisions of Armenia, and other eastern countries, passing his time amidst the bishops and other prelates of the church. He is a man of holy conversation and religious, a man of few words and circumspect in his behavior, for he does not speak at all unless when questioned by the bishops and religious men; and then he tells of the events of old times, and of the events which occurred at the suffering and resurrection of our Lord, and of the witnesses of the resurrection, namely those who rose with Christ, and went into the holy city, and appeared unto men. He also tells of the creed of the apostles, and of their separation and preaching; and all this he relates without smiling or levity of conversation, as one who is well practiced in sorrow and the fear of God, always looking forward to the coming of Jesus Christ.

Numbers come to him from different parts of the world, enjoying his society and conversation, and to them, if they are men of authority, he explains all doubts on the matters on which he is questioned. He refuses all gifts that are offered to him, being content with slight food and clothing. He places his hope of salvation on the Lord who, when *suffering prayed for his enemies in these words, "Father, forgive them, for they know not what they do."*

Jon frowned and put the manuscript down. At that moment, Sean came back into the room. Jon hadn't realized he'd left.

"They're going to Bruges," Sean said.

Izzy nodded. "They're taking Bryce to the chapel. We'll need a plane."

"A plane?" asked Jon.

"You finished?" She turned to him abruptly. "What do you think?"

He blinked, trying to switch gears. "It's interesting. The language is consistent, at least as far as I can tell. Texture of the paper, appearance of the ink, layout on the page. See these other markings? Faint letters reversed on the page? That tells us it's been inside a book for a long time, such that the acids in the ink burned into the paper on the other side. It all looks authentic. I wouldn't be able to verify it completely without running some chemical tests."

"Okay. So it might be real. What about what it says?"

"Like I said. Interesting. But to tell you the truth, it doesn't seem all that important."

"We'll need a passport, too," she said to Sean. To Jon she demanded, "How can you say that?"

"What am I missing?"

"Jonnie, please. Think! Who was Joseph of Arimathea?"

"He was a member of the Sanhedrin. Secretly a follower of Jesus. He asked for Jesus' body and buried Him in his own tomb. That's about it."

"What else?"

"There is nothing else. Not in the Gospels, anyway."

"There is one more story of Joseph of Arimathea. He also collected the blood and water of Jesus when the Roman pierced His side."

"Yeah, I read that."

"You read that in here," she said, tapping the manuscript. "But it's not the first time you've heard of Joseph of Arimathea."

"Of course not. He's a popular figure in second century literature, mentioned in The Gospel of Nicodemus, The Acts of Pilate, most notably. The Narrative of Joseph. And much later, in Robert de Boron's *Joseph d'Arimathie*, as part of the Arthurian cycle." He bent forward and picked up his coffee mug. He was about to take a sip when understanding dawned. "Are you serious? You're talking about the cup of Christ. The Holy Grail?"

"No. Not the cup. Everyone's so focused on the cup, they're missing out on the real story. The cup isn't important. It's what's in the cup that matters. Even the *Flores Historiarum* describes it. Roger of Wendover gives us the origins of the Grail legend, telling us of the basin he used to wash the body of Jesus. But within that basin was mixed the blood of Jesus Himself."

"Okay. What's your point?"

She looked exasperated. "The blood of a man who could heal anyone, even raise the dead, if the legends were true."

"Wait a second. Izzy, these aren't legends. The miracles that Jesus did—the resurrection itself—these are historical facts. They're not in doubt for those who actually look at the evidence."

"All the more reason, then! According to this document, Joseph of Arimathea is the Wandering Jew—the whole legend of Cartiphilus and his curse is a red-herring. It was always Joseph. He came into contact with the blood of Jesus, and therefore, he is still alive today. The Grail legend itself says that within the Grail lay the power to heal, even give life. *In* the Grail. Not the Grail itself, but inside it. The very Elixir which Paracelsus sought, which Joseph hid from him. *That's* what they're after."

He ran a hand through his hair, feeling exhausted. "The blood of Jesus? Really? You think all this stuff is really true?" He suddenly realized just how much like her brother Isabel Kaufman had become. Steven Kaufman was always on the lookout for the next big find, the obscure and sensational. Eventually, it got him killed.

Maybe he could steer her in a safer direction. "These are just myths that grew up around the person of Christ. Nobody takes this stuff seriously. It's simply too wild to believe. And it certainly isn't based on the strong evidence the gospels are based on. The documentary evidence is just simply too far removed to be trustworthy."

"Whether you believe it or not," said Sean, "the men who've taken your friend believe it. And they'll stop at nothing to possess it."

"We cannot let them have it, Jonnie."

Jon leaned back into the couch, sipping his coffee. "Let them search, then. There's nothing to find."

"We can't run that risk," she said.

"You can't. I can. I only want to get Bryce back."

There was a crash from the front window. Jon whirled, surprised by the noise, but found himself pulled off his feet. Sean flung himself at the couch, overturning it on top of them. A second later, the room exploded.

SEVENTEEN

"THIS MAN," SCHAUMBERG pointed a finger at Joseph, "is the Wandering Jew."

"Ridiculous!" spat Harry.

"And what would you accept as proof? We've shown you the photographs of his internment in Dachau."

"That proves nothing. He is simply older than he looks."

"Mmm. Sadly, the world has only recently embraced the scientific technique with its rigorous standards of evidence; otherwise, proofs would have endured through the ages. It is easy for you to reject it now, because you believe it to be impossible. It is for this same reason many reject belief in God. It is too easy to dismiss evidence that our paradigms cannot logically assimilate. You believe the world to be one way. You cannot accept evidence that challenges your notion, because to do so would pull the entire construct you call reality down upon your head. So rather, let us start with the inconsistencies in your worldview. Tell me, doctor, do you believe in God?"

Harry frowned. Was this man really going to try and talk him into this? "Well, I suppose so," he said. "I've never given it much thought."

"But you are a religious man."

"After a fashion. I am a member of the church. I attend infrequently, but well enough to keep myself in good standing with—you know." He aimed a finger heavenward.

"So for you, faith is a matter of insurance. Just in case."

"If there is a God, I don't want to run afoul of him."

"Indeed. And what do you make of Jesus?"

"Son of God, according to the Bible." He struggled to remember his catechism. "You know, Virgin Birth, crucifixion and resurrection, all that."

"And do you believe it to be true?"

"You mean literally? I don't know. My friend Jon does. But I've always approached the stories as metaphor. I look at religion for what it has to teach us about ourselves."

"You see, Doctor? That is precisely where your problem lies. You are not a believer. You only think you are. Now, our friend Joseph here, he is very much a believer." Schaumberg rested his hand on Joseph's shoulder. Joseph shrank from his touch. "In fact, not only is he a believer, but he is also an eyewitness of the majesty and glory of the Lord. The last living apostle, as it were. For Christ Himself said, 'There are some who are standing here who will not taste death until they see the Kingdom come with power.' Is that not so?"

When Joseph didn't answer, Schaumberg turned back to Harry. "Cat's got his tongue. Joseph knows that he must testify to the truth. He cannot stop speaking what he has seen and heard. Not when your salvation is on the line."

"You have no right to talk about salvation." Joseph's

harsh whisper seemed foreboding. The look he gave Schaumberg raised hairs on the back of Harry's neck.

"Oh but don't I? Like you, I am also a believer."

"You believe God is one, you do well," Joseph quoted. "Even the demons believe, and they tremble."

"So they do. But I am not a demon. I am, however, a man who takes the words of Jesus literally." Schaumberg moved away from Joseph and took a seat across the aisle. "When He says, 'Some will not taste death,' I know of whom He speaks. I know He did many miracles, even raised the dead. His power was in His touch, such that even a woman who had a hemorrhage for twelve years had merely to touch the hem of His garment, no doubt coated in His sweat, and she was infected by Him and thereby cured. There never has been, nor will there be again a man like Jesus of Nazareth, a man who could heal with a touch, and bring back the dead with a prayer.

"Where did He get such magical power? From God? God doesn't do magic. He does not break His own laws. Therefore, He must work His will through the laws of nature, which means there must be a mechanism through which this healing power was manifested. Now, the scriptures tell us again and again salvation is in His blood. That's where His power lay, within His blood, suffused within His very body. And how many times, Dr. Bryce, have you kneeled before the priest as he placed the wafer on your tongue and uttered the phrase '*Hoc est enim corpus meum,*'? This is His body. This is His blood. Such a precious gift, poured out upon the world, to bring it healing? Perhaps things didn't turn out as planned."

Harry watched as Joseph fumed beneath Schaumberg's words. The old man's angry stare bore into the geneticist, but Schaumberg showed no signs of stopping. Perhaps his heart was already frozen beyond warming by a heated counter-argument.

"The Christ suffered under Pontius Pilate, was crucified and buried in this man's tomb." Schaumberg wagged a finger at Joseph. "But what became of the precious blood that could heal, cure any disease? All four Gospels tell us that Joseph of Arimathea asked for the body of Jesus and washed it and laid it in his own tomb. And you know, it's still there. Joseph's tomb. They built a church over it, of course, which is just fine, because I don't suppose he'll Joseph will ever need it."

He turned to Joseph. "But that's where it happened. The first real communion. What was it Jesus said? 'Whoever eats my flesh and drinks my blood has eternal life.' Did you remember those words as you prepared His body? You took that most Holy Communion. Can you now call it a curse, because the consequences were exactly as Jesus said they would be?"

Joseph raised himself up in his seat. "You accuse me now of cannibalizing Christ? It's not the first time that accusation has been leveled at Christians—"

"Indeed," said Schaumberg.

"—And it was false then. It is false now!"

Harry intervened. "Dr. Schaumberg, this is really quite

absurd. Your ignorance is inexcusable! The Wandering Jew and Joseph of Arimathea are two completely unrelated myths. The Jew's name was Cartaphilus. He was a porter in Pilate's service, or possibly a cobbler, and when Jesus was going to be crucified, he said, 'Go faster, Jesus, why dost thou linger?' According to the myth, Jesus looked at him and said, 'I will go on, but you will linger till the last day.' Later, Cartaphilus became a believer, was baptized and given the name 'Joseph' by Ananias. But for the coincidence of their names they are unrelated. Why you don't know this is beyond me. My freshmen could have learned that with a little research."

"In which case, doctor, they would have learned precisely what was meant them to learn, the misinformation my former employers have been feeding to the world for centuries. You say my ignorance is inexcusable? I say it is yours that needs excuse."

Schaumberg opened Joseph's shirt. "Look again, doctor. You know what this is." He pointed to the symbol tattooed on Joseph's chest, a seven-pointed star.

Harry scowled. "He could've gotten that anywhere."

"Now who's being ignorant?"

"Fine then. Joe, where did you get the tattoo?"

"Yes, Joe," Schaumberg sneered. "Where did you get such a symbol? Tell us the truth."

"Truth?" Joseph fumed. "You wouldn't know Truth if He stood here in the room. You think you can demand the gift of God, that you can rape the Holy Spirit of His power, and take by force what does not belong to you? You reach out to the heavens, but you will be thrust down into the depths."

Schaumberg narrowed his eyes. "We shall see, wanderer. Dr. Bryce, this symbol. What do you know of it?"

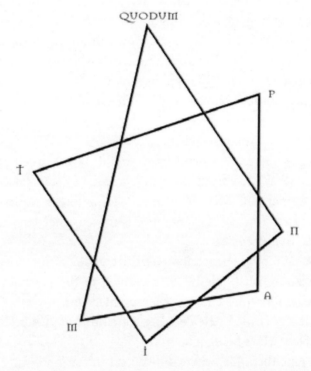

"Ah, well, the septagram is an ancient symbol. Inverted, it's been abused by pagans and Gnostic pretenders like Alistair Crowley, but originally it was an ancient symbol of Christian protection, which is why the septagram is still used in law-enforcement today."

"And what of this one?" Schaumberg persisted.

Harry stared into the darkness outside the windows, feeling suddenly out of his depth, despite everything he knew. Schaumberg's arguments were perversely logical, but plainly preposterous, the product of a deranged and desperate mind. Surely there couldn't be anything to them. He cleared his throat and said, "It appears only a few times in literature, usually in obscure documents, such as those belonging to alchemists like Newton or Bacon. Always it depicted an ancient order of the Church, obscure enough to rival the secret societies of Europe. An order whose existence predates even the council of Nicea, said to protect... the Grail." He looked up, studying Joseph. "They were thought to be extinguished by the Muslims. Some say by the Knights Templar. Some say they became the Knights Templar, after Hugues de Payens and Godfrey de Saint-Omer convinced them to take up the sword in defense of Christendom."

"And what else?"

He shrugged. "That's it. That's all I know. It's just a legend, really."

"What of the word? Quodum? It's Latin. What does it refer to?"

"I have no idea."

"The letters at the points?"

"I said I don't know!" Harry threw up his hands. Schaumberg opened his mouth, as if he wanted to say something further, but then closed it again. Instead, he pulled a photograph out of his back pocket and handed it over to Harry. It showed a small child with a large, bald head, wide eyes, and a faint smile. His skin looked wrinkled.

"My son, Collin, from my second marriage." Schaumberg said. "He suffers from Progeria."

"Progeria." He felt sorry for the boy. "This is why you're so adamant."

"Yes," he sighed. "It causes advanced aging. He was seven when that photograph was taken. He turns eleven this September. And he hasn't much time left."

"I'm very sorry for your... it must be quite painful." He wanted to add, "But that's no excuse," then thought better of it.

Schaumberg took the photo back. "I've spent the last ten years looking for a cure. We've identified the cause. A single mutation on the Lamin A gene renders his cells unstable. The nuclei in his cells cannot hold together, leading to the appearance of premature aging. They've been making advances with farnesyltransferase inhibitors. The drugs show promise in correcting the cell defects that cause the disease. They're conducting human trials..."

"Weren't you able to get him on the trial?" asked Bryce.

"It was one of the first things I did. But that's when I learned the awful truth. It was a double-blind study. My son was receiving the placebo." He looked at his hands. "There was nothing I could do. Take him off the trial, he loses hope. Switch the drugs, and we lose the study. I had to look elsewhere." He nodded at Joseph. "And that is what led me to you, my ancient friend.

"I was researching aging. Reversing its effects. We had

breakthroughs with various genes, telomere lengthening, following on the excellent research coming out of Sierra Sciences, but then we hit a brick wall. This led me to Triprimacon. I tried to get them to fund Dr. Andrews' work on the matter, but they wouldn't hear of it. Something about proprietary research. At any rate, Triprimacon believes they can best prepare for the future by studying the past. I was willing to try anything. They showed me there is no reason to dismiss ancient miracles besides pure prejudice. Simply because we have not encountered the mechanism by which miracles operate does not mean they cannot happen. Nor should a scientific explanation invalidate the miraculous. On the contrary, it establishes it. The simple reality is this: even God follows natural law."

"Or rather, natural law follows God," corrected Joseph. "He created it, after all."

"Either way, as I said, He does not do magic. He does not suspend His own laws. How could He, if He is eternal? So if Jesus could heal the sick and raise the dead, there must be a mechanism by which this operates. I'll admit, I was as skeptical as the doubt I see written on your face, Dr. Bryce. At first we thought it must be a virus or a prion, something that interacts with our DNA that gave Him this power, but we could find no evidence in the blood we tested."

"The blood of Christ?" exclaimed Harry.

"Yes. Samples taken from the Shroud of Turin, the Sudarium of Oviedo, the Image of Edessa—but the DNA was too degraded. The proteins had collapsed. There remained, however, another possibility: a supply of blood still in serum form. That is what we hope to find. And if we do, we just might save my son." He turned to Joseph. "I know you know where it is. You will help me find it."

EIGHTEEN

JON ROLLED OVER on the floor, his head pounding, a shrill tone ringing ceaselessly in his ears. A moment later, the room filled with a noxious, opaque cloud. His eyes and throat burned as he tried to crawl away from the blast. He coughed, but it did nothing to ease the raw fire in his throat. Through the milky veil in his eyes, he saw Sean lying face down on the rug, unconscious. The floor vibrated with heavy footsteps. Someone dressed in black had thrown Izzy over his shoulder and was carrying her out. The urge to defend her pulled Jon to his feet, but a sudden blow to the back of his head drove him to his knees. He saw stars, then nothing.

When he opened his eyes again, Sean was gone. He groaned and pushed himself into a sitting position. The lights were out, as was the fire, and a cool breeze blew through the room. The front door hung wide open, swaying gently in the morning breeze. He rose to his feet and shut it, then turned on the overhead lamp and surveyed the damage.

The couch was still upended from when Sean had flipped it on its back. The remains of the coffee table lay on the floor in a splintered heap. The percussion grenade had shattered the picture window. Fragments of glass littered the floor and carpet like landmines of shiny crystal daggers. He stooped down and started picking them up.

"Don't bother." Sean stood in the hallway, holding a blood-soaked rag to his forehead.

"This *DuChamp* did this, didn't he?" Jon dropped the fragments where he stood and glared at Sean. "How'd they find us—?"

"Don't know."

"You have to know." He waved angrily at the room. Why'd he take Izzy? All he wanted was the manuscript. Why didn't he just take it and go?"

Sean winced at his verbal assault and replied in a quiet voice. "He did. Taking Izzy might've been his way a' rubbing her nose in it, yeah? He'll rightly interrogate her—try to find out what she was after. DuChamp's arrogant, but he's sharp as a knife to whit. He made both our safe houses, took us out the second time without tipping his hand. I'll give him this: he's a quick study, that one is."

Jon removed the rag from Sean's head and examined the wound. He'd have a scar for certain. Sean held up a pair of butterfly bandages to him.

"Now what do we do?" Jon asked as he applied the bandages to the wound. "We're supposed to be looking for Bryce, and now we've got to find Izzy, too?"

"Aye. That about sums it up. But here's the thing: don't be underestimating the lady. She's always a step or two ahead. She'll know we'll try to get her back, which means she'll lead them exactly where we were going anyway. It's our best chance of finding her."

"And where is that?"

"Bruges, Belgium. It's where they're taking your friend Bryce."

"How do you know?"

"It's best you don't know. Let's just say I've a friend what owes me a favor. He's been keeping tabs on 'em for me."

Jon shook his head. "What's in Bruges?"

"God knows. But as that's where they've gone, that's where we'll need to be heading, yeah?"

They left the house in a hurry, not even bothering to close the doors or lock up. Sean grabbed a narrow strip of metal from the trunk of the Volkswagen and tossed the car keys into the bushes, then led Jon on foot for a block before stopping beside a small Toyota. Jon watched, curiosity turning to fear as Sean inserted the metal strip down the edge of the passenger side window, unlocking the car with a quick turn of his wrist. The mercenary scrambled across the front seat, popped the ignition switch, and a moment later, the Camry roared to life.

Jon blanched. Now they were car thieves? "What about the Beetle?"

"Either bugged or bombed. Can't take a chance either way."

"But stealing a car?"

"Can't be helped. Get in."

Jon hesitated, but Sean grabbed his arm and tugged him inside, and then tore away from the curb.

He pulled onto the expressway, following I-94 west into Chicago. Three-and-a-half hours later, they turned north just past the Gary-Chicago airport into East Chicago and pulled off into a desolate stretch of empty warehouses and weed-strewn parking lots, where Sean parked the car. Jon shifted nervously in his seat, wondering just what sort of area Sean was taking them. From all appearances, it looked just like the kind of place he generally preferred to avoid.

The street was dark, save for a single streetlamp casting pale light across the pitted concrete and asphalt. Beyond the streetlight's reach, inky shadows lurked behind brick corners and weathered street awnings. Sean glanced down either side of the alleyway before leading Jon farther into the blackness. He stopped before a nondescript, steel door with narrow bars across its boxy window and pounded it hard. The noise resounded through the alley. It would doubtless draw attention to their presence, if anyone besides the rats were watching. Jon wished he'd stayed in the car. "What is this place?"

"The reason I don't go to East Chicago." Sean pounded a second time. An instant later he raised his fist to hit it a third time, but a fluorescent light winked on in the rear of the shop.

"It's about bloody time," Sean muttered.

A moment later the sound of four locks turning echoed in the alleyway, and the steel door ponderously swung open.

On the other side, a squat man in a T-shirt and boxers, wide glasses, and a thin bathrobe gave them a disgusted look, then turned to one side and let them in.

The shop's interior was a dingy array of cheap candy, booze, cigarettes, and porn. The shopkeeper closed and locked the door behind them and stood regarding them for a long, silent moment, his arms folded.

"Well," he finally said. "Ain'tcha got nothing to say?"

"Hello, Dad," Sean replied.

Jon sat in the basement of the shop, trying to reconcile the disparate images of Sean and his stepfather, Patrick O'Shaughnessy. The two couldn't have been more dissimilar, and he wondered if Sean took after his father, and if that wasn't why Sean's mother had married such a different man. A lot of unpleasant history had passed between Sean and his stepfather. Jon found himself on the outside of most of their conversation, barely able to follow it.

"How's Mum?"

Patrick snorted. "Getting along. She'll be pleased as pie to see you. Tell you that for nuthin'."

Sean shook his head. "I'm sure she would be, but we have no time. You understand."

"Understand? Aye, more than you know." He took a long swig from a bottle of Glenlivet and looked him in the eye. "You need to quit this business, Sean, afore it takes your life, like it took Daniel's."

"Daniel died fightin' for what he believed in, which is a lot more than can be said for a sot like you," he shot back.

Patrick chuckled, apparently taking this in stride. "Ah, Sean, my boy. Still angry after all these years."

Sean made an unpleasant and anatomically impossible suggestion.

"Oh," exclaimed Patrick. "It touches my heart to know how much you care."

Sean shot to his feet. "This is pointless," he muttered. "Come on, we'll go someplace else."

Jon rose uncertainly. Patrick thunked the bottle down on the table. "Now why would ya be rushing off? Just as I was warming up to your company."

"Because we haven't got time for you and your shenanigans, Patrick! We've got a woman what's missing, and we've got to be about finding her, now, haven't we?"

"A woman is it? Why didn't you say so in the first place? Let it never be said that Patrick O'Shaughnessy refused to help a damsel in distress."

He ushered Sean back into his seat and began rummaging through the drawers in his workbench. Jon leaned over and whispered to Sean.

"Just curious. How much is this gonna cost?"

Sean shook his head. "Nothing. He'll do it for free now. There's two things you can bank on in this world," he ticked them off on his fingers, "Patrick O'Shaughnessy's love of the drink and his Irish pride."

"So all that was an act? To get him to help us?"

"Oh yeah. Of course," he muttered.

Patrick turned around. "Here we are," he said, holding out two passports. "Now, you don't breathe a word of this to your mum, hear?"

"On my honor," Sean replied, accepting the passports.

Jon opened his, staring at the face inside. "Who's this?"

"That's you," Patrick replied.

"This guy looks nothing like me."

"Well, we don't all age gracefully, do we?"

ΠΙΠΕΤΕΕΠ

I ZZY WOKE WITH a start and stared without recognition across the room at the dresser against the far wall. It was built of oak and ornately designed, with an antique mirror mounted above it. A silver-handled brush and matching comb lay atop of the dresser, next to a ceramic pitcher and teacup. She looked up, seeing a canopy above, and realized she was in a four-poster bed with cotton sheets and a floral comforter. Beside the bed stood an end table with a silver alarm clock ticking on one side and an easy chair next to an unlit fireplace. She frowned, remembering neither the room nor how she came to be in it.

The clock read eight a.m., and daylight streamed through the lace curtains over the window. She pushed her legs off the bed, stunned to realize she wore a silk nightgown. Her cocktail dress had been cleaned and pressed, and was draped over the back of the chair, along with her undergarments. Flushing with embarrassment, she dressed quickly and moved to the window, which was locked. Two stories below, a manicured lawn stretched to a hedge of cypress trees, thick with Spanish moss, which grew just past a high stone wall at the far end of the yard.

She turned and leaned against the wall. Whoever

kidnapped her and brought her to this southern plantation had wanted her to feel at least somewhat comfortable, but putting her in a nightgown and washing her clothes was less about comfort than control, under the guise of civility.

On a nearby table, an unmarked envelope caught her attention. She opened it.

Checkmate. Breakfast will be served promptly at eight o' clock. P.D.

Pierre DuChamp.

She crumpled the note in her fist, strode resolutely to the door, and flung it open. She poked her head into the hallway, looking both ways before catching a whiff of crepes, bacon, and fresh coffee. Her stomach rumbled.

Whatever his faults, DuChamp's ego would not permit him to serve less than the best. No doubt he found this whole thing rather humorous and was looking forward to gloating.

She followed her nose, navigating through the empty hallway to a flight of stairs winding down. At the bottom was an empty foyer with a glass front door looking out on a stone walkway. Across the hall stood a pair of closed, wooden double doors. The smell of breakfast emanated from within.

She hesitated. Undoubtedly, the front door would be unlocked, and if she chose to run through it and make her escape, no one would try and stop her. DuChamp had what he wanted. He had the page from the *Flores Historiarum*, even if he didn't realize its significance. What he was offering was something else—the opportunity for her to be recognized as a worthy, if defeated, competitor.

She glanced between both doors, and smiled when she

realized which would give him less satisfaction. Shaking her head, she pulled open the door to the dining room and stepped inside.

At the far end of an elegant table filled with steaming, covered dishes and sterling silver flatware sat Pierre DuChamp, dressed smartly in a sport jacket and sweater. He spoke discreetly with one of his servants.

She clapped loudly and slowly, drawing their attention. DuChamp glanced up, and his expression flashed disappointment before broadening into a wide smile.

"Miss Kaufman! How kind of you to join us."

"Congratulations, Pierre."

He waved it off with false modesty. She knew it was what he really wanted to hear. "Oh, come now, have some breakfast. You must be hungry. You've had quite a night."

"Have I? Would you care to clarify?"

"Whatever do you mean?"

"I woke up in a nightgown, Pierre. That's low, even for you."

"Oh my dear Isabel, on my honor I took no advantage at all. I merely wished you to have clean things to wear."

"Why do I find that hard to believe?"

He blushed and grinned sheepishly. "Well, I confess that I did enjoy the view, but I promise that is as far as it went."

"You're a pig."

"My dear, I am a man. And you are far too beautiful a woman to not appreciate, given the chance."

"Nice try. You're still a pig."

He scratched his ear. "Would you like some coffee?"

"I'd like to know what happened to my men."

"Oh, you mean the two gentlemen who were with you? We left them unmolested, which is a lot more than I can say for what you did to mine. Honestly, Izzy, blowing up the house on them? That's excessive, even for you."

"It's not like you left me much choice. You came after me with armed men."

"Of course I did. You have a face that would launch a thousand ships, my dear. Sending a small strike team after you seems restrained, if you ask me. At any rate, you did have a choice. You could have conceded the inevitable long before it came down to this. Now you've lost two houses and the manuscript. Whatever will you do?"

She crossed her arms. "So what happens now?"

"Now? Now is time for breakfast. Please sit and eat. The eggs are getting cold and the coffee is quite good."

She rolled her eyes and came around the table to the place-setting at his right hand. Pierre snapped his fingers, and the waiter came forward, poured her coffee and uncovered the plate of Eggs Benedict, bacon and crepes. He served her a generous portion, then retreated to the background.

"I'm so glad you could join me," said DuChamp.

"Cut the crap, Pierre. What do you really want?"

"Well, now that I have your manuscript, I wonder what you'd be willing to pay for its return."

She scowled. "You want me to pay to get my own property back?"

"Delicious, isn't it?"

"What do you want for it?"

"Hmm." He ogled her chest. "I could think of some interesting methods of payment, but what I'm most interested in right now is information."

She picked up her knife, fingering the edge. It was unfortunately rather dull. She put it down again. "What kind of information?"

"Isabel Kaufman, sister of the late archaeologist Dr. Steven Kaufman—a known fraud—burst onto the antiquities scene two years ago, procuring a fortune by selling off pages of very old New Testament manuscripts. Some reputed to be the oldest ever found. Through this she becomes extremely wealthy, extremely popular, earning her the attention of several well-known, very eligible bachelors—all of whom she turns down—as she gains her confidence by dabbling in modest purchases in the art world. Nothing too extravagant. Nothing terribly discriminating or discerning. Clearly an amateur who has been incredibly lucky.

"Then quite suddenly, without any explanation at all, she dumps a load of pages on the market, earning herself a sizable fortune while at the same time diminishing the value of the earlier pages she has already sold—a move even a fourth-rate accountant would advise against—all of which suggests she is amassing a slush fund. But for what purpose?

"She makes no purchases for the next six months, until at long last she shows up at Sotheby's in London and makes a bid on a rare and probably spurious thirteenth-century manuscript, for which she pays an enormous sum, massively outbidding even the most determined investors.

"All of which brings us to my question: why? Tell me that, and I will gladly return your manuscript."

She gaped at him. "You did all this to satisfy your curiosity?"

"Yes. And I would do it again."

"You could've just asked me."

"Truth is a rare and costly commodity. One simply does not give it away. It must be earned. If I had simply asked you, you would have thought up a clever lie and expected me to be content with your deception. After all, simple truth does not allow someone to remain loyal to a known fraudster, or to acquire a hoard of precious manuscripts." He took a sip of coffee. "Now that I possess what you have struggled so hard to acquire and paid so dearly to own, I think you will tell me the truth. Because if you do not, you will never see your precious manuscript again."

Izzy leaned back in her chair. DuChamp may have liked to play hardball, but he had no idea what he was up against. On the other hand, he just might be of use after all.

She leaned her elbows on the table. "What if I told you that you could keep the manuscript?"

He choked on his coffee. "Oh, you *are* into something deep, aren't you?"

She leaned over seductively and traced a single finger across the flaccid skin of his cheek. "If you want to know why, Pierre, you're going to have to offer me more than something I no longer need…" she tapped his lips and he trembled, "or have ever desired."

DuChamp leaned back in his chair and grinned, "Oh, my dear, this is going to be so much fun."

TWENTY

Peter Schaumberg left the back of the plane and returned to the cockpit. He sat in the co-pilot's seat next to Evelyn.

"That was dramatic," she said.

"Perhaps. Think he bought it?"

"Which part? The part about Joseph being the Wandering Jew, or the part about you believing he's the Wandering Jew?"

"That one."

"Maybe. I almost began to believe it myself. You missed your calling. You should've been an actor."

"Hmm. All those years wasted as a geneticist. Saving people's lives." He nodded at the intercom. "Are they talking?"

"Starting to."

He slipped on the second pair of headphones and listened intently.

Harry shook his head. "The man is desperate."

"Grief will do that," Joseph agreed. "What he said about me, it isn't true."

"Of course it isn't true. Don't be ridiculous." Harry fidgeted in his seat. "Out of curiosity, what is the truth? About you? Your…"

The old man smiled. "My name is Isaac. It's also Joseph. I had it legally changed when I came to America. Isaac Lake. According to family legend, I am the sixteenth generation from the original Isaac Lakedion, who was himself descended from Joseph of Arimathea."

Harry stared. "Are you serious?"

Joseph nodded. "It's a legend only, passed down from father to son. Dr. Schaumberg has confused it with history."

"Go on."

"There isn't much more to say."

"Oh, that's a matter of perspective, isn't it? How did Schaumberg learn of your family's legend?"

"I don't know."

"There must be more."

Joseph laughed. "Yes, I suppose so. You're a historian, yes?"

"I am, after a fashion."

"According to the legend, history only tells half the story. My family's story is sweeping. So many myths are wrapped up in it. It is hard to separate truth from fantasy."

"Well, this is part of what I do, as a historian and a student of the Middle Ages. Tell me about your family."

"The family legend says the Holy Grail really exists, or rather, it did for a time. If they found it today, they would not recognize it. It would not do what they wished. Joseph, my alleged ancestor, collected and preserved the blood of

Jesus in a pair of cruets. He brought them to Glastonbury, England in 97 A.D."

"Yes, I've heard this part."

"Indeed? I've never looked to see if any of this was true."

"Yes," said Harry, sitting up. "This legend is told by John of Glastonbury, and also William of Malmesbury, in his Chronicles of the English Kings."

"Interesting. At any rate, before Joseph died, he entrusted the cruets to a fellow disciple, Saint Maximim. Maximim founded the order in which Joseph's grandson would later take part. Seven disciples devoted themselves to protecting the cruets of Saint Joseph, for which purpose they chose a seven-pointed star, as much because there were seven of them as because of the seven days of the week. The number meant they would not slumber nor rest while the cruets lay in their keeping.

"Eventually it was decided to secure the cruets in a safe location, originally a cave in a mountain, as my father told me, allowing the keepers to rest. Each new generation is given the star at their maturity, the star which reveals where the cruets are kept."

Harry held up a finger. "Are you telling me this is the origin of the myth of the Seven Sleepers? Or of the six knights of Barbarossa, the king under the mountain?"

Joseph pursed his lips. "It's possible. I only know what my father taught me. But as to what it means? I am as much at a loss as you or anyone. It's only a legend now, anyway. And it will die with me, as it should. If there ever were relics, then let them be lost forever. I doubt they should ever have been kept in the first place. They have caused my family no small amount of trouble. Perhaps as we end, so should they."

"In all those years, if these relics were such a cause of trouble, why not find them and destroy them?"

"They are not mine to destroy. They did not belong to any of the seven, either. Even if I possessed such hubris, as I told you, I don't know where they are."

"You said they were in Glastonbury."

"I said they were brought to Glastonbury, yes. But they did not stay there."

"So what happened to them?"

Joseph shrugged and fell silent, and after a moment, Harry decided not to press him on the matter. He turned around in his seat and stared out the window, wondering how long before he'd be able to get home again.

Frederick closed the door to his condominium and locked the deadbolt. He then swung a heavy, iron bar over the door and latched it into place. It didn't matter if the company had a key or not—which he was sure they did—they weren't getting into his home without his permission.

He turned to a panel on the wall beside the door and switched on a recorded loop. Six months ago he'd discovered the redundant video and audio feeds coming from the electronic bugs scattered throughout his home. It had taken him better than two weeks to find them all, and two months more to successfully hack into their individual feeds and plant an audio-video loop of himself doing practically nothing for a week. The playback days were randomized, meaning no two weeks of recordings were ever exactly the same. He supposed a careful analysis of the captured data might expose his cover up, but that was unlikely. More to the point, who would confront him about it? The spying was supposed to be a secret. That they hadn't managed it successfully was hardly his fault—and what would they think of him if he did discover their surveillance and failed to act accordingly?

With his home and privacy secure, he swept over to the bar and poured himself a straight shot of vodka. He'd acquired the taste during his assignment in Russia, where he'd also hired Vasily and seen to it the former agent was properly equipped.

Watching himself in the mirror, he toasted the agent and smiled wickedly. It had been a long night, toying with Casper, watching the man wriggle and fret as his scheme came apart. After driving around town for the better part of the evening while Casper burned off steam, he'd finally convinced the old man to let him take him home. The sun was just starting to brighten the horizon when he finally got away, hiking across town to his own condominium.

In a way, he'd almost pitied the man. Casper was clearly out of his depth. The old man was all about control, but he failed to understand what would happen when he played against an equal partner. Let alone a superior player.

Frederick always lost at chess when he played Casper. Deliberately. This led the old man into a false sense of security, a belief that he knew all the possible moves Frederick might make, ignoring the strategies Frederick actually employed because he believed them beyond Frederick's imagination.

There were twenty distinct possible moves in chess after the first piece was played. The next possible combination jumped to four hundred. After seven moves, the numbers exceeded three billion. Such possibilities were beyond Casper's thinking, which explained why he could not imagine that he, Frederick, prompted Schaumberg to defect in the first place. How could Casper know that Frederick had manipulated the drug trial, ensuring that Schaumberg's son Collin received the placebo, and then had made the information available for Schaumberg to find?

Already he was three moves ahead before Casper even realized the game had begun. And now, with Vasily sent to "assist" the Cleaners in Europe, his black knight would ensure that Schaumberg would complete his mission and deliver the formula, where he, Frederick, would become its sole possessor.

Everything was proceeding according to plan.

Alexandre Dumont put down his Blackberry and took a long sip of coffee. He stared across the promenade at the row of cars parked along the *Torhoutse Steenweg* on the outskirts of Bruges. Behind him, a lone train waited on the tracks for someone to notice it. It had been there for days, he knew, and would not likely be moving any time in the near future.

Above him, the sky was a deep, azure vault, with only scattered clouds gracing the mid-afternoon air. He vented a long breath and glanced at his watch, silently cursing the men in their suits for this vulgar inconvenience. The train had all the time in the world. He did not.

A little more notice might have given him more time to prepare, to act accordingly. Then he could have taken his stroll at an earlier hour and not lost this moment, the one highlight to his day. As it was, the clock continued its interminable sweep, ticking the seconds away into minutes, eroding his break.

They should never have moved the company to the States. Already they'd adopted the American bad habit of rushing, of wanting things now. Soon all beauty, poetry, and meaning would be swept away by the American passion for efficiency, replaced by cold pragmatism. Did they think it was easy, cleaning up after their mess? He and his men practiced their art with a delicate precision, removing targets with a minimum of fuss, stress, witnesses, or blood. Such precision took careful planning.

Quel est l'amour? C'est quoi création? C'est quoi aspirent? Quelle est une étoile? he thought, remembering his Nietzsche. *What is love? What is creation? What is longing? What is a star?*

These were *la dernière hommes,* the last men. That was who he worked for. Men of *ennui*, bereft of all that makes men men. They had no concept of the difficulties of his job, nor how their petty interferences made life difficult for all.

He glanced at his watch again. He was out of time.

It made no difference. The day was spoiled already. He picked up his Blackberry and forwarded the email with its attached jpegs to a select contact list with a simple message. *L'aéroport. Immédiatement.*

Tossing the half-drunk beverage in a waste bin, he climbed into his Audi and tore off down the street, heading west.

TWENTY-ONE

JON STRUGGLED TO keep up with the mercenary. The man moved like a snake, weaving through the arriving crowds of business men and women, tourists and students, dodging human obstacles as he thrust forward toward the car rentals. Above them, the ceiling of *Brussel Nationale Aéroport* curved in a gentle arc of gray, tubular girders beneath a corrugated steel roof, making Jon feel as though he were walking through a large, tricked-out drainpipe. The polished floor tiles caught the reflections from halogen ceiling lights and pink neon signs, written conveniently in English. All along the corridor, yellow arrows pointed the way to various arrival and departure terminals. Far above, banners of happy people drinking beer smiled down upon them, inviting newcomers to imbibe and support the local economy.

Jon caught up with Sean as he slowed before the Hertz counter. One couple stood ahead of them.

"Can't believe you told them that," Sean muttered.

"It was all I could think of!"

"Rule number one." Sean held up a finger. "You never draw attention to yourself. You don't tell a customs agent 'we don't all age well,' under any circumstances."

"What else was I supposed to do?"

"Nothing. Act normal."

"That was normal."

"Normal? You even looked guilty."

"That's because I am," Jon hissed. His voice seemed to echo from the floor and steel.

"Yes, but you don't think about it. You think about why we're here. Stay focused on the mission. It will keep you calm."

"Sorry. It's just that last time I jumped a border I was hiding in a car being chased by a madman. Oh wait, that was you!"

"Don't get cute."

Jon bit back an appropriately sarcastic reply. Sean's tone was dark, grimmer than usual. He'd been that way ever since they left Patrick O'Shaughnessy's shop. Jon wondered if Sean was genuinely worried for Izzy, or if it was something else.

The couple ahead of them moved on, and they stepped up to the counter. Sean obtained the keys to a Mercedes and looked pointedly at Jon when the clerk asked for a credit card.

"Are you serious?"

"I don't carry credit cards, for obvious reasons."

"How do you get around?" he asked. Sean grimaced, and Jon remembered the Toyota. "Never mind," he said, retrieving his wallet. Fifteen minutes later, they were on the road.

The plane touched down a little after three in the afternoon. Harry and Joseph had quit talking shortly after sighting the coast of France an hour earlier. Once on the tarmac, the plane taxied to a private hanger. The Schaumbergs hustled Bryce and Joseph into a private car with tinted windows and drove toward the city.

Bruges rose before them as a centuries-old assemblage of storied brick buildings with red, gabled roofs. Baroque cathedrals punctured the heavens with jagged towers, asserting their faith to the constant sky. Cobblestone homes brooded over placid waterways, while gray brick streets meandered by gaily painted shops and eateries.

Billed as the Venice of the north, the city took the rough shape of an egg. Long ago, the residents dissected the remains of the Reie River into four canals of green water, the Langerei, the Potterierei by the shipyards, the Spiegelrei and the Spinolarei. The canals now bordered and split the city, compelling low, arched bridges of stone to stitch the community together and append it to the surrounding countryside.

Harry sat sandwiched between William and the door, with Joseph on the other side. Dr. Schaumberg rode in front, and Evelyn drove. Harry briefly considered opening the door and flinging himself onto the pavement to get away, but their relative speed dissuaded him. *That*, he thought, *and they've probably engaged the child safety locks.* Instead, he stared around at the city streets until his curiosity got the better of him. "Where are you taking us?"

Schaumberg glanced over the seat. "St. Basil's Chapel."

"Do you think maybe we could get some food while we're here?"

"This isn't a sightseeing trip."

"No, of course not. It's just that I am diabetic, and it's been awhile since I've eaten." His voice grew fainter toward the end.

William piped up, "I could go for some grub."

Schaumberg shot him a dark look. Evelyn touched her grandfather's arm. "It's not a bad idea."

He grimaced. "We'll see what we can do."

They entered the city from the southwest, passing by t' Zand Square, an open expanse of brick pavement on which a set of four bronze sculptures beside bubbling fountains drew tourists and amateur photographers. Turning up the Zuidzandstraat, they followed it past the cathedral of Sint-Salvator, where the street plunged northward past the Grote Markt. Here, a panoply of sixteen flags fluttered around a central court with a large statue in the center. Along the northern perimeter, an array of eateries and cafés with green awnings and numerous tables beneath red, yellow, gray, green, and burgundy umbrellas invited them to stop.

Evelyn parked the car near the Provincial Court, an imposing castle of arched windows, flying buttresses, and layered balconies, and climbed out. Harry tried his door, confirming his suspicions from earlier. It was locked. William tapped his arm.

"Don't be getting no ideas, now," he growled.

Evelyn returned a few moments later with two bags of burgers and fries. Harry unwrapped his sandwich, took a large bite and said, "Nothing quite like European cuisine."

"Just eat," Schaumberg sighed.

"Seriously. We've come all this way. We're in Belgium, of all places. You'd think we could at least get something besides fast food."

"Hey," Evelyn said, "it's food, okay? I did the best I could."

They ate quickly, but not quite sufficiently for Harry's taste, and then climbed out of the car. William took both Harry and Joseph by the arm and steered them both forward. Schaumberg led them a short distance down a narrow alley named Breidelstraat, and then to the massive, stone basilica that opened up before them on the right.

The Heiligbloodbasiliek, or Basilica of the Holy Blood, was a Romanesque chapel built of dark stone with polished gilt statues above a large door. A second, smaller red door stood locked beside it. The façade of the building was dwarfed by the massive, whitewashed brick of the town hall immediately to its left, replete with statuettes of Thierry of Alsace and other royals of antiquity.

The group thrust their way into the main, upper chapel of the basilica, ascending the stairs into a gilded hall, crowded together like a pack of tourists. Harry stared at the room, his breath taken away. Grapevines painted on the columns and arched ceiling supports glowed with the light from the stained glass windows. Every conceivable surface of the walls displayed garish images of saints and royalty. Even the support beams of the ceiling were lined in gold. Immediately before them sat an enormous altar, featuring a replica of a cathedral with numerous peaks housing images of the apostles and Belgian royalty. In the center was the crucified Christ. Six candles graced the sides, three on each side, and just in front of it sat the reliquary housing the Holy Blood. The reliquary resembled the ark of the covenant, with two cherubim above it in gold. A pair of gold cabinet doors stood beneath the cherubim. Within it, Harry surmised, lay the vial containing the Holy Blood.

Or what was reputed to be the blood, anyway.

"So," he said, "this chapel houses the relic of the Holy Blood? Washed from the body of Christ by Joseph of Arimathea," he glanced at Joseph, "and preserved for over a thousand years until Thierry of Alsace happened to stumble upon it during the Crusades? It makes you wonder. How much did Thierry pay for it, and was the king of Jerusalem laughing all the way to the bank? Or perhaps some enterprising Moor?"

Schaumberg glanced back as the last of the other tourists disappeared down the stairs. "We've already confirmed the blood is real."

"So what do you need me for?"

"Clues, Dr. Bryce. The basilica is a clue. We know that much. We don't know what the clue is, or where it points us. That's why you're here."

Harry gaped. "I'm just supposed to figure out a clue from all this?" He waved around at the chapel. "You're not giving me a whole lot to go on."

"Then try this: *Sanctus fontis ex Brugge fluo*," said Schaumberg.

"The sacred fountain from Bruges flows," Harry translated. "What's that from?"

"An unpublished manuscript of Paracelsus."

"That could mean anything!"

"Dr. Bryce," Evelyn approached. "Assume for a moment the sacred blood has been preserved, but not just here. Assume also that Thierry of Alsace at least knew where the cruets were being kept, and that he built this chapel to point his descendents to it."

"Thierry of Alsace fought in the Second Crusade," Harry muttered, "bringing back the relic after their defeat by the Turks." His voice trailed off, then frustration took over. "There are so many relics! No less than thirty nails are venerated as being one of the three or four used to crucify Christ. Holy Blood relics are found in France, Germany, Italy, and Spain," he pointed to the reliquary, "not to mention, Belgium! What makes this place so special that it stands out against Weingarten Abbey, or the Basilica di Sant'Andrea di Mantova?"

"Both Weingarten Abby and Mantova claim their blood from the spear of Longinus. He is said to have pierced Christ's side with the lance, and even to have assisted Joseph in washing the body," Schaumberg replied quietly.

"But Longinus is a myth," Harry rejoined. "The name derives from the Greek Longche, meaning 'spear.' The name wasn't even mentioned until the fourth century." He glanced sidelong at Schaumberg. "You've already ruled them out."

"Rather, Paracelsus did. His quest for the Elixir of Life

took him through all these countries. And always, he was disappointed. Until he realized Thierry of Alsace never possessed the blood, but only wished to point to where it was located."

"And so you think this chapel is the clue."

"A veritable compass, if you know how to read it. And I suggest," he said as he pulled out a gun, "that you try."

TWENTY-TWO

ARRY STARED AT the gun, realizing that Schaumberg just might use it, no matter what assurances Joe had given him on the plane. *Not a killer, indeed*, he thought. Joseph came up beside him, glaring at Schaumberg. "Why don't you put that away?"

"Cooperate, and there'll be no need for it."

"You want him to cooperate? Can he even think with you waving that in his face?"

Evelyn stepped over to her grandfather and whispered something in his ear. He pressed his lips together, and then holstered his gun. Harry let out his breath. He hadn't realized he was holding it.

"All right," said Schaumberg. "William, guard the door. Let's give these gentlemen a chance to think."

William and the Schaumbergs retreated to the back of the chapel and took their own seats, yielding them some space. Joseph steered Harry into a chair and sat beside him.

"I can't do this, Joseph," Harry said, staring at the floor. "I don't know how to find what they're asking me for."

Joseph put a comforting hand on his shoulder. "It is all right. Truly, I would help you if I could." Conspiratorially he whispered, "Except, of course, it would mean helping them."

"You mean you could help, but you won't."

Joseph shrugged. Harry pressed his lips together. Joseph wouldn't give up the information, and he *had* to know what they were looking for. He hadn't gotten that tattoo at a shop in Queens. Harry knew only one way Joseph would have even known about it, let alone had the symbol stained on his chest.

Joseph belonged to a secret society.

But if that meant anything, it meant he wouldn't reveal the secrets even under pain of death. Such strictures were common stock for secret societies, especially one as old as this. He'd probably already told them as much as he was permitted. It didn't surprise Harry that he feigned ignorance now.

Harry sat back and wracked his brain, trying to remember what he knew of the order. There was scant detail in the sources he'd read—whispers of a holy order predating the Knights Templar, dedicated to protecting the Grail. On the whole, he'd dismissed the accounts as somewhat mythical in nature. He never expected to run into someone wearing their seal on his chest.

On the other hand, just because Joseph bore the seal did not mean he was, in fact, a part of the order. Perhaps he only knew about it, or wished to reconstitute it for the modern era, not at all unlike those who claimed to be Wiccans while really following the 1950s imaginings of Gerald Gardner, or even the Freemasons with their pseudo-Egyptian heritage.

He stared up at the ornate ceiling, following the line of images to where they converged on the fresco painted over the back wall of the church. Two paintings composed the fresco. The lower painting showed Thierry of Alsace receiving the blood relic from the Patriarch and King of Jerusalem, and then in another panel giving it to the chaplain here in Bruges, surrounded by his wife and children. Above this, a much larger painting detailed the crucified Christ, embraced by a red-robed figure representing God the Father and gazed upon by the dove of the Holy Spirit. Two angels sat on either side, one above Bethlehem and the other above Jerusalem. Around Him, seven angels waited with chalices, collecting the blood that flowed from his hands, his lanced side, and his feet. Beneath Christ, a fountain flowed, providing water for the sheep at His feet to drink. A verse from the first chapter of Ephesians, stenciled in Latin, ran around the wall beneath it.

Harry stared at the angels, a new thought forming. He turned to Joseph. "The order you serve—it's based on seven protectors, is it not?"

Joseph shrugged.

"Look at the angels."

Joseph studied the painting. Then he said, "Well, I'll be."

"Seven angels—protectors—receiving the blood of Christ. And there's your fountain."

"Perhaps the legend is true."

"At least, someone wanted us to think so. This painting

was finished in 1905. If this part of the story is true, then maybe more of it is as well."

"Meaning?"

"Meaning your tattoo is the key. May I see it again?"

Reluctantly, Joseph opened his shirt, revealing the septagram emblazoned on his chest. Harry pulled out a thin, spiral notebook and pen from his jacket pocket, quickly redrawing the septagram and the symbols that accompanied it.

Harry glanced up when he felt a presence at his elbow. Schaumberg had come over. "Well?"

Harry took off his glasses and polished them on his coat sleeve. "We have two pieces of a puzzle. Joseph's tattoo is one piece. And this," he pointed at the mural on the wall behind them, "is another."

"What about it?" Schaumberg studied the painting.

"Count the angels."

"There are nine."

"Two of them are over the cities of Bethlehem and Jerusalem, covering Jesus' birth and resurrection. What are the rest doing?"

Schaumberg nodded a moment later. "All right. I see your point."

"Do you? Because we're missing another piece. At least. We have no connection between the septagram and the angels. And I don't think we're likely to find one, either."

"And why is that?"

"Because several hundred years have passed since this chapel was built," he blurted. How could this man not understand this? "Unfortunately, whatever clue linked the chapel and Joseph's septagram have likely been lost to time. It isn't here anymore. It doesn't exist."

"What about the lower chapel?" asked Evelyn.

Harry shook his head, and then shrugged. "It's possible."

Schaumberg smiled grimly. "Then why don't we find out?"

Together, they left the upper chapel with its bright colors and garish décor and headed down the steps to the lower chantry. The austere chapel below lay in stark contrast to the gaily-painted room above. Gone were the decorative flowers and ornate stenciling, replaced by drab, gray rock and dark wooden benches arrayed before the altar on a floor of stone. Off to one side, a stone statue of Jesus, bound with ropes, languished beside a row of candles. If the chapel above celebrated Christ triumphant, it was built with the lower chapel as its foundation, revering Him as the Suffering Servant.

Schaumberg and Evelyn held back while Harry surveyed the perimeter of the room. Joseph took a seat on a bench, his head bowed, hands fingering his rosary. Harry wandered through the nave, each of the side aisles, the choir room, and the apse. He spent several minutes poring over the sculpted tympanum of Saint Basil's baptism and the statue of Mary with the Christ Child in the right aisle, as well as the Chapel of Saint Yves, which housed the relics of Saint Basil himself, built in 1504.

After forty-five minutes, he came back to them, shaking his head. "I give up," he announced, and flopped onto a bench.

Schaumberg swore. "It must be here!"

"I tell you, it's gone."

"It can't be."

"Well, I don't have much do go on, do I? Can you tell me anything more? What was it written in that book you quoted earlier, the one by Paracelsus?"

"*Sanctus fontis est Brugge fluo.*"

"Is that it? There isn't more to it?" he asked. Schaumberg and Evelyn exchanged glances. Harry threw up his hands. "Well, that's it, then. I'm afraid I can't help you further."

"That is very disappointing, doctor." Schaumberg's tone was quiet and grim. A veiled threat. Harry wasn't buying it.

"What more could you possibly expect? You have drugged me, flown me halfway around the world, dropped me in a medieval church built to honor a forgery, and asked me to solve a mystery I know little about, with nothing more to go on than a cryptic phrase and a lopsided tattoo!" He threw his hands in the air, feeling his blood-pressure spiking. "I mean: *sanctus fontis ex Bruge fluo?* Seriously? Y-you don't even know if it has anything to do with the chapel. This whole thing is ridiculous. You wanted my opinion. There. I've given it to you."

Schaumberg had dropped into a chair when Harry started his rant, clearly exhausted. But when Harry said this he raised his head. "What did you say?"

"I said this is ridiculous."

"No. What did you say?"

Harry wrinkled his brow. "That you abducted me and dragged me halfway around the—?"

"No. Something else."

"That you don't know what the hell you're doing?"

Schaumberg snapped his fingers. "That was it. Or close enough."

Evelyn turned to him, her eyes widening. "It isn't the chapel."

"The sacred fount from Bruges flows. They were wrong!"

"What?" asked Harry. "Who was wrong?"

Evelyn pulled out her iPhone, swore, and started for the stairs. Schaumberg motioned for them to follow.

"What? Where are we going?"

"Up," Schaumberg replied. "She needs a better signal."

At the top of the stairs they crowded around Evelyn, who was viewing an ancient map of the city of Bruges. "I've got it," she said. "It's the Gheerhaert map, from 1562." Holding her phone up to Joseph, she met his eyes. He glared back.

"Open your shirt!" Schaumberg demanded.

Joseph frowned grimly and began undoing the buttons. Bryce tried to offer his drawing of the tattoo, but Evelyn brushed him aside. Impatiently she grasped Joseph's shirt and tore it away, sending buttons popping onto the floor. She pushed the I-phone next to his chest, aligning it with the tattoo.

"My God," Schaumberg muttered.

TWENTY-THREE

ALEXANDRE GAZED OUT the windshield of his silver Audi at the *Grote Markt* in the heart of Bruges. In front of him, the *Belfort*, a medieval bell tower, soared eighty-three meters over the square, while all around him traffic and pedestrians surged, making it difficult to keep watch, let alone hear anyone's approach. He'd sent his advance team to the chapel only moments before. Surveillance only. He sneered. Those were the new instructions. He'd protested, of course. His men were fully trained and capable of handling the situation as originally tasked, but *la dernière hommes* in America were very clear on this: under no circumstance was he or his men to engage. That would be left for Vasily.

He shuddered at the name. Vasily. A cold-blooded assassin of brutal methods, utterly lacking in the subtleties for which Alexandre prided himself. The company employed him when they didn't want things covered up or made to look accidental, when they wanted to send a clear message. He'd heard of the man, of course, but they'd never crossed paths. Those who did, rumor had it, did not live to tell about it. There was always the possibility that his reputation was only a ruse—something to keep others in line, but

Alexandre couldn't be certain. That he was to make contact now unnerved him. Doubtless, the company wanted to prevent anyone from linking them to the assassin, should anything go wrong. He studied the height of the bell tower, wishing he could climb its steps and keep an eye out for the man. At the very least, it'd help to get above the crowds and the noise.

His heart lurched when his passenger door opened and a silver haired man stepped into the car. The man—undoubtedly Vasily—shut the door, glancing at Alexandre momentarily before his eyes lost focus. Alexandre opened his mouth to protest, but instead found himself staring at the man's left eye. The eye glared back at him, an unnatural disk of blue, with something glinting in the pupil.

The man didn't acknowledge him, but moved his gloved hands, as though typing on an invisible keyboard. After a moment, he dropped his hands and faced him.

"They are in chapel?" he inquired.

"You must be Vasily." Alexandre swallowed the lump in his throat. "I was told you would make contact."

Vasily's face registered no reaction. Against the dark orb of the artificial eye, Alexandre thought he could see tiny letters changing shape, scrolling across the lens. He shuddered and turned away. "My men are reconnoitering. They should be back *une moment*."

"They are in chapel," he repeated.

"*Oui, oui*. We will know more once my men return."

Vasily smiled flatly. "*Dah*. We go now."

He climbed out of the car, slamming the door behind him. Alexandre struggled to undo his seat belt and pursue.

"Wait," he said. "That is—those are not my instructions!"

Vasily barely glanced behind him. "New instructions. Come."

"But—!"

"Stay, then."

He opened and closed his mouth, then pulled out his keys and pressed the lock button on the remote. The car chirped and flashed its lights. He turned and raced to catch up with the long strides of the Russian agent.

Sean parked the Mercedes off the *Vismarkt* near *Brambergstraat.* Jon glanced up and down the idyllic street, struck by the Baroque beauty of the buildings and homes crowding the brick pavement. He'd purchased a travel book in the airport and read up on the town. What he'd seen in its pages didn't compare with what he saw around him. White, ocher, and burgundy facades warmed the alley, while brooding statuettes on tall towers frowned upon the delighted tourists exploring the shops beneath. Bruges had once been the crown of Flanders, built on the economic advantages of an inland seaport. But when the Zwin channel silted up and the boats couldn't get through, the town fell into despair, earning it the title of "the Dead City." Other population centers surpassed it, bounding into the new century with modern construction and opportunities for expansion.

All of that came to a halt when World War II broke out, and the Nazi war machine steamrolled Europe. Bruges escaped, largely unscathed due to its utter insignificance. Neither the Axis nor the Allied powers wasted their munitions upon its quaint cathedrals and quiet streets. Its chocolate shops and beer halls contributed almost nothing to the war effort either way, and when the dust finally settled, the people of Bruges found themselves uniquely positioned to remind Europe of all they had lost. Tourism surged and the city recovered. Its charm was its best commodity, and the city fathers recognized and protected what they had.

Sean and Jon passed by the gray peristyle housing the town fish market, where the smell of seafood overpowered the otherwise pervasive aroma of chocolate and beer. Around them, crowds still mingled—tourists sampling the local fare and residents shopping for the best deals, utterly oblivious to the drama in which he and Sean partook. Together, the two crossed a narrow bridge over a green canal, approaching the chapel from behind. In the water below, a long tour boat glided gently beneath the stone bridge, barely clearing the arch. Jon watched as it passed, then hurried to catch up to Sean, who hadn't missed a stride.

"You think they're in there?" Jon studied the back end of the chapel. He wondered if Sean was right. Had Izzy been brought here by her captor? And how on earth would they get her or Bryce free?

Sean didn't look back. His eyes were fixed on their

destination. "Could be," he said. "We get inside, we'll ask around a bit, see if anyone remembers seeing them. If so, our next trick will be a wee bit harder—figuring out where they've got to now. 'Course, we could always get lucky and find them waiting for us, yeah?"

"And what happens then?"

This time, Sean glanced back. What Jon read in his eyes didn't make him feel any better.

"What is it?" Harry pushed between them to see.

"The gates," Evelyn replied. "Bruges has seven gates. *Dampoort, Ezelpoort, Boeverierpoort, Smedenpoort, Katelijnepoort, Gentpoort* and *Kruispoort.*" She pointed out each of them on the map. "And if we line Isaac's tattoo up with them, like so, we get this."

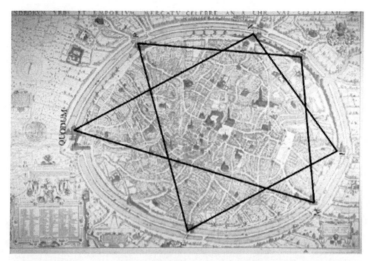

"Amazing," Harry muttered. "I thought there were nine gates. Yeah, here they are." He pointed to the two neglected gates marked on the drawing.

Schaumberg shrugged. "There's still nine angels."

"But only seven gates are directly connected to land," Evelyn explained.

"And only seven angels receiving the blood. All this time," murmured Schaumberg, "they were looking in the wrong place."

"Who?"

"My former employers. The heirs of Paracelsus." He shook his head. "Hundreds of years they searched—all based on the interpretations of Gerhard Dorn. What fools they've been!"

"They never stopped to question him," Evelyn said. "But what about these letters? They mark places on the map."

"The first word is *Quodum*. The rest of the letters are P, T, N, A, M, and I."

She keyed in the word and said, "*Quodum* is Latin. A conjunction. What meaning could it possibly have here?"

"Perhaps it is just introducing the cipher? 'Whereas the following'… you know?" suggested Harry.

Schaumberg snapped his fingers. "It's a code key. We need a *tabula recta*."

"A *tabula recta*?" repeated Harry.

"Yes," Schaumberg murmured. "Invented by Johannes Trithemius in the early sixteenth century—"

"Yes, I know what a *tabula recta* is," Harry huffed. "It was perfected later by the Italian Bellaso a few decades later, though the Frenchman Vigenère received credit. Why do you need it?"

"To solve the cipher, of course. What we have here is a little different, but it should work. Most encryption involves a longer phrase. This," he tapped Joseph's chest, oblivious to the man beneath the tattoo, "concerns a single word."

"I've got it," Evelyn said. She held her phone up for them to see. The screen was filled with a table of letters. Both the top and left-hand column showed the alphabet in their traditional arrangement, but each subsequent row and column were shifted to the left or top by one letter, while the beginning letters were shoved to the end.

```
    A B C D E F G H I J K L M N O P Q R S T U V W X Y Z
A | A B C D E F G H I J K L M N O P Q R S T U V W X Y Z
B | B C D E F G H I J K L M N O P Q R S T U V W X Y Z A
C | C D E F G H I J K L M N O P Q R S T U V W X Y Z A B
D | D E F G H I J K L M N O P Q R S T U V W X Y Z A B C
E | E F G H I J K L M N O P Q R S T U V W X Y Z A B C D
F | F G H I J K L M N O P Q R S T U V W X Y Z A B C D E
G | G H I J K L M N O P Q R S T U V W X Y Z A B C D E F
H | H I J K L M N O P Q R S T U V W X Y Z A B C D E F G
I | I J K L M N O P Q R S T U V W X Y Z A B C D E F G H
J | J K L M N O P Q R S T U V W X Y Z A B C D E F G H I
K | K L M N O P Q R S T U V W X Y Z A B C D E F G H I J
L | L M N O P Q R S T U V W X Y Z A B C D E F G H I J K
M | M N O P Q R S T U V W X Y Z A B C D E F G H I J K L
N | N O P Q R S T U V W X Y Z A B C D E F G H I J K L M
O | O P Q R S T U V W X Y Z A B C D E F G H I J K L M N
P | P Q R S T U V W X Y Z A B C D E F G H I J K L M N O
Q | Q R S T U V W X Y Z A B C D E F G H I J K L M N O P
R | R S T U V W X Y Z A B C D E F G H I J K L M N O P Q
S | S T U V W X Y Z A B C D E F G H I J K L M N O P Q R
T | T U V W X Y Z A B C D E F G H I J K L M N O P Q R S
U | U V W X Y Z A B C D E F G H I J K L M N O P Q R S T
V | V W X Y Z A B C D E F G H I J K L M N O P Q R S T U
W | W X Y Z A B C D E F G H I J K L M N O P Q R S T U V
X | X Y Z A B C D E F G H I J K L M N O P Q R S T U V W
Y | Y Z A B C D E F G H I J K L M N O P Q R S T U V W X
Z | Z A B C D E F G H I J K L M N O P Q R S T U V W X Y
```

"All right," she said. "Now what?"

"We have to narrow it down. There are six letters in *Quodum*, and six letters at each remaining point of the septagram."

Harry frowned. "What does that have to do with the gates?"

Evelyn and Schaumberg exchanged glances. Joseph glared at him. "Why are you helping them?" he demanded.

Harry flinched and moved back. "Sorry. Got a thing for puzzles."

"He's right," muttered Schaumberg, ignoring Joseph's outburst. "Seven gates. Start with the first letter of each gate."

"But *Dampoort* is labeled *Quodum*."

"Let's leave that out."

"Right. Oh, look. *Kruispoort* and *Katelijnepoort*. Two 'K's' and two 'U's'." She traced her finger along the line of K's until she came to the column U. "E," she said.

"Two 'E's'," Schaumberg said. "Now we just need the remaining four letters." He pulled out a scrap of paper and started writing down the different combinations.

BV. Ez. G. S.	Q	R	U	W	I
Katelijnepoort	U	E			
BV. Ez. G. S.	O	P	S	U	G
Ez. G. S.	D	H	J	V	
Kruispoort	U	E			
BV. Ez. G.	M	N	Q	S	

He frowned. "Both 'B' and 'S' intersect with an 'E.'"

"They would've used the 'K' for that." Evelyn pointed out.

"Right, which means we can eliminate those choices. The 'D' and 'M' in *Quodum* must refer to either *Ezelpoort* or *Gentpoort*, because only the 'Q' and 'O' can refer to either *Boeverierpoort* or *Smedenpoort*." He scratched out the letters and their combinations.

BV. E̶Z̶. G̶. S.	Q	R ̶ ̶ I
Katelijnepoort	u	E
BV. E̶Z̶. G̶. S.	O	P ̶ ̶ G
EZ. G. ̶	D	H J ̶
Kruispoort	u	E
B̶V̶. EZ. G.	M	̶ Q S

"What do you think?" Schaumberg murmured. "Reph something?"

"Maybe the name of an angel?" Evelyn offered.

Harry stared at the letters, then his eyes widened. "Oh!"

Evelyn and Schaumberg whirled on him. "What is it?"

Just then, William rushed in, speaking feverishly to Schaumberg, whose face contorted as he shoved William back. "Then stop him!" he bellowed.

TWENTY-FOUR

WILLIAM'S EYES BARELY flickered. "That'd be a mite harder than you'd expect. You don't know this man like I do."

"I don't care, though, do I?" Schaumberg turned to Harry. "What did you find, doctor?" His voice was breathless. Anxiety etched lines on his face. Harry wondered what all the excitement was about.

A gunshot shattered the window behind them and stifled Harry's response. William tackled Schaumberg, pulling him down and to the left.

"What the devil?" Harry stepped into the aisle. William grabbed the back of his coat and yanked him down as well. Harry hit the stone floor of the church even as shards of glass impacted the tiles around him.

A second shot rang out, splintering the chair in front of them. Evelyn screamed.

"That way!" William pointed right, in the general direction of the museum.

"Someone is shooting at us?" Harry asked.

William grabbed Harry and Joseph, thrusting them toward the museum. "Run!" he barked. They nearly bowled Schaumberg over in the process. William pulled his weapon free and fired blindly toward the rear of the chapel, covering their escape.

"*Non!*" cried Alexandre.

Vasily's eyes flickered in his direction before returning to the scope on his AK-103 assault rifle and sighting in on his prey. Already it looked as though his first two shots had gone wild. He'd misaligned his scope, moving it off center by a fraction of a degree–enough to throw off his aim. Made the whole thing look entirely too real. Of course, if he'd wanted them dead, they would be.

"I have orders to surveil alone!"

Vasily gritted his teeth and squeezed off another round. Another miss. He swore for effect. Alexandre was turning beat red beside him, his eyes bulging.

"*Arretez*! Stop shooting at them!"

They were running into the museum, out of his line of fire. Vasily rose from his position to follow, barely glancing at Alexandre. "Tell your men to close the net," he ordered.

"*Que*? Are you not listening?"

"We go now. Come."

"What's going on?" asked Jon.

"Someone else." Sean jerked Jon down behind the railing.

"Obviously." Jon had caught sight of Bryce as he

disappeared with the others around the corner. The shots were coming from somewhere to their left. "But who is it?"

"Bloody hell, how should I know?"

"They're going out through the museum."

Sean nodded, tugging Jon to follow. "Come on, then. We don't want to be late for the party, now, do we?"

"What? You're going *toward* the guns?" That didn't make any sense. People got hurt that way.

Loud cries rang out from the front of the chapel. Jon glanced back to see a gaggle of priests dashing into the sanctuary, waving their arms in distress, human shields between the gunman and their sacred house. Another bullet tore out, splintering the wood above the exit to the museum.

Reluctantly, Jon followed Sean down the steps and out through the façade in the front. Sean ran with his gun held low, out of the sight of the crowd gathering on the street outside. In the distance, sirens of the local police wailed in alarm as they raced toward the scene.

Sean stopped at the edge of the museum, raising his gun and firing in a single, smooth motion. The glass window of the museum shattered, and Jon ducked and cringed.

"What are you doing?!"

He grinned. "Just keeping 'em on their toes, yeah?"

Another shot, this time from their side. Jon glanced inside the museum as five figures ducked out the far side of the building, heading away from the basilica. One of them turned and pointed something at him. He felt a stiff arm shove him to one side just as a bullet tore through the air inches from his head.

"You might wanna keep your head down, yeah?"

He stared up at Sean and swallowed. "Thanks."

Rising from his crouch, Sean raced around the perimeter of the museum, Jon pursuing breathlessly. As they rounded the far side, he saw Bryce climbing into a boat with two older men, a bald man with a gun, and a redhead.

"Hold still you lymey bast—" Sean fired, but the bald man ducked and fired back. One of the old men fired a second gun, the shallow crack of a revolver sending a bullet wildly into the air. From the basilica, rapid-fire rounds punctured the earth just above the canal, sending clods of dirt flying into the air. The woman screamed.

Sean cursed. The boat engine rumbled, and the water behind it frothed and gurgled as they cast off the lines. A moment later, the bald man opened the throttle. The boat roared down the channel.

A lone man, dressed in black, with white hair swept back from his face, raced across the ground. He fired a semi-automatic toward the departing boat. A final burst, and he threw the weapon behind his back, where it dangled from its strap. He dropped down the same steps and climbed into a second boat. Within seconds, the engine grumbled to life, and he tore after them.

"Come on!" Sean bellowed. He led the way around the back end of the basilica toward their car. Jon followed him over the bridge to the other side of the canal. But here Sean turned and led him down a set of steep, narrow steps to a long boat moored to the dock below.

"What about the car?" Jon asked.

Sean ignored him and searched under the seats and in the compartments beneath the steering wheel. He emerged a moment later, triumphantly holding a set of keys tied to a miniature buoy. He turned the key in the ignition. Glancing back to the car, Jon gave up and hopped onto the deck. He tore off the bow line and moved to the stern to do the same there, but fell to the deck as Sean floored it. The rear mounting groaned and snapped clean off, trailing wood fragments from the boat behind it as it skipped across the water.

Jon scrambled to his feet, stumbling into the passenger seat as the boat surged down the waterway. He stared ahead at the boat driven by the man with white hair, not three hundred yards ahead of them.

"Friend of yours?" Jon hollered over the throb of the engine.

"Who?"

"The guy we're chasing!"

Sean shook his head. "Never saw him before."

They roared underneath the narrow bridge, ducking their heads until they cleared the other side.

The Rolls-Royce Phantom rolled through the intersection of Katelijnestraat and Oude Gentweg, gently gliding past numerous shops, bars, restaurants, and delicatessens, heading north by northwest into the heart of the city.

DuChamp sat in the back with Izzy, staring idly through the windows at the fanciful streets and architecture.

"This really is a splendid little town, isn't it?"

Izzy said nothing. She'd been little better than sullen the entire flight out—such dull company that he was seriously minded to drop her off on the side of the road and have done with it.

They approached a narrow bridge over the canals, where Katelijnestraat ended and Mariastraat began, just as two long boats roared through the canal, thrusting enormous wakes behind them and startling the bicyclists and tourists who clogged the street.

A moment later, a third boat tore under the same bridge, its pilot desperately trying to control the craft through the frothy water.

Sean? Izzy rolled down her window, staring through.

DuChamp bolted upright. "Who was that?"

She turned, a wry smile playing upon her lips. "That would be your competition."

He stared over her shoulder as the boats disappeared around a bend, then he tapped his driver. "Turn around. Follow them, quickly!"

"It's a one way street, sir."

"I don't care!"

Gritting his teeth, the driver hit the gas and whipped the wheel around, causing panic on the street around them. A loud bang shook the windows as a truck plowed into a car that had stopped to avoid them. Heedless, they surged past, honking as numerous drivers swore at them, waving obscene greetings from their windows.

They turned into a narrow alley and surged through, passing the canal again. In the waters below, the wake of the boats trailed away toward the Minnewater.

"They're getting away!"

The Rolls turned up a side street and then down another, heading toward the park. Ahead of them, the boats raced away.

DuChamp undid his seatbelt and climbed into the front seat. He slid open the sunroof and poked his head through for a better look. "Hurry. We must reach them before the canals split!"

He slapped the top of the car and laughed aloud. *Now this is fun!*

Schaumberg stared over the prow of the boat, then glanced behind. The white-haired gunman hadn't gained on them, but they hadn't lost him, either.

"Can't this thing go any faster?"

"Throttle's full on," came the reply.

He dropped back into his seat. Turning to Bryce, he yelled over the roar of the motor, "Tell me what you saw!"

A spray of bullets flew over their heads, shattering the windshield. Bryce cowered on the bottom of the boat. Heedless, Schaumberg pressed his face closer. "What was it?" he demanded. "What did you see?"

"The letters," Bryce stammered. "It's Latin for Ephesus!"

Something large splashed behind them. Schaumberg looked up and realized that Joseph was not in the boat. Schaumberg swore, pointing in the water. A frail form bobbed in the canal. A moment later, the second boat swept past him and he was lost to view.

TWENTY-FIVE

L OOK!" JON CRIED, pointing in the canal.
"We'll lose them!"

Jon barely glanced at Sean, but already the mercenary pulled back on the throttle, steering the boat alongside the floating figure. It was one of the older men who'd fled with Bryce and the others. The wash from their boat swamped him, and he came up, sputtering and choking.

Jon leaned over the gunwales and grabbed the man by the back of his shirt, hauling him up. He fell into the boat, vomiting canal water.

Jon nodded to Sean, but then turned suddenly. Had someone called his name? He looked up at the street on the far side. A dark sedan rolled by. Someone leaned out the sunroof, while another figure waved frantically at them from the window, calling his name. The car pulled away, following the road.

"Who is that?"

Sean swore. "It's Isabel!"

"Are you sure?"

"She called my name, didn't she?" He hit the throttle.

Jon braced his hand on the dashboard and frowned. "I thought she called my name."

"Ask her when you see her." Sean turned the boat away from the Beguinage, pulling into a narrow channel that split off to the left of the main canal. Jon glanced back as the canal swept out of view.

"What about Bryce?" Jon demanded.

"First thing's first!" He glanced back, catching Jon's scowl. "Isabel knows more about the men what got your friend than either of us. We need her help."

They ducked again under a low canal and Sean cut back on the throttle, scanning the roads to the left between the buildings. Jon turned to the boat's newest occupant. "Are you okay?"

The man had taken a seat in the aft section, looking dazed and confused. He ran a shaky hand over his face and pulled his soaked shirt tighter about his frame. "I'm all right." Water dripped from his nose. Jon took off his jacket and wrapped it around the man's shoulders. He sneezed.

"Do you need us to take you to a hospital?"

The man's eyes narrowed. "You're American."

"Yes. Those men in the boat—one of them is a friend. Dr. Bryce. We're trying to help him."

"Jon. . ." Sean growled a warning.

"You're friends with Harry?" asked the old man.

Jon chose to ignore Sean. He nodded. "We work together at the same university. Colleagues for years, actually."

The man brightened and introduced himself. "My name is Joseph. I was kidnapped by the same people who took your friend."

"Do you know why? What do they want with him?"

He shrugged.

Jon frowned. He'd hoped to learn something helpful from the man. Sean called him to the front.

"Don't be getting cozy with your friend," he warned. "We don't know what side he's on."

Jon glanced back and snorted. "You kidding? I don't even know what side I'm on."

Alexandre grimaced as he drove around a pair of cyclists pedaling through the narrow streets. He pressed the Bluetooth headset into his ear, vainly hoping for new instructions. That white-haired maniac took off without him, phoning him from a boat he'd stolen and telling him to collect his men and follow. Arrogant *bâtard*! He called his superiors, but was coldly ordered to do whatever Vasily asked. Vasily was in charge.

Stupid Americans. That's all they were now. No honor or sense of propriety. Just cold, efficient stupidity.

Packed together in the back seat, his men sat together silent and uncomfortable. Sulking. Already they'd complained vociferously about being sidelined with surveillance while the Russian blasted the hell out of everything in sight. He agreed with them, and but for his orders would have taken them up on their suggestion to eliminate the Russian and run the op themselves. They could easily have taken out Schaumberg at least ten different times and ways before the Russian showed up and spooked him. Why even use them at all if they weren't going to do anything? He'd ordered them to be quiet, but couldn't help but wonder whether *la dernière hommes* hadn't lost control of the situation, the way they'd seemed to have lost control over their agent. If that was the case, he might benefit by showing initiative. If he could take charge of the rapidly evolving situation on the ground, he might demonstrate his usefulness to the company once and for all. And then? Who knew where his career might land?

Static crackled in his ears. He glanced at the GPS to confirm the direction, and then glanced in the rearview mirror at his men. "They are headed for the outer canal, near the Minnewater."

No one so much as glanced in his direction.

He pulled into the street, nearly running into a Rolls Royce Phantom that barreled past, heading in the same direction. Frowning, he followed.

Isabel pulled away from the window as the gap between their car and the boat with Sean and Jon widened further. She glanced at DuChamp's backside as he stood arrogantly through the skylight, shouting directions to his driver and laughing like a child.

Moving in her seat, she peered through the windshield as they bore to the left, then right, heading due south.

"Get us to the bridge!" DuChamp hollered. "We can cut

them off if they come this way, or chase them down on the expressway."

As the Phantom rolled onto the bridge, Izzy grabbed the wheel and jerked it sharply to the right. The chauffer cried out and pushed her away, but it was too late. Snapping through the frail wooden guardrails, the car careened off the bridge and plunged into the river below.

The impact knocked them forward and back, slamming them against the seats. Water gushed through the open sunroof and windows, soaking them. Izzy grabbed DuChamp, dragging him back into the car and climbing over his body through the open sunroof. He clutched her ankle, but she kicked hard with her other foot, smashing him in the face with her heel. DuChamp collapsed into the back seat, and she was free.

Sean pulled the boat into the green waters of the Reie, steering toward the fleeing craft ahead of them. Just then, Jon grabbed his shoulder and pointed in the opposite direction.

"There!"

He looked and saw a Rolls Royce disappearing beneath the water, with a woman and two men, one of them bleeding profusely, swimming away from the wreckage. Whipping the boat around, he crammed down the throttle, pushing the boat between the woman and the men.

Jon bent over the side of the boat, offering his hands to

Isabel, helping her into the boat. Once she was onboard, he yelled to Sean, "Let's go!"

Sean turned the boat around and resumed the chase.

Watching with his head just above the waterline, DuChamp slapped the water in frustration. Somehow, despite his superior machinations, Isabel Kaufman had outwitted him and engineered her own escape under his very nose.

And to top it all off, he was bleeding from where she'd unceremoniously kicked him in the face while she climbed out over the top of him.

His chauffer bobbed up in the river beside him, sputtering water. "Are you all right, sir?"

He wiped the blood from his face. "No, Maurice. I'm not all right at all."

Together they struck for shore. As they climbed up the embankment, a team of men in a silver Audi waited for them at the top. "*Bonjour*," their leader greeted them.

William shoved the wheel hard to the right, bringing the boat around a tight bend and throwing a huge wave onto the crowded sidewalk above the canal. Passersby yelled in protest. He gunned the motor and fled down another side canal. A moment later, the second boat carrying the white-haired maniac followed.

"I can't shake him," he yelled over his shoulder.

"Lose him," Schaumberg returned.

"No good. He sees our wake and follows it every time."

Schaumberg glanced back, seeing the white, greenish water trailing behind them, the wash clearly marking their path.

"Then we need to get off this boat," he said.

"What?" exclaimed Harry.

"Look for someplace we can hide."

"Found it," William cried triumphantly. Ahead of them, another stone bridge loomed low over the canal. "We've got to jump free just as soon as we clear the bridge."

"You must be joking," said Harry.

"Count of three," William said as the bridge neared. "One, two." The bridge passed overhead, briefly thrusting them into shadows. "Three!"

Harry hesitated, but William grabbed his shoulder and leaped with him into the water. He tumbled headfirst and came up spluttering. William clamped his hand over his mouth and pulled him over toward the shore.

Scant seconds later, the other boat roared through the overpass, spraying them all with an angry wave. Their own boat continued ahead several yards until it smashed into a distant bridge with a resounding bang that echoed back along the canal.

Schaumberg waited with Evelyn on one side of the bridge abutment, and William guarded Harry on the other. Two minutes later, the second boat returned, motoring slowly along the river way, its white-haired captain scanning the waters for any sign of them.

Quickly, they ducked under the waves, holding their breath and hiding in the brackish water until the boat rumbled past. Then they came up, drenched and breathless, scrambling for dry ground.

Schaumberg motioned to William, telling him to wait on that side. William tugged Harry up the embankment. At the top, they stood dripping on the pavement until Schaumberg and Evelyn joined them.

"What now?" William asked.

Schaumberg wiped his face on his sleeve. "Just get us out of here."

TWENTY-SIX

EAN SAW THE second boat trolling toward them at a slow pace. He steered toward a mooring in the channel and commanded everyone to get down. Pulling his gun, he peered through the windshield, watching as the white-haired man floated past. In the distance, sirens wailed, their impatient whine growing louder each moment.

He turned to the others, nodding in the assassin's direction. "He must've lost 'em."

"It's time we got lost, too," Izzy returned, "before DuChamp gets himself another car."

They raised their heads, sitting up to look around.

"What about Harry?" asked Jon.

"Can't be helped," Sean said.

"We've got to do something!"

"Aye. Would you happen to have a suggestion?" When Jon didn't answer he continued. "Look, the best we can do right now is step back a wee bit and take stock of our options. We may have lost the round, but we ain't out of the fight. Not just yet anyway."

"Sean's right," Izzy said. "We need to collect ourselves,

get me some dry clothes, and get some answers to our questions. Like, who our new friend is."

Together, their heads turned to study Joseph, who shrank from the attention. "I am no one."

Jon patted his arm reassuringly. "Don't worry. We'll figure it out."

Izzy took charge of their situation, dismissing the men's concerns with a wave of her hand. She'd hailed a taxi and asked for Sean's phone, and then made a quick call to her bank. Directing the taxi to a wire transfer service, she sent Jon in to collect the money. He protested at first, but she pointed out that she had no identification, and seeing how Sean was still on Interpol's watch list, it wouldn't do to show his face to a camera while collecting a large amount of cash. Bereft of further objections, Jon walked into the shop and retrieved the money, surprised by the amount she'd requested.

"Are you sure you want to be carrying around this much cash?" he asked.

She pulled a strand of hair away from her cheek and smiled at him. "Trust me. We won't be carrying it long."

She ordered the cab to take them to a clothing store, where she insisted on purchasing new clothes for Joseph despite his objections, and then took them to a local hotel. Here she showered and changed, inviting Joseph to do the same while she ordered dinner.

Once Joseph was safely out of earshot in the shower, she said, "So. Who's our friend?"

"His name is Joseph," Jon began.

She interrupted him. "Yes. He told us this in the car."

"And he says he was kidnapped by the same people who took Harry."

"And?"

"That's it. That's all we know."

She pressed her lips into a thin line. "You're not very good at interrogation, are you?"

He shot her a dark look. "I might be a bit rusty."

She let it slide and turned to Sean instead. "DuChamp infiltrated our safe house. I'd like to know how."

Sean folded his arms. "You and me both, luv."

"Well, until we find out, I suggest we avoid any of the usual channels. I don't like him getting ahead of us so easily."

"Does he know what you're after?" Jon asked.

"Not yet. But now that the stakes have been raised, he'll want to find out. He won't take kindly to the bath I gave his car."

"Sorta makes up for your houses, yeah?" Sean grinned.

"He'll just try to hit back harder."

"Aye, but we take our joys where we find 'em."

"What else do we know?"

"Not much," Jon said. He glanced at Sean. "I think I'm speaking for us both. By the time we got to the chapel, the shooting had already started. We don't know if they found what they were looking for or not. What *were* they looking for?"

"A clue. A part of the puzzle we don't have. There's an old manuscript by Gerhard Dorn that quotes an unknown work of Paracelsus. *Sanctus fontis ex Brugge fluo*."

"The sacred fountain flows out of Bruges."

"Dorn believed it was the Basilica of the Holy Blood. We cross-referenced his name with some of Triprimacon's earlier holdings and came up with a seventy-two percent match."

"Meaning he was a member."

"More than likely. Triprimacon has no formal membership list—at least none that we've found. The only way to identify members is to cross-reference their names with the shell companies and other holdings. The more hits you come up with, the greater probability they're part of the inner circle."

"So if Dorn believed the secret lay within the chapel. . ."

"Then so does Triprimacon."

Jon cocked his head and furrowed his eyebrows. "You were guessing."

"Guessed right," Sean returned. "There's one more thing. The bald man with them? I know him. His name is William Higgs. Done work with him in the past. Not the most reliable sort. Had to fire him."

"They've hired a mercenary?" asked Izzy.

"Aye. But Triprimacon's got guns of their own, and what with his dubious résumé, I find it hardly likely they'd have brung him on board."

"There's been a rift."

"Might explain a lot, including that white-haired gunman."

She nodded slowly. "Jonnie? Maybe you could ask your friend Joseph if he'd be willing to have a chat with us?"

He blinked and rose to his feet. "Yeah. Kinda surprised he's still in there." He moved to the bathroom door and knocked gently.

"Joseph?" he called. "Are you all right in there?"

Swearing, Sean bolted for the window and threw it open. He looked out and cursed again as he swung over the edge, then dropped out of sight.

Jon frowned and banged louder on the door, and then jiggled the handle to no effect. He came over to Izzy at the window and poked his head out, looking past her shoulder.

Sean had scampered across the fire escape to the narrow ledge running along the exterior wall and was creeping closer to the old man who'd plastered himself against the wall and was inching away from them, hanging on by his fingertips.

"Joe!" Jon called. The old man turned, saw Sean coming toward him, and with a little cry tried moving faster. His hand slipped and he dropped. Joe's feet scrambled on the wall, finding scant purchase on the brick. He flailed about with his arm, trying desperately to find a handhold.

"Hang on!" Sean bellowed, moving almost within reach.

Jon tore away from the window. He dashed to the bathroom door and smashed it open with his foot. It slammed against the bathroom wall. Inside, the shower still ran, but the bathroom window hung wide open. Jon tore the shower curtain down, quickly tying the curtain and the liner. "Izzy!" he yelled, "bring the sheets!"

Izzy poked her head briefly through the doorway. She returned a moment later with the top and bottom sheets from one of the beds. Jon grabbed an end and tied it to the shower curtain. She tied the opposite end to the other sheet. "More?" she asked.

"Hope not."

He looped an end around the pedestal of the sink and tied it off. Sitting on the window ledge, he called down, "Sean!" and tossed the makeshift rope down to him.

Sean gave the line a harsh tug, making the sink's pedestal grate against the floor, and strapped the sheets around his shoulders. Kicking off the ledge, he swung around, coming behind Joseph. At that moment, Joseph lost his grip, dropping straight down. Sean caught him just under the armpits.

The sink groaned and broke loose from its pedestal, flying toward Jon at the window's edge. Jon ducked at the last second, then grabbed the ceramic basin just before it flew out the window. The sheets strained against the window ledge. Behind him, Izzy dealt with a spewing fountain, furiously twisting the valves on the broken lines. Water seeped across the floor, making the tiles slick. Jon stumbled, now hanging onto the sink and makeshift rope for balance as he struggled to regain his footing.

Suddenly, the line of sheets abruptly fell back into the bathroom. The weight on the other end was gone.

"No!" Izzy rushed forward as Jon pushed the sink off

his chest. He scrambled to his knees and peered over the window ledge. On the fire escape, Sean ushered Joseph back up the steps toward their window.

Izzy dashed back to the bedroom, leaving Jon soaked in the corner. Grabbing a towel off the rack, he dried his face and pants, turned off the shower, and followed. In the bedroom, Izzy was helping Joseph through the window. A moment later, Sean reappeared through the same.

"Well, now. That was a bit of an adventure, yeah? Where might you have been running off to, old man?"

Joseph ducked his head. "I just want to go home."

"You and me both," Jon muttered.

"We'll be happy to take you anywhere you wish to go," said Izzy, "but first we need your help."

Joseph sat back and looked askance at her.

"You don't believe me?" she asked.

"He's already been kidnapped and held against his will once, Izzy." Jon came up beside her. "I think we should just let him go, or we're no better than they are."

"How can you say that? You know what we're after."

"They're after the same thing."

"But not for the same reasons."

"What difference does it make?" Jon insisted. "We aren't judged good or evil by our intentions, but by our actions."

"He's got a point, luv. Not unlike that time in Naples."

Izzy shot Sean a dark look, but he met her gaze evenly. Jon wondered what happened in Naples, but hesitated to ask, and finally chose against it. Izzy turned to him. "I suppose you'll want to go, too."

"Not without Harry."

"All right." To Joseph she said, "I guess we'll get you to the airport and try to find you a way home. You'll need a passport, but I'm sure we can arrange something. Or, if you want, we can take you to the American Embassy and you can explain the situation to them."

Sean hissed through his teeth. "Embassy means Interpol. That'll complicate things."

"Just a minute ago, you were all about doing the right thing."

"I'm about keeping it simple, boss."

She turned to Joseph. "What would you like?"

He measured her with his eyes. "You'll let me go? Just like that?"

"Yes," Jon said.

After a moment, he said. "Harry is in grave danger. Dr. Schaumberg will stop at nothing to get what he wants. He won't hesitate to kill him if it serves his purpose."

"Dr. Schaumberg?"

"He is desperate to save his son," said Joseph. "He will do anything. I can tell you where they are going. It is the least I can do."

TWENTY-SEVEN

THE PLANE TOUCHED down at Esenboğa International Airport a little after three in the afternoon, Ankara time. Nicky ran a hand over his face as he plodded through the terminal, feeling drawn and spent—and utterly lost. He stared askance at the signs on the walls, grateful that at least half of them were in English. The rest was in a language and alphabet he didn't recognize. Probably Turkish, he thought, before realizing just how stupid that sounded.

"Of course it's in Turkish. You're in Turkey," he muttered to himself.

He'd only been on the plane for ten hours, but had somehow lost a whole day. Bright sunlight cascaded through the skylights in the ceiling, filling the interior of the airport with a warm, happy glow. He frowned at the light, wishing it was night. The hour conflicted sharply with what time his body said it should be. *Maybe I could pick up one of them sleeping masks with some of the money from Joe's lock box.* Some of that currency was bound to be Turkish money—not that he could recognize it from anything else.

Then again, that would be stealing. Joe might've meant

the money for him, but maybe not. His note didn't say either way. Which meant Nicky wasn't going to touch it one way or the other without permission. Even if it meant he had to find some other way to get some shut-eye.

He'd tried to sleep on the plane, but found his mind restless, wandering. He played endlessly with the medallion Joe had given him, startled to find at one point, if he held it loosely from its chain that it worked a little like a compass, duly pointing north and turning every time the pilot made a course correction. Still, it was unlike any other compass he'd ever seen. Though the lodestone aimed northward, the markings on the medallion pointed in a different direction, like it was meant for something else. But what that was, Joe's letter hadn't said. The note only told him to bring it back to Ephesus at all costs.

And that was another matter. Ephesus didn't exist. At least, not anymore. He'd only had a general idea of its importance from his Bible study with Joe, but when he tried to find it on a map, he came up empty. Joe had told him to tell no one where he was headed or why—a promise he kept to the letter—but it did involve a side trip to the New York Public Library to figure out where he was supposed to be going.

And then there was that little matter of the parole violation he incurred by leaving the country under a false name. He was sure that would land him in hot water big time if he were caught. Ex-con drug dealer travelling out of the country under an alias? There's only one way Customs would read that—and it would spell DEA and a short trip back to the pen. Fortunately, he knew a guy who did papers pretty good, and for a thousand bucks he'd fitted Nicky with some convincing ID. He'd only had to hold it together through security and while passing by the air marshal seated in the front row of the plane. Once they were in the air, he was home free.

But Joe's strangest request by far had been the tattoo...

He shook his head, placing his hand over his left breast, where the pricks of the artist's needle still stung his flesh. He wished he could've asked Joe about that. He'd read in scripture once that God's people weren't supposed to be marking their bodies like the heathen. He still bore more than a few reminders of his old life in certain parts of his anatomy he preferred not to mention.

But Joe's instructions had been quite specific, and since the old man wasn't around to explain it to him, Nicky had decided to take it on faith and just obey. Still, the design didn't exactly fit with any of the other artwork he'd had done. At least the artist had picked up on the fact that he was in a hurry, and resisted any embellishments in the design.

As he passed through the mezzanine, he began thinking about the phone call he'd made before leaving. The man on the other end hadn't even spoken English, answering the phone with a cryptic *"Merhaba?"* It took Nicky a moment to remember to recite the phrase Joe had written phonetically for him. Even then, he'd botched it badly. There was a rustle on the other end, and then someone came on the line who spoke English... sort of.

At any rate, they were supposed to meet him at the

airport, hook him up with a place to crash and some food—and maybe someone who could explain what the hell he was supposed to be doing. Whoever they were.

He looked up as he approached the far side, both relieved and uneasy about the man he saw. The bearded figure stood almost six feet and wore a brown monk's robe. He held a sign with Nicky's name misspelled in block letters across the front. Nicky made a beeline for the monk, desperately trying to remember the greeting Joe had written out for him. When he was five feet away, he stopped. Clearing his throat, he plunged in. *"Care is who min kai aye ren ae apoh the-oo patros haymoan kai coor ee oo yay soo kristoo."*

The monk smiled quizzically as he spoke, and then laughed. "That was terrible. Your Greek is very bad."

Nicky deflated, his shoulders sagging. "Knew I butchered it."

"Yes," the monk agreed. "My English is not so good, too. I am honored you try. My name is Brother Davut. You must be Brother Nicholas." He held out his hand.

Nicky shook it. "Wow. Only my mom has ever called me Nicholas. And then only when I was in trouble."

Brother Davut furrowed his brow. "Is not your name?"

"No, no. It's my name. Just that most everyone calls me Nicky."

"Nick-ee. Is good. Suits you. Come, Nick-ee. I have a car waiting."

"I still don't understand," said William. "Why aren't we flying?"

Schaumberg glanced back, giving his mercenary a baleful look before turning around again without answering. William gritted his teeth. The only response he'd gotten to his question so far was something Schaumberg mumbled about how it was too dangerous. *Ridiculous*, he fumed. How on earth did they expect him to work security like this? He'd already complained once about not being kept in the loop. True, the position had belonged to Andre, but what with the Frenchie taking a tumble out the door back in the States, William figured that left him in charge. At least, he saw it that way. Why didn't the old man?

He was about to ask again when Evelyn said, "We're being tracked." She walked beside him, her shoes marking a staccato rhythm with every step. Between them marched Harry, carrying the insulin kit the Schaumbergs had purchased for him before leaving the States.

"Tracked?" William questioned. This was an interesting development. He wished they'd said something sooner. "How?"

"Probably through the plane," she answered. "What difference does it make?"

"Bloody hell lot of difference, if you don't want them following you." William shook his head, surprised by their ignorance. It always amazed him how people supposedly so smart could be so foolish at the same time. "You could have a chip planted in your luggage or in your cell phone—practically anywhere and probably more than one. Five or six redundant chips are usually adequate. More if your quarry's smart. That's how I'd do it, anyway." He shrugged. Maybe they'd start paying him some proper mind.

Schaumberg stopped and studied him. "How would we get rid of them?"

William rubbed his chin, warming to the subject. Now that was more like it—treating him like the professional they paid for instead of some dumb hunk of muscle. "Scan for 'em," he said, "'cept we ain't got a scanner. You could tear everything apart and look for them—either way you're taking a chance that you got 'em all. Usually there's only one thing you can do."

"And that is?"

"Dump everything and start fresh."

"Everything?" Evelyn paled.

After a moment, Schaumberg nodded. "Do it."

"Not everything!"

Schaumberg turned a smoldering glare toward his granddaughter. She clutched her handbag defensively.

"It's Versace!"

He pried it from her hands and handed it to William. "It goes."

William grinned and opened the bag, pawing gently through its contents. He always wondered what a woman carried in her purse.

"Do you mind?" she protested.

He pulled out his knife and slit the lining on both sides, not too surprised when the blade's tip clicked against something that should not have been there. "Hallo." He pulled the lining further away, tearing the stitching. Reaching inside, he withdrew a slender microchip with a tiny battery attached. He held it up so they could see.

"Yeah," he said, "How you like the look of that? Micro transmitter. Very clever. This little beauty sends a signal over whatever carrier is closest to it. In your case," he pulled out her iPhone, "your cell. Long as you kept it in your purse, it had no problem accessing the signal, telling them right where we were at all times." He handed the bag back to her. "It's clean now."

She snatched it from his hand, pouting at the shredded seam.

"All right," said Schaumberg. "Now what?"

"Like I said. You can either ditch everything and start fresh, or spend a day or two fumigating all your stuff."

"Then we ditch everything," he said, grabbing the handbag back from Evelyn. "Clean or not. And be quick about it. We haven't much time."

Evelyn opened her mouth to protest, but then closed it again, evidently thinking better than to argue. Instead, she pulled out her credit card. "So I assume we're going shopping?"

Schaumberg glanced at William, who shrugged. "Can't hurt," William said. "It's not like they don't already know we're here."

"Right. New clothes for everyone. Then we're done. The train leaves in an hour."

TWENTY-EIGHT

FREDERICK AWOKE TO the sound of his cell phone buzzing frantically by his ear. He frowned and rolled over, checking the time before answering the call. He'd been asleep for four hours. What could possibly have happened that merited waking him up like this?

"What is it?" he mumbled into the phone.

"You're late." Casper's voice grated in his ear. "The meeting started a half hour ago."

"Meeting? What meeting?" *Casper,* he groaned inwardly, *what are you up to now?*

"The meeting to discuss your dismissal. The entire board has been assembled, and is here waiting for you to explain yourself."

He sat up. What *was* Casper up to? He could curse the man for not needing sleep. He must've been far less tired than Frederick had realized. Looking at his watch, he said, "I can be there in fifteen minutes."

"You're already a half hour late. We'll have to do this over the phone."

He snorted and rubbed his eyes. So, this was what it was. A power play designed to put him off balance. So like Casper. He could deal with this. "Put me on speaker, then."

"You're already on speaker."

Of course he was.

"Then gentlemen, I apologize for keeping you waiting. I did not receive notice there was a meeting scheduled."

"We sent you an email two hours ago."

"I was sleeping."

"Of course you were," Casper's tone was snide. "Your failure to show up on time for work is the least of your concerns, I assure you."

"Given that I was up all night driving around town with you, Casper, I'm sure it would be. But perhaps someone there could explain why I'm being dismissed?"

There was a moment's silence, then the voice of another board member came over the phone, Ellis Gramsci, one of Casper's cronies straight from the Old Country. "It has to do with the situation in Bruges."

Bruges? "Which situation is that?"

"We've received a very disturbing report from our man there, Alexandre Dumont. He informs us that he was told not to take action against this Schaumberg fellow, but to wait for a Russian hitman, one Vasily Ivanovich."

"Go on."

"I don't know what you're playing at, young man, but this is not how we do things. Discretion is the better part of valor."

He'd moved off his bed and into his kitchen, where he

loaded a shot of espresso in his Keurig coffee maker. "I'm afraid I'm still not getting the whole picture just yet."

"Things went badly in Bruges, Frederick. It's all over the news. Gun battles in the city? A shoot-out at a historical church? The whole continent is in an uproar! Interpol is breathing down our necks. The media—"

"A church, you say? The *Heiligbloodbasiliek*?"

After a telling second, Ellis answered. "Yes."

Frederick smiled, pulling his espresso from the coffee press and taking a sip. "So it's true then. Schaumberg is after the cruets."

"Schaumberg is not our concern at the moment. We—"

"Schaumberg is precisely our concern! Don't you get it? While the lot of you dither about in your paneled offices and sip your gin and tonics, fretting about your reputations, Dr. Peter Schaumberg is going after the prize—the Elixir that has eluded you for centuries! What would your forebears think of you? Playing your fiddles while the city burned?" He crushed the phone to his ear, the caffeine shot loosening his tongue. "Gentlemen, my job, as it was explained to me on the day that you hired me, Casper, is to put my best efforts into achieving the objectives of this company. Now we are faced with a crisis none of us have foreseen—a potential disaster which would render our final objective forever beyond our reach. If Schaumberg reaches the cruets and develops the Elixir before we can attain it, *we will never possess it!* A thousand years of hard work and research washed down the drain. So please, tell me exactly how I'm overreacting?"

"Well that—that's not right," said a mousy voice Frederick guessed belonged to Miles, from accounting. "Dr. Schaumberg is bound to us by contractual obligations. Anything he develops is, legally speaking, ours."

"Schaumberg's contract only applies to work he performs while in our employ," Frederick retorted. "His contract terminated the moment he went rogue, when Casper decided to fire him."

He heard two things at once, which told him he was in no further danger of being fired. The first was several voices demanding to know if this was true, and the second was Casper sputtering an explanation. It was time to draw the net.

"As I said, gentlemen," he broke in, "Schaumberg's defection is something none of us could have foreseen, much less that he would personally go after the cruets and attempt the formula on his own." In reality, he had predicted this exact set of events. He was only surprised by how quickly, even how easily, it was all coming to pass. "Were Schaumberg an ordinary man, Casper's actions would have been sufficient to resolve the matter. He can hardly be blamed for misperceiving the gravity of our situation.

"But now that we know who and what we are up against, we have to pull out all the stops. We cannot risk anything less. This is why I sent Vasily after him. Evidently, he was even more than the Russian had anticipated. He won't miss a second time, though. I'd stake his reputation on it."

There was a moment of brief discussion he strained to hear, then a clearing of throats telling him they'd come to a decision. It was Miles who spoke. Frederick raised his eyebrows. Who knew the accountant had such courage?

"I move that we immediately place Frederick in charge of this operation. If there are no objections?"

"Now wait a minute!" Casper broke in.

"Yes, Casper? Something you'd like to add?" This came from Ellis. His voice was terse. He'd never heard him use that tone with Casper before. Not ever. A heavy silence brooded over the phone. He could almost see the trickle of sweat running down Casper's face.

Finally, Casper's voice came through. Tired. Defeated. "I have no objections."

"Then we are in agreement?"

"Gentlemen, I accept your offer." Frederick tossed back the last of his espresso, feeling now fully awake and alive.

"Excellent, Frederick. Now, what can you tell us about DuChamp?"

He stopped celebrating, his mouth hanging open. "Who?"

Jon pulled the car to the curb and parked. He looked through the passenger window across the Boulevard du Régent at the beige office building rising four stories above the sidewalk on one side and seven stories on the other. The right half of the building looked much like a seventeenth-century bank, with straight, no-nonsense lines capped by a Mansard roof—a rather dull example of second empire architecture. The left side struck a discordant note. It was an addition, a modern nightmare of steel and glass, with strong, horizontal lines bracing large windows in its face.

If it weren't for the fact that the buildings were attached and each sporting an American flag, he wouldn't have known they were both part of the same embassy. Somehow, it was a suitable testimony to the American penchant for function over form. There was no attempt to blend in with the surrounding environs, testifying to his nation's hegemony in Europe, as if the superpower simply expected the city to abandon its history and adapt to the U.S. presence. He snorted. No wonder Europeans thought Americans were arrogant.

The drive from Bruges to Brussels had taken longer than he'd anticipated, a fact which didn't help his argument to Sean that they should take Joseph to the embassy before grabbing a flight to Turkey. Sean pointed out that they were in a hurry, but Jon insisted. It didn't hurt to have Izzy back him up, but it put the mercenary in a sour mood.

Jon had dropped them off at the airport first, and then backtracked to the heart of the city. Traffic was mercifully light, and within fifteen minutes he was parked in front of the embassy.

He turned to Joseph, who was unbuckling his seatbelt. "All set?"

Joseph flashed him a wan smile, nodding. "It will be all right now. Thank you."

"It was the least I could do."

"It was more than that. Now go, find your friend. And may God be with you."

"And with you."

Joe nodded once more, and then opened the car door.

Jon watched him cross the street, heading for the embassy's entrance. After a moment he started the car, pulled back into traffic and headed for the airport.

Joseph watched him go. Once the car was out of sight, he turned abruptly, walking away from the embassy. He turned up Paleizenplein around Maier Von Rosenau Park, weaving through a maze of side streets, passed the Stadhuis Brussel and up the Rue au Beurre, finally pausing for breath in front of the Église Saint-Nicolas. Built in the eleventh century, the Église Saint-Nicolas was the oldest church in Brussels, and one of the few cathedrals of Europe still in continuous use.

He only hoped they remembered.

Intricate stained glass windows brooded from the white stone of the outer facade. So much had changed since the church was constructed. The building had seen its share of pain, not unlike the Bride of Christ down through the centuries. There was even a cannonball still lodged in one of its pillars from the French bombardment in 1695. *We must fill up what is lacking in regard to Christ's afflictions*, he thought, remembering Saint Paul's words to the Colossian Christians.

Crossing the sidewalk, he tugged open the wooden door and crossed the threshold, feeling a sudden sense of warmth as he did so. He smiled. Entering a church always felt like coming home.

"Excusez-moi, la masse est fini pour la journée." The parish priest rushed down the aisle, telling him mass was over.

Joseph held out his ring so the priest could see it and asked for his help. *"J'ai besoin de votre aide, mon frère."*

The priest's brow furrowed as he examined the ring. An expression of shock and surprise filled his eyes. *"Incroyable!"*

†WEN†Y-NINE

IS ALL THIS really necessary?" Pierre DuChamp cocked his head to one side, listening carefully. With the blindfold that covered his eyes and the dark hood that covered his head, he wasn't even sure anyone was there. Beside him, he could still feel Maurice slumped against him on the bench.

The men in the Audi had been surprisingly discourteous, and when Maurice objected to the blindfold and hood on the grounds he was claustrophobic—which, DuChamp knew from his many years of service, happened to be true—they'd answered his objections by pistol-whipping him into submission before stuffing the hood over his head anyway. After that came a ponderous drive through many twists and turns in the trunk—the trunk!—of the Audi, until at last he and Maurice were manhandled up a flight of stairs into a dank, moldy room.

He wouldn't have been half-surprised to see a single light bulb dangling from a wire and blacked-out windows with rats crawling in the corner. If only he could see! By far the worst of it was how utterly predictable it had all been. His captors displayed no imagination at all. Forty years of building wealth through any means necessary had taught

DuChamp the value of a proper interrogation, and he'd refined the technique to a delicacy few could appreciate. He was able to elicit intel from the most unwilling subjects with a minimal amount of discomfort, merely by finding the appropriate kind of leverage. Sometimes it was a payout. Sometimes it required more provocative measures involving a set of pharmaceuticals used in the correct proportions. It almost never involved dark hoods, mysterious drives, isolation in abandoned warehouses and beatings. Not if he could help it, of course.

He was about to raise this objection yet again when he heard the door open and a collection of heavy boots rumble into the room.

"Finally," he said as rough hands untied the hood around his head. "I was just going to say how—"

"*Bezmolvie!*" The deep voice sounded Russian.

"I-I'm sorry. What?"

The blindfold fell from his eyes. He blinked in the light and saw the fierce glare of a silver-haired man pointing a finger at him. There was something remarkably odd about the man's eyes, particularly the left one. Behind him, the men from the Audi stood at attention, guarding the doors and windows, submachine guns nestled in their arms. One of them, the man who'd addressed him at the riverbank, was speaking rapidly into a cell phone. He didn't look happy.

"Shut up," the Russian growled at DuChamp, drawing his attention back.

He tried to smile. "Shu-shutting up."

The man straightened. "I ask question. You answer. You do not speak unless I tell you."

"I understand."

The man swung a gloved fist hard against DuChamp's jaw. Pain exploded across his face and he saw stars. Gasping, he gave the man a bewildered stare.

"What I say?" the man bellowed.

"D-do not speak unless you t-tell me."

"Dah. Is better. Now. Tell me about Schaumberg."

"I—" He cocked his head, unsure how to answer. "I don't know who that is."

With a throaty growl, the man reared back to hit him again. Too late, DuChamp turned his head to absorb the blow, which sent him reeling to the side. The chair tipped. He crashed to the floor and cut his tongue. Blood filled his mouth, and he spat it onto the floor. Crouching, the man gently lifted a strand of hair out of DuChamp's eyes.

"Do not lie to me."

"He can't tell you."

DuChamp's eyes flickered to Maurice, who'd turned his head in DuChamp's direction, as if he could see through the hood.

The man whipped the hood and blindfold off the driver's head. DuChamp gaped at the battered face of his servant. Maurice looked drawn and haggard, with one eye swollen shut and a trail of dried blood running down from his broken nose to his split and swollen lips.

"He can't tell you because he doesn't know."

The man eyed them both, as if considering the possibility

they were telling the truth. "Then, tell me how is it you come to be here?"

"We weren't following this Schaumberg. We were following Ms. Kaufman," Maurice explained.

"Kaufman. And who is this Kaufman?"

"Isabel Kaufman," said DuChamp. He struggled for a moment to sit up from the floor before giving up the attempt. "She is a wealthy collector and seller of ancient manuscripts. Antiquities. That sort of thing. We'd acquired a certain scroll from her—"

"Stole it, actually," said Maurice.

"Yes. Well. All's fair in love and war. We were bartering for its return when she offered us something much more interesting in exchange."

"So you are a thief," said the man.

"I prefer to think of myself as an opportunist."

The man stepped over to him and lifted him upright with one hand. The chair landed on the floor with a bone-jarring thud. Leaning in close, the man wrinkled his nose. "You are a thieving capitalist pig. Tell me why I should not kill you now?"

"That would be a mistake."

"Why?"

"Isn't it obvious? You don't know who we are. You know nothing about Kaufman, what she's capable of, who she's got working for her. This game is far more complex than you are aware. Unless you know the players, you won't succeed. I suspect that would be a disappointment to your employers. Am I right?" When the man didn't answer, he hazarded a further comment. A suggestion, really. "I know it would be if you were my employee."

At this, the man's eyes grew hard. He'd picked up on the subtle invitation, but he shook his head, refusing it. "You know nothing of me."

"Oh, that's not true. Not entirely. I may not know your name, but I know your type. I've hired men like you before. You're Russian. Probably former KGB, now unemployed, forced to work for the *capitalists* you once despised. Still despise. But what can you do? You've still got to eat. Bills have to be paid. One sympathizes. In the end, you have no real stake in this. You're just a hired gun, doing what you were trained and paid to do. The only real question is: how much are they paying you? Is it enough? Whatever it is, I'll double it. Don't think I can't."

"You make me sick."

DuChamp swallowed blood. "I didn't ask you to sell out your principles. You already did that. I'm just offering you an opportunity to renegotiate—"

With a growl, the man raised his hand to strike again, but a cry from the man with the cell phone stopped him.

"Vasily, *écoutez!*"

Vasily turned around, studying the phone that the man held out to him. He sneered at the man, snatching the cell phone out of his hand and holding it to his ear. After a moment, he hung up and tossed it back. When he turned around, he wasn't smiling.

"Appears it is your lucky day."

He turned around and stalked out of the room,

grumbling toward the other men still standing there. "We are friends now. Clean them up."

After the application of a styptic pencil, bandages, and some heavy-duty painkillers, DuChamp brushed away any further attentions from his captors and now studied the man in front of him.

His name was Alexandre Dumont. He'd brought DuChamp into a different room in the building with a plain table and a pair of chairs. DuChamp still couldn't tell where they were, but the building they occupied had the feel of an abandoned warehouse. Alexandre leaned toward DuChamp with his elbows on his knees. "Before we begin, please accept my apologies on behalf of my co-workers. Especially Vasily. We have not worked with him before. He is, how you say, a loose cannon? Oui?"

"It would mean more if it came from him."

Alexandre smiled. "Regrettably, that is unlikely. The man is uncivilized. Can I get you anything? Coffee? Perhaps something stronger?"

"Tea, if you have it."

"I will send someone for it. Your name is French, but you are American?"

DuChamp pursed his lips. Alexandre was trying hard to be solicitous. DuChamp decided to play along. The men had brutally interrogated him and Maurice, and that was a debt he'd require from them sooner rather than later. But for now, he saw no way to get back into the game unless he made an alliance here. "I am. My family has been in America for fourteen generations. We were some of the original settlers of the Louisiana Territory. Long before the Revolution. Before we get too far, though, there is the issue of my car."

"Ah yes. You drove it into the river."

"An unfortunate consequence of the struggle. It is, however, a Rolls Royce."

"A quality automobile."

"Indeed. I am understandably concerned. I should like to send Maurice to look after it. He is my driver only. He has no further use to me except in that capacity."

"I shall have to have that approved."

"Naturally. But please be expeditious. I am...distracted... with concern."

"Perhaps I can arrange for one of my men to accompany him."

"As you wish."

Smiling broadly, Alexandre leaned back and tapped on the door. When it opened, he spoke quickly to the man in French, then added in English, "And some tea as well."

"Thank you," DuChamp said.

"Now. To business. You present a peculiar problem for us, Monsieur DuChamp. We do not know what you want."

"And you cannot properly ask me without tipping your hand."

"That is correct. So you see? You are an unknown variable in the equation."

"Yet I am hardly your biggest problem."

"Yes. This Ms. Kaufman you spoke of. Do you know what it is she is after?"

DuChamp smirked. "I haven't the faintest notion."

"And yet you are in pursuit? I suspect you are not being truthful, Monsieur."

"On the contrary. I pursue Ms. Kaufman for my own ends, not for hers. *Q'uelle c'est 'mour?* The heart has its reasons which reason cannot know."

"Pascal. Ah, you are in love!"

"I am in pursuit."

"Spoken like a true Frenchman. You are a credit to your lineage. I am prepared to make you this offer. We shall make our pursuit together, as it appears our quarries' trails have converged for the moment. In the event Ms. Kaufman breaks off pursuit, you must do the same. For our part, I promise we shall take no deliberate action to harm Ms. Kaufman, excepting, of course, any inherent risks. For the duration of our arrangement, we shall offer mutual assistance to one another. Is this arrangement suitable?"

"We have an accord."

There was a knock at the door. "Ah," said Alexandre, "our drinks have arrived." He opened the door and passed the tea over to DuChamp. "To love?" he offered, raising his cup.

"What else is worth living for?" DuChamp took a sip. He smiled thinly, keeping his eyes fixed on Alexandre. *Soon*, he promised himself, *the tables will turn.*

THIRTY

THE JOURNEY FROM Bruges to Selçuk by train would take a little more than two days. Evelyn had a heated discussion with her grandfather before boarding the train.

"You can't be serious," she exclaimed, staring at him wide-eyed, uncomprehending.

He grabbed her arm and pulled her close so she could hear him whisper. "What choice do we have? Mmm? We need his help. His expertise. Evie, everything is on the line now. The houses. Cars. Your apartment in New York. All our resources are funding this expedition. If we can't produce the formula then it all goes away. Is that what you want?"

He knew better than to play the sympathy card with her. But everything was still in his name, and unless he produced the formula and recouped his investment, then she'd inherit nothing when he died except the attention of some very determined collection agents.

"All right. Fine. If that's what you want, I'll do it."

"It has to be this way."

"Just remember this. I don't come cheap." She turned to walk away, but he grabbed her elbow, spinning her toward him. His eyes warned her that he was not about to apologize.

"Be convincing," he hissed.

She tore her arm away. "You make me sick."

For most of the first day, Bryce sat in the compartment staring out the window. Dr. Schaumberg had booked them first class—something Bryce had hoped would provide him a decent place to stretch out and relax after the ordeal in Bruges. His legs and back hurt from the exertion of running and being tossed about in a boat, let alone plunging into the river to escape that white-haired, gun-toting lunatic. But rather than relaxing in a large compartment with plenty of room, he found himself in a T-4 Couchette, with nothing more than a pillow and a blanket with which to sleep, and a bunk not much wider than the couch in his office.

For a man his size, it was decidedly uncomfortable.

No less uncomfortable was the silence between them. Evelyn sulked about her ruined purse and abandoned clothes. William fretted about the mercenary he'd seen in Bruges, the one who at first appeared to be working with the white-haired assassin, but then couldn't have been. He'd discussed it aloud for the first two hours of the train ride, coming to no useful conclusions—in effect, talking in circles—until Schaumberg finally told him to shut up, at which point he fell into muted consternation.

Schaumberg was as caustic as ever, snapping at the others for real or imagined offences, and at the porter who brought him tea a little colder than he preferred. Eventually he, too, fell into a morose silence, pulling a photograph out of his wallet and staring at it for hours.

Toward evening, Harry's stomach started rumbling loudly enough for the others to hear. Finally, Evelyn said, "Dr. Bryce, would you like something to eat?"

"No thanks. I'm fine."

His stomach growled, and William smirked, "I beg to differ." Both he and Evelyn snickered. She rose from her bunk and offered Harry her hand.

"Come on. We'll go to the dining car. You'll feel better."

Reluctantly, he slipped off the bunk and stood, still feeling a little unsteady on the moving floor. Evelyn took his arm and helped him to the door.

"Go with them," Schaumberg ordered William. The bodyguard dropped from the top bunk. Evelyn asked her grandfather if he wanted anything, but he shook his head. She bent forward and whispered in his ear, then led the others from the compartment.

In the dining car, Evelyn steered Harry toward a two-person table, leaving William to find his own seat a few rows down. Around them, the conversations of other passengers and the tinkling of glasses mingled with the sound of a piped-in string quartet. Waiters in white coats with black bowties moved easily with the gentle sway of the train, while out the window the countryside slipped by under the cover of night, the landscape only briefly illuminated by the flash of ambient window light as the train passed.

Their server filled their water glasses and offered them each a menu, speaking first in French and then switching to English when Evelyn furrowed her brow.

"Never could get the hang of French," she confessed.

Harry chuckled. "I read it better than I can speak it, but I can manage, I suppose." He settled on a heavy meal of prime rib, baked potato, and asparagus tips with Béarnaise sauce, topped with a French Merlot. Evelyn watched him order, bemused. She settled for a salad and coffee.

"I feel like I haven't eaten in days," Harry spread his napkin in his lap.

Evelyn said nothing, wondering if she could do what her grandfather had asked of her. She looked across the table at the sweaty, obese man in front of her. How could Grandfather ask this? It was so unfair! Maybe she wouldn't have to go that far. The attention itself might be enough. She gritted her teeth, swallowed her pride, and pasted on a smile. "I wanted to tell you how sorry I am that we dragged you into this."

"Hmm? What?" Harry looked up from the menu he'd kept reading, even after ordering. The man was obsessed with food! No wonder he was so fat.

"This wasn't my idea, you know. And uh, well, I only wanted to say that I wish we'd met under different circumstances." She traced her finger along the back of Harry's hand. He stared at it, a bead of sweat forming on his brow.

"Oh dear," he said.

Unbelievable, she thought. The man was a pushover. Instinct told her less was more. She pulled her hand away and drew a lock of hair from her face.

"When we first met, did you..." she made her voice small.

"Go on," he urged.

She bit her lip and looked away. "I'm sorry. I'm being a fool. You're a man of accomplishment and learning. And what am I?"

"No. It's all right." A slight grin playing beneath his mustache.

"It's just that, I've never met anyone quite like you before. And when we met, I was just wondering whether you... you know... if you... felt... something."

"Felt something," he repeated.

"For—for me."

"You felt something?"

"It's stupid. I shouldn't have brought it up."

"No! No, not at all." He grabbed her hand. She could feel the sweat of his palm. "I-I did feel something. It's just... I dismissed it. And in all the chaos, of course, I just never thought you'd feel the same."

She looked out the window, deliberately avoiding his gaze. "If only things had been different. If our need weren't so dire, it would've been nice to get to know you. We could have had dinner, perhaps."

"We are having dinner."

She laughed. "Yes, I suppose we are."

Their food arrived then, and Harry's attention turned to his plate. He greedily sliced through his steak and lifted a large piece to his mouth. An expression of pure bliss washed over his face. Her grandfather seemed to have chosen the wrong temptation. She turned to her salad. "Perhaps when all this is over... if it ever is over."

"You sound despairing."

"I suppose I am. I've been trying to figure this puzzle out, and I'm just not getting anywhere. It's so enigmatic."

He grunted his assent and took another bite.

"If only we could just solve it and get it done."

"Why do you stay with him?"

"Hmm?"

"Your grandfather. Why do you stay with him?"

She looked at her fork. The question was unexpected. Finally, she confessed, "He needs me. And maybe I need him. He's all I have, you know."

"What about your parents?"

"Gone. They died when I was young. Grandfather took me in. Raised me as his own. I was with him when his first wife died, my grandmother. He remarried ten years ago, but then Collin was born, my uncle, technically. There were so many complications with his disease, it tore them apart. Grandfather became obsessed with finding a cure.

That's probably what ended their marriage. I'm all he'll have left, once Collin is gone."

"Do you believe him?"

"I believe in him, if that's what you mean."

"Not precisely."

"I don't know whether or not he'll find a cure in the past, in the plasma he hopes to find. I don't even know that it still exists—but I've seen enough to make me believe it existed at one time. And many miracles have been attributed to its efficacy. I'm unwilling to discount them. So, I suppose it's a calculated risk. If he fails, we'll lose everything."

"I see."

"That's why we need your help, Dr. Bryce." She leaned over, taking both his hands in hers, trapping his fork to the table. "Why I need your help. Grandfather is an expert in his field, but when it comes to Middle Age mysteries, we are rank amateurs. Not like you. You are so brilliant and strong and—and I can't even speak French!"

"Yes, well I—"

"Oh thank you, Harry, thank you!" She rose over the table, grabbed his face in her hands, and planted a long, lingering kiss on his greasy lips. "I knew I could count on you."

THIRTY-ONE

JON LOOKED OUT the window seat of the Cessna Citation X as it banked through the air. He leaned back in the leather chair, drumming his fingers on the burled wood of the table.

They'd taken off a little more than an hour ago, having spent the better part of the previous day securing a passport for Izzy, who had come in on DuChamp's private plane and didn't have one on her. Sean worked his connections to procure the appropriate papers, but it took longer than they'd expected. He mentioned that he'd burned a lot of bridges when he started working for Izzy, as if that explained everything.

Once they got in the air and reached a cruising altitude of 30,000 feet, Jon began to relax. They were en route to Selçuk, Turkey. Though the chartered corporate jet could reach speeds approaching Mach one, Izzy had instructed the pilot to take his time, as they were not in a hurry.

Nothing could've been further from the truth, but the story she'd told the charter company was that they were on holiday and wanted to see the ruins in Turkey. Everything was supposed to look casual. He felt a twisting knot in his gut. Everything was far from casual. How could he have gotten so close to Bryce, only to miss him again? He chewed his lip thoughtfully. Already this "holiday" had gone on a lot longer than he'd intended. He'd felt certain they'd be able to rescue Harry in Belgium—especially once he saw him there. But now? Now it was guesswork. He only hoped the old man's information about Ephesus was correct.

Izzy came back to his table and offered him a tall glass of champagne. He shook his head. She set it on the table and sat across from him, resting one foot on the seat. A few rows back, Sean poured over maps of the ancient ruin.

"You know," she traced a finger along the back of his hand, "you really should take time to appreciate the finer things life has to offer."

He blew out a breath, still staring out the window. "I have no objection to champagne. I just don't feel like celebrating."

"You're worried about Bryce?"

"Yep."

"We'll find him."

"Hope so."

She pulled her hand away and propped her chin on her palm, resting her elbow on her knee. "Thank you, by the way, for coming after me. You didn't have to do that."

"Didn't I? You didn't offer me that much choice last time." He turned from the window and met her eyes.

She sipped her champagne. "You're not still sore, are you?"

He studied her, unsure whether or not to take her

question seriously. How did he feel about her, anyway? After falling back into his life two years ago in the midst of her brother's greatest archaeological discovery and ultimate, untimely death, she'd relied on Jon to rescue her from crisis after crisis, all the while plotting to steal the discovery out from under his nose and leave him holding the bag when the authorities arrived. She was unpredictable and disruptive, dangerous, even. Living life at full volume.

Now she'd kidnapped him in the middle of the night, forcing him to help her in this bizarre quest—and here he sat on a chartered plane, flying across Europe. It was just the sort of thing that would never have happened to him in his simple, cluttered office surrounded by his beloved manuscripts and dusty tomes. An utter contrast to his carefully manicured life. In spite of himself, he laughed. "What am I going to do with you?"

She shrugged, a wan smile tugging at the corners of her lips.

"You really are impossible. You know that, don't you?" he asked.

"But you like it. Admit it."

"I admit nothing of the sort. It only encourages you." They shared a laugh, then he said, "How'd you get mixed up in all this, anyway?"

"Oh, I don't know." She traced a pattern on the table with her fingertip. "I'm always on the lookout for the next adventure. It was Stephen, really. Something he'd been working on for years."

"Figures."

"He'd heard of Triprimacon in various circles. Legends connecting them to Middle Age alchemists in their pursuit of ancient prizes, that sort of thing. That's why I recognized the name at Sotheby's. Otherwise I might not have paid much attention to them. When I went through his notes, I found he'd done far more research into the company than I'd previously imagined. But there was so much misinformation. He had this enormous wall chart all rolled up, and when I spread it out, it was a nightmare of arrows pointing all directions, scribbled out names, circled or underlined. A few photos glued carefully in place. And in the center, the big question: Who are they?" She took another swallow of champagne. "I'd never realized he was so obsessed. But I suppose it suited his personality. My brother would pursue the most unlikely threads, tugging at them until the tapestry unwound, revealing the truth."

"Truth," Jon repeated. He wondered what she knew of the truth.

"Yes. He used to say that the construct we call reality is but a blanket thrown over our eyes. Stephen always wanted to pierce the veil. See what was on the other side."

"And even if our gospel is veiled, it is veiled to those who are perishing. The god of this age has blinded the minds of the unbelieving."

"What's that from?"

"Saint Paul. Second Corinthians four verses three and

four. He's describing taking away the veil that keeps people from recognizing the truth."

"Really? How fascinating."

"He also says the veil is only removed in Christ." He met her eyes again, hoping to pierce the veil over her own heart. If only just a crack.

"Yes. I suppose he would say that. Well," she said, pulling back, "we'll be landing in an hour or so. I guess I'll make arrangements for a vehicle."

She rose and left for the cockpit. Jon watched her go. He glanced at his wristwatch. The flight was supposed to take around three and a half hours. They still had two hours to go. Every time he brought up faith, Izzy fled in the other direction. He wondered what she was running from. What about God scared her so much?

"You'd have better luck nailing the wind as trying to pin that one down, yeah?"

Jon turned to see Sean studying him from the back. He rose from his chair and joined him in the next row. "What do you mean?"

"Means she likes to make her own way. Pains her to ask for help. That's why you won't find her saying 'yes' to Jesus. She won't be asking. She don't want saving."

"Really."

"You have no idea how hard on her it was, asking you for help. And when you wouldn't return her phone calls— it cut her deep."

"Well, isn't it great she had you to turn to."

Sean narrowed his eyes, but a grin toyed with the

corner of his mouth. Jon wondered if he'd take the bait, but instead he said, "I've learned a lot from her in these past few years. And a lot about her. All her life she's lived in the shadow of her brother. He's gone, and now she's the man on top. She wants to prove she's as capable a man as he."

"Woman."

"What's that?"

"Woman. You said, 'man.'"

"You're missing the point, lad. Point is, she's got to believe it herself. Believe in herself. That's why she took on DuChamp. Why she's after Triprimacon. It's always the next adventure with that one. Anything to prove her point."

"You'd think with all this she'd feel successful."

"Och. This? This don't matter. She knows it was you what won the prize. This is all stolen goods, so to speak. Stolen from you, no less."

"Hardly. I wouldn't have tried to profit off the autographs."

"Be that as it may. It still ain't her success. It's yours. Now she wants to have something of her own. That's all that matters to her, now." He frowned then, turning back to his maps.

Jon bit back the question that had plagued him since he'd discovered Sean worked for Izzy. It nagged at him, making his heart beat a little faster than it should.

It was bad enough that Sean was in her employ. How they came to be partners mystified him. But what exactly was the nature of their relationship? Evidently, they'd connected shortly after Izzy took the autographs two years ago. What had happened in the intervening years? Were they just partners, or was there something more?

He shook his head, silently berating himself for thinking this way. There was no cause for jealousy. What he and Izzy had shared died a long time ago. It certainly didn't need resurrecting now.

"And what about you?" he interrupted Sean's map-study. "Do you need saving?"

Sean chuckled. "Och. I'm finding me own way."

"Is that a fact?"

"I know where you're coming from, doctor. I'm just not there yet."

"Okay. But think about this. There's a reason we keep crossing paths. And it's got nothing to do with earthly treasure."

He didn't wait for Sean to respond, but stood and returned to his seat. They had no further interaction for the rest of the flight. Izzy never reappeared from the cabin. Sean finally put his maps away and reclined his seat, closing his eyes. And Jon continued to stare out the window, wondering how he managed to wind up in a chartered jet flying back into a country from which he was permanently banned.

Two hours later, they were on the ground.

THIRTY-TWO

OSEPH ENTERED THE main concourse at Esenboğa International Airport, fully exhausted from the flight. At his age, he really shouldn't be flying. It was simply too much on an old man. Then again, he was the one who had tried to climb out a window and across a fire escape. In his younger days, he'd have made it, too. There'd have been no embarrassing slippage and need for rescue.

Like his disciple, he too once lived on the wrong side of the law. It was the nature of his order to seek out those least likely to serve. Thieves, addicts, the indigent. As Saint Paul himself said, "But God hath chosen the foolish things of the world to confound the wise; and God hath chosen the weak things of the world to confound the things which are mighty; and base things of the world, and things which are despised, hath God chosen, yea, and things which are not, to bring to naught things that are, that no flesh should glory in His presence."

Oddly enough, this same class of people had the requisite skills to keep the secret safe from any and all who would seek to profit from its possession. He only hoped Nicky was just a man. Only one thing would really prove it, but he prayed it would not come to that.

Had Nicky made the flight? And if so, what did he think about it all? There was so much to explain—so much he hadn't told him yet. Couldn't tell him, actually, until he was ready. Nicky had never travelled out of the country before. Surely all of this was expanding his world at an uncomfortable pace. He just prayed it wasn't too much for him to handle.

Through the concourse, he finally saw him. Nicky's face lit up with relief, and the monk who stood beside him nodded placidly. Nicky crossed the corridor in what seemed like two steps, hefting Joe into a tight embrace.

"I am so glad to see you!"

"Oh, put me down, Nicky. You're crushing me!"

Nicky released him. "Where've you been? Did they hurt you? I swear to God, I find them, I'll—"

"Nicky, it's all right. I'm okay." He patted the younger man's shoulder.

"You scared me, you know? What you ever go with them goons for anyways?"

"I thought it best. I did not want any harm to come to you."

"To me?" He rolled his eyes. "Aw Joe, you know I can take care of myself."

"Yes. I know. I just did not want you to have to. Not on my account."

"I can't think of anyone better to do that for, y'know? You're like a father to me. You really are. Ain't many people I'd go to the mat for, but you're one of them."

"I know. Thank you."

"Then don't ever do a thing like that again. You hear me?"

Joe smiled and said nothing. He wondered what Nicky would have thought about his recent escape. He strode toward Brother Davut. Nicky fell into step beside him.

"So you're all good? They didn't do nothing?"

"They only wanted some information."

Brother Davut waited patiently for them near the exit, but his eyes kept watch on the crowds. Joseph felt a tiny bit of relief wash over him. The man understood the danger, even if he didn't know the reasons why.

"Information?" Nicky asked. "What, they couldn't like call or something? They had to kidnap you? Geez-Louise. So what happens now? We going home?"

"Unfortunately, no." He stopped and faced him. "Nicky, you must understand. Events have been set in motion that cannot be undone. You must trust me now."

"Of course," Nicky replied, but Joe had already moved on to the monk.

"Oğlum Davut, biz bir yer isteriz," he said. Nicky furrowed his brow.

The monk nodded and motioned with his hand. *"Benle gel. Benim bir yerim var."*

Joe took Nicky's arm and urged him forward. "Come," he said. "We have much to discuss. Brother Davut has a place nearby."

Together, they left the airport.

Brother Davut drove them around the city to the south-west quarter, passing by a myriad of buildings and homes until turning onto a side street bordered by tall structures with red tile roofs. He pulled in front of a nondescript house with a vegetable garden behind a wrought-iron gate.

As they climbed out of the car, Nicky cast his eyes up and down the street, mulling over the uniform houses. *Geez-Louise, and I thought Queens was bad. I ever get lost here I'd never find my way home.*

Brother Davut clapped his shoulder. "It is safe here. Many Christians in this place. No harm will come to you or the Abbot."

Nicky frowned. *The Abbot? Did he mean Joe?*

Brother Davut led them through the gate and up the steps. He rang the doorbell and waited. Nicky continued to look around, still feeling uncomfortable. Brother Davut's reassurances, far from comforting to him, brought home the possibility that someone might still be after them. Now he felt eyes on the back of his head, like someone was watching them.

Presently, the door opened to a middle-aged woman in a scarf and traditional dress. Her face lit up when she saw Brother Davut, and she began speaking rapidly in Turkish.

Brother Davut put a finger to his lips and replied in a lower voice, using his hands to indicate Joseph and Nicky.

With a look of surprise, she opened the door and beckoned them inside.

"*Sen bazı çaylar ister misin?*" she asked, then, on catching Nicky's confusion, she switched to stilted English, "Ah, tea?"

"Yes, thank you," said Joseph. He glanced at Nicky and gave him a slight nod. Nicky took that to mean he should say yes as well.

"Uh, yeah. Me too. You have a nice house, Mrs… uh, I'm sorry I don't know your name."

Brother Davut smiled painfully, and turned the woman toward the back of the house. She followed him with a stricken look, muttering something under her breath. Nicky looked to Joseph, feeling helpless.

"What I say?"

"It is not your fault," Joseph explained. "In this culture, we do not compliment people on their possessions. They will think you envious. Custom dictates they give you what you envy, to ward off the evil eye. Otherwise the house will be cursed."

"Evil eye? What, so now she has to give me her house?"

Joseph grinned. "Something like that. I suggest you find something wrong with it. Criticize it. This way she will know you do not envy the house."

"Seriously?"

"Yes. Also, you should not inquire about her marital status."

"Marital status?"

"You called her Mrs. and asked about her last name."

"This is a problem? I ain't asking the lady out, y'know? She could be my grandma."

Joseph took his arm as he explained. "The Christians in this country have had a hard time at the hands of their Muslim countrymen. There are those who would impose Shariah on even the Christians—such that a married woman cannot be in the presence of a man she is not related to without her husband present."

"Jeez-Louise. This is crazy."

Joseph chuckled. "The world is full of many different peoples, languages and customs, my son. It can take some getting used to."

He led Nicky into the other room. He glanced at the woman, who smiled at him nervously. He nodded and said, "Yeah, it's a nice house. Little too—um—Turkish—for my tastes, though, y'know?"

Relief washed over her face, and she welcomed him to a chair around the table. He nodded sheepishly and took his seat. A moment later, she served them tea, and then disappeared into the back.

"Brother Davut," Joseph began. "Thank you for your assistance. Brother Nicky is a novitiate in my order. He must be tonsured and take vows before I can fully initiate him into the mysteries."

Davut nodded, but Nicky leaned back and held his hands up. "Wait a second, tonsured?"

"It is nothing," said Davut. "A tradition only. We give you a—" He made a clipping motion on his head.

"A haircut?"

"Yes!" Davut was delighted. "Tradition." He rose and whispered something to the woman. She nodded and disappeared into another room.

"An important tradition," Joseph replied. "As many are. But you must understand this: it is completely up to you. Taking vows is a serious matter. It is not something to enter into lightly, no more than one should get married too quickly. I meant to wait until you were ready, but I find, after so many years, that now I am suddenly out of time."

The woman reappeared with a large towel and a razor. Nicky looked askance at the razor, and then at Joe, wondering what had happened to him since he left the mission so many months before. "You're starting to creep me out, y'know?"

"You must take vows before I can reveal the secrets to you. But if you choose not to—"

"No, no. I'll do it. I mean, how hard can it be?" He laughed nervously, and then swallowed when neither Joseph nor Davut showed any signs of levity. "Wow, that bad, huh? Okay. I mean, uh, fire away, y'know?"

Joseph bowed his head and made the sign of the cross, beginning the ritual. "*In nomine Patri, et Fili, et Spiritu Sancti, amen.*"

THIRTY-THREE

"Come," said Vasily. "It is time."

Andre looked up from his tea with a question in his eyes. "So soon?"

DuChamp studied them both, unsure how to reconcile their relationship. Dumont appeared to be in charge, but the Russian agent preferred to give orders anyway. Almost like they were working for two different employers. He wondered if he could make use of that.

"I have not received notification," Alexandre protested. Just then, his cell phone rang. Vasily smirked and left the room as Alexandre answered it. He set the phone down and sighed. "He is correct. We must depart. Our quarry is en route to Selçuk. Can you tell us why?"

DuChamp shook his head. "I have no idea. But Selçuk is near ancient Ephesus, and if Ms. Kaufman is going there, you can be sure something of value awaits."

Vasily poked his head back in, his face a mask of frustration. "*Toropit'sya!*" he demanded, tapping his watch. Even without a translation, his meaning was clear. DuChamp took another sip of his tea and rose to follow.

In the next room, Andre's men were busily stuffing

their bags, vacating the warehouse. Evidently, Vasily had lit a fire under them with his urgency.

"If you don't mind my asking," DuChamp said, "how do you intend to get there?"

Vasily didn't look at him as he grabbed a duffel bag. "We leave for airport. I have ordered tickets for us. We fly in two hours."

DuChamp frowned. "Airport? You don't seriously mean to use an airline, do you? Fly the friendly skies and all that? You'll never get there in time! Not when Ms. Kaufman has this much of a head start on us. And I can't even imagine the headaches with security."

The Russian straightened, studying him with his normal eye. "And what would you do, instead?"

"Obviously, I'd charter a plane, if I didn't have one of my own."

"Of course we have such a plane, but it is being serviced in Germany. And there are no charters available. I have already checked. If we go to Selçuk, we must take airline."

"My dear fellow, you've misunderstood me. I said, 'If I didn't have one of my own.'"

Vasily relaxed, sitting on the edge of the table. "You have a plane." Alexandre came around, motioning his men to wait.

"Of course." DuChamp lifted the last of the tea to his lips. "We can be fueled and wheels up in an hour."

"How soon before we arrive?" asked Alexandre.

"The flight should take a little less than three hours. We

might even arrive in time for dinner. Or, if you prefer, I can arrange to have dinner served in flight."

Vasily glanced at Alexandre, who said, "You truly are a civilized man, Monsieur DuChamp. Your years in America have not harmed your pedigree." To Vasily he said, "I have no objection."

Finally, the Russian nodded. "Dah."

"Of course," DuChamp cut in, "I'll need to contact the pilot. Let him know we'll be leaving. He'll need time to fuel up and file a flight plan, and—"

Vasily responded by reaching in his breast pocket and tossing DuChamp his phone. He caught it and gave a thin smile. "So glad we're friends now."

He typed a quick text message, informing the pilot of their intentions, and CC'd Maurice with instructions to assemble a team of his own. Newfound friendship or no, it was time the tables turned in his favor.

"All set," he said, pressing send, and quickly deleting the text history. Satisfied, they finished packing and left.

Casper sat in his office at his desk, idly pushing away from the burled oak surface and spinning in his leather chair. He'd been at it for almost an hour now. Stewing, his mother would have called it.

He knew better.

His mother never was a good judge of character, which

was why she chose to remain with his father, even though the man savagely beat her at the slightest whim.

He stopped spinning a moment and stared out the window of the seventh floor office at the parking lot and reflecting pool on the ground below. A brace of ducks took flight from the pond, startled by some noise or movement or waft of scent rising on the wind. They circled in the air for a moment, then returned to the pond, their fears allayed.

Not at all unlike Mother.

He smirked. She had tried to leave his father. Only once did she take Casper with her, bundling him up in his winter jacket and trudging with him down to the station where they waited for hours for a train that never came—couldn't come, because his father had phoned the railroad and gotten them to hold it until he could retrieve his son from the station. She'd come back with him, then, knowing full well what waited for her at home.

The next time she ran off, she left Casper behind. She was gone two days. Then she returned, just like the ducks returning to their pond. She tried it two more times. The last time she came back his father threw her down the stairs, and told the detectives investigating the scene that she fell. Nobody asked any more questions after that.

No one questioned his father.

Casper watched all this as he grew up, and slowly determined he would surpass his old man. One day he would seize the throne of his father at this company and punish him for what he did to his mother. Unlike strength, weakness held no virtue.

It would've been a simple thing to physically beat his old man. He could've done it himself, or hired it out—but that wouldn't satisfy. His father had not simply smacked his mother around. He'd psychically overpowered her. He dominated her mind, her will, her choices—that's why she had kept coming back, begging forgiveness all those years, accepting her punishment as just and deserved.

Casper had made his father grovel, the same way his mother groveled before. And he made sure he did it when the old man was at the top of his game—the pinnacle of his career. That's when Casper struck. In one day, all his father's assets, his money and wealth and political influence—all of it collapsed. Deplorable video cassettes of child pornography were found in his basement. Thousands of films implicating the old man in an international pedophile ring. This, combined with a precipitous loss in the very stocks that made up the old man's massive wealth portfolio, did more than anything to destroy him. Not only did he wind up in jail, but he also lost his ability to mount an adequate legal defense. After that, all Casper had to do was visit the man in prison, and announce loudly what the old man was accused of doing.

The inmates did the rest.

Frederick lacked such ruthlessness. Of this, Casper was certain. There was nothing in the young man's background to give him such an edge. Nothing to fire-harden the steel in his heart. To that end, he still remained pliable to Casper's maneuverings and manipulations.

This did not, however, mean he wasn't dangerous. In this latest round, Frederick had outmaneuvered him; masterfully planted his black knight right in the middle of the action and checked him even while Casper tried to set up his own trap. The boy was frustratingly brilliant. It was his greatest asset.

And his greatest fault.

Despite Frederick's brilliance in recruiting Vasily, he was still just using him to drive Schaumberg closer to the goal. He wondered how Frederick would react once he learned the truth—that everything he'd hoped to accomplish had only served his master's ends.

He spun away from the window and picked up the phone, speed-dialing Alexandre. He left him a simple command. "Eliminate Vasily at your best opportunity and take possession of the artifact at all costs."

"And the American?"

"Dispose of him as you see fit."

Frowning, Frederick put down the cell phone. He'd cloned all company cell phones some time ago, when he'd overseen the upgrade to the newer 4G models. It simplified the process of monitoring his bosses. Triprimacon routinely scanned their offices and phones for listening devices and other Cold War technology, but few of the men in the upper echelons seemed to grasp just how easy it was to spy on someone without bothering with such expensive, low-tech devices.

So, Casper arranged a move against Vasily. It would backfire badly. Still, the Russian was growing instable. His death might be beneficial. On the other hand, if Frederick didn't warn him of the threat, and if Vasily survived, that could prove equally disastrous. Frederick could maintain good faith with the man with one simple text message.

The only real risk was in whether or not Vasily would move on the intel too soon, while they still needed Alexandre's team to contain this DuChamp fellow and whatever other players were involved. Vasily generally resisted micromanagement, especially when he was in the field. But this time he'd just have to manage.

THIRTY-FOUR

GETTING TO SELÇUK was comparatively easy. Knowing what to do once they arrived–that was a wee bit harder. Or so Sean thought, anyway.

He sat on one of three beds in their hotel room and peered past the wrought iron planter to see out the window. Scraggly trees competed with harsh grasses on brown hill-sides, while squat buildings of stone or clay brick hugged the loose gravel roads. Outside, the temperature was a balmy seventy-six degrees. The wind carried with it the salt-scent of the Aegean Sea, scant five miles away.

By far, the hardest part of their trip had been convincing the Selçuk-Efes Airport to let them land. The tower attempted to divert them to Adnan-Menderes in Izmir five times. It was only when he dumped the fuel and convinced the pilot to call in a mayday that the flight controller relented and cleared the runway so they could touch down. But after one look at the mile-long runway and single-engine prop planes that dominated the airstrip, he'd wished they'd listened to reason instead. Izmir was only fifty-five kilometers north, and a darn sight larger. But Isabel insisted on landing as close to Ephesus as possible.

And it didn't get no closer than the airfield right next to the bloody ruins.

Speaking of which–he checked his watch–Jon and Izzy were due back at any moment. The minute they'd arrived, Izzy had wanted to dash off to the ruins to investigate, but both men prevailed upon her to step back a bit and approach the question methodically.

The simple fact was they didn't know what they were looking for. All they knew was that this Joseph fellow they'd rescued had told them the Schaumbergs were en route to Ephesus. And they knew from their own research that the Schaumbergs were after the Grail—or something to do with the Grail, anyway. Izzy thought it had to do with what the Grail allegedly contained.

But that still didn't leave them a whole lot to go on.

In the end, they decided to divvy up the responsibilities. Jon and Izzy would inspect the various historical and archaeological treasures, of which there were several, and Sean would use his contacts over the internet to try and track something down.

At least, that's what he'd told them. In reality, he wanted more information on Joseph. He'd already started a dossier on the man during their flight, beginning with the partial fingerprint he'd lifted from the hotel room and the number he'd seen tattooed on the old man's arm. Almost immediately, however, he sensed something wasn't right.

The number corresponded to tattoos given in Dachau, but the name he came up with didn't match the identity derived from the print. And the man he'd pulled off the ledge in Bruges couldn't possibly have been that old anyway. So either Joseph's tattoo wasn't real, or the man wasn't who he claimed to be. And it was far more likely the latter.

Not that choosing a new identity following the Holocaust was unheard of. A lot of people rewrote their lives after the turmoil of those years. Perhaps "Joseph" had stolen the identity of the real man in Dachau, though why he'd do that remained a mystery. Motives abounded, not the least of which was money, though there may have been other reasons. Speculation led him nowhere.

Even tracking down his information through the fingerprint proved elusive. From what he could gather, Joseph Lake had changed his name dozens of times through the years. Anyone who needed that many aliases raised more red flags than he cared to consider.

Joseph must've been a wee bit more than a mere victim in this whole scrap—he might've been an operative himself, in his time. Mayhap his ghosts had returned to haunt him in his old age.

Sean shook his head. The man was a riddle wrapped in a mystery inside an enigma, as the phrasing went. He put the research to one side and turned his attention to Ephesus itself. This proved equally frustrating, but for the opposite reason. Whereas with Joseph he suffered from too little information, with Ephesus he floundered under too much.

The city of Ephesus predated classical Greece. It was one of the twelve major cities of the Ionian league, the first alliance of city-states in the region. Its founding dated as far back as the fifteenth century, BC, though the surrounding countryside had human habitation at least as far back as 6,000 BC. At various times it was under the control of the Greeks, Cimmerians, Lydians, Persians, Greeks, Romans, Byzantines, Ottomans, and finally, of course, the Turks. It was famous for its temple to Artemis, the many-breasted goddess of the Greek pantheon, as well as temples to Hadrian and Domitian, whom the Romans worshipped as gods. Ephesus also had the library of Celsus, a major theatre, and a bath complex supplied by an advanced system of aqueducts.

As far as Christianity was concerned, the city played a prominent role in both the book of Acts and in the book of Revelation, and it even had its own epistle penned by St. Paul. Sean read every biblical account before deciding that the answer to his question did not lie within Holy Scripture. Not surprising, either, given the scant attention the Bible paid to the Grail—or non-existent attention, as Dr. Munro insisted. Historically, Ephesus continued to be significant to the Church—with a tomb reputed to belong to Saint John, the nearby grotto of the Seven Sleepers, and an ancient house that some claimed to be the final resting place of Mary, Mother of Jesus. A spring close to the site, said to be miraculous, often refreshed pilgrims.

Jon and Izzy had gone to the Mary house with its sacred spring first, and then to the tomb of Saint John. All to no avail. Next they were to inspect the grotto of the Seven Sleepers.

When he heard the room key in the door, Sean grabbed his pistol and spun around, then put it away when he recognized Jon's voice.

"I understand," he was saying, "I do. But there just aren't that many records."

Izzy walked in ahead of him, a girlish pout creasing her lips and brow. Sean shook his head, knowing what was coming next.

She grabbed a pillow and flopped onto the bed.

Jon sat down beside her and put his hand on her shoulder. "We might as well face facts. We're at a dead end. I think it's time you face the possibility there is no Grail. There never was."

"Tell that to Triprimacon."

"Triprimacon may have gotten caught up in the myth just like everyone else. You tell a lie long enough, you can start to believe it yourself."

"I don't buy that. I believe in the Grail. And in everything we've done. You can't tell me it's all for nothing. You just can't."

"Whether you believe it or not doesn't alter the—"

"Professor—" Sean warned. Too late.

"You may not believe it, but I do!" She whirled around and faced Jon. "The Grail is real. And it's here! Maybe not the cup, but what was in it. It's here. And we'll find it. We just don't know where to look."

Jon looked helplessly to Sean.

"Well you're right about that," Sean said. "We don't know where to look, or even what we're looking for. Which leaves us but one option. We wait for the Schaumbergs to show us the way."

"We don't even know if they're coming here. Or where exactly they're headed."

"True enough, which means we've got to make them tell us, haven't we?"

"How do you propose we do that?" Izzy sat up on the bed.

He grinned and held up his cell phone. "Back channels, love. Professor, you remember that mercenary they hired?"

"Yeah, you said you knew him," Jon said. "You think you can get him to turn?"

"Nah. But I can get him to answer his phone, and that's good enough."

Izzy relaxed her shoulders. "Make it happen."

At his computer, Sean logged into a secure site through a back channel password. "Interpol uses cell towers to triangulate an active cell phone. It should give us a rough idea of their direction and speed. Let us know when they're coming and how. All we need to do is give the program the phone number, and make the call. The rest is automatic."

"You're hacked into Interpol?" Jon asked.

Sean ignored him. He pressed send on his phone and waited. A moment later, a voice said, "Hello?"

"William. How are you, mate?"

"Sean? Is that you? What you be calling me for?"

"Ah, seeing how we're working the same job, now, I

wanted to offer you a chance to parley. Avoid any unnecessary unpleasantries, yeah?"

"Unpleasantries, is it? You mean like abandoning me in Ankara two years ago without even my bloody passport?"

"I suppose I owe you for that one, now, don't I?"

"You're bloody right you do. You can make good on it by staying clear of me now. It was you then what took shots at me there in Bruges, yeah?"

"Aye. Among others."

"Then you know what you can do with your parley. You come at me now, Sean, I won't hesitate."

"Is there no way we can come to terms, then?"

"None that I can see. You've got nothing to offer."

"Then may the best man win. Good luck to you, William."

"Keep yer luck. You're gonna need it."

Click!

Sean studied the screen, reading the output from the cell towers on an overlaid map. He turned to the others. "I wouldn't have thought it. They're taking the bloody train. Looks like they're en route from Izmir now. Should be getting in about five, I'd say."

Izzy glanced at her watch. "Then we haven't got much time. Well done, Sean."

She hurled off the bed, grabbing her purse on the way. "Now where're we going?" Jon sputtered.

Sean clapped his shoulder on the way out the door. "Give you three guesses."

THIRTY-FIVE

ARRY STARED AT the Gheerhaert map, holding it next to the drawing of Joseph's tattoo. He tilted Evelyn's iPhone so he could get a better angle on the map. Ever since the previous evening he'd been studying the puzzle, trying to find a clue.

He tried to tell himself that it wasn't because she'd come on to him, but just natural curiosity that motivated him. That and the fact they'd probably kill him if he didn't produce something useful. Still, he couldn't stop thinking about the taste of her lips on his, the thrill that had run down his spine and awakened feelings long dormant. Of course, it was entirely possible she was playing him, trying to motivate him to do exactly what he was doing now. But was it really that implausible, the idea that a woman half his age would be attracted to him? Stranger things had happened, though not to him.

Then again, everything in his life had taken a strange turn, lately.

The train had passed the borders of Turkey sometime early that morning, heading full steam into Istanbul. Here, they'd changed trains again, finally stepping off the Eurorail for the Turkish State Railway. They were scant hours away from Ephesus, and he was no closer to solving the mystery of where they were going or what they were looking for once they got there.

The clue, he was certain, had to be in the letters at each point on the star. Using the *tabula recta* had yielded no further clues. Nor had variations on the word *Quodum*. There were 720 variations on the letters P, T, N, A, M, and I, and the only combinations that made any kind of sense were PITMAN, TIPMAN, and MANPIT.

He'd hoped the map would give him the secret—perhaps something in the order of the letters. But even putting the letters in the correct order of the gates that spelled out Ephesi yielded nothing further than MAPTIN, and that made even less sense.

He shook his head. The only thing that did make sense was that he didn't have all the information. He stared out the window, studying the terrain that flashed by, pondering the age of the earth—the generations and empires that had lived, thrived, and died on this soil before it was paved over by the modern era.

There was a piece of the puzzle still out there, something Joseph hadn't revealed to them, buried under the history of the land. Without it, they were lost.

The *dolmuşe* swept along the D-550 highway past verdant orchards and fields on the left, and limestone hills on the right. Not quite a bus or a van, the *dolmuşe* was designed to provide a modicum of comfort for western tourists en route to the historical sites and beaches of southwestern Turkey. But even with refreshments on board, it still didn't compare to a limo. DuChamp sat in the back seat between two gunmen, trying to drink his tea without constantly spilling it. The ride was fairly smooth, but the large men on either side of him evidenced no concern—nor even awareness—of just how much room they took up, or how little DuChamp was left with. He pressed his elbows into his ribs and lifted the tea to his lips, taking a gentle sip before setting the cup back down on the saucer in his lap. His knees were pressed close together, had been for more than an hour, in fact, and he dearly wished he could stretch them out.

"Monsieur Dumont," he called up front in his best French accent and asked how much longer until they arrived. He found Dumont more cooperative and gregarious when he at least attempted to speak his native tongue.

Dumont glanced back, a bored expression creased on his face. He checked his watch and said, *"Vingt minutes."*

He nodded. Twenty minutes. Surely he could handle that. He settled back in, jostling the shoulder of the brute next to him, earning a glare, and giving him a wan smile in return.

The mercenaries had shown very little gratitude for the flight he'd arranged, nor any interest in the alcoholic beverages or delicacies he'd provided, which, given that he'd ordered them laced with tranquilizer, proved most disappointing. The white-haired Vasily hadn't even let him speak to the pilot alone, which hampered his ability to communicate with his own men. He'd wanted to verify that Maurice had received his text and confer on how many men to bring, but there was no way to do so. All he could do now was trust that Maurice would come through.

He took another sip of his tea, which had grown cold now, and frowned. Ever since Isabel had dumped his car in the canal, things had been going wrong. Now he was caught between a rock and a hard case, with no way out. And that just did not sit well with him at all.

Twenty minutes later, they pulled into the bus station and disembarked. Alexandre turned to him and said, "Now, monsieur, if you please."

DuChamp furrowed his brow. "Please what?"

"Where will we find this Miss Kaufman?"

"I have no idea."

Vasily moved menacingly toward him.

"But if I were to hazard a guess, I'd say she was holed up in a hotel. There can only be so many in this city."

"And you propose we check them all?"

"Something like that, perhaps? Unless our friend here can narrow things down a bit?"

Alexandre turned to Vasily, who glared at DuChamp for a moment and slipped on his gloves. He began typing at an invisible keyboard, staring at something they could not see. After a moment, he mumbled, "*Eto zaĭmet neko-toroe vremya,*" and walked off.

Alexandre smiled at DuChamp and explained, "He will need some time."

Vasily strode purposefully to the sidewalk café beside the bus depot, putting distance between Dumont's men and the American collector, all the while logging into a secure chat room to speak with Frederick. He sent a text message to the man while he ordered his coffee, and then took a seat near the street, where he could keep an eye on the others. He removed a pencil-thin camera from his coat pocket and switched it on as he set it on the table. A moment later, a window opened in his eye-screen, showing an image of himself watching himself in the café. He smiled, amused. *Now I am omnipresent as well.* The effect was mildly disconcerting. He angled the camera to get a view of what was behind him. Omniscience was preferable to omnipresence. This way no one could sneak up on him.

A second window waited, the laptop camera of Frederick's computer. He considered switching it on remotely, then thought better of it. Frederick was fanatical about his own security and quite capable of causing serious damage if Vasily crossed that line—not that Frederick would survive should he actually attack. The most Frederick could do was cause Vasily some difficulty—perhaps by feeding him misinformation, or affecting his online status or the dummy accounts Vasily had set up just for that purpose. None of it would keep Vasily from putting a bullet through the man's head if it came down to it. But there was no reason for it to come to that. Let the man have his illusions of security. He still had his uses.

Presently, Frederick's screen flickered, and his face came into view. Vasily activated his earpiece and said, "I was beginning to wonder if you received my call."

"Of course I got it," Frederick huffed, "but not all of us are permanently wired in like some people I could mention. What is it you need?"

"Information. We have arrived in Selçuk, but the French-American DuChamp does not know where in this city of 29,000 people to look."

"And you were hoping I could tell you."

"Dah. I have searched all the usual places. I have scoured the internet for intelligence, but I do not have time wade through the garbage to find the truth. My study of this Kaufman woman has not turned up anything of use. She is new to the antiquities market. She has employed a mercenary of dubious reputation as her personal bodyguard and assistant, and she is forbidden to enter the country. Her associate is wanted by Interpol."

"Which means there's no way they're staying anywhere under their own names."

"We could spend our time looking for them. Or we could go straight for the prize."

"Schaumberg has to reach the artifact first. I thought I was clear on that."

He shrugged. "It does not matter one way or the other. I merely suggest we lay in wait for him. Let him take possession. Once the artifact is secure, then I can perform the service for which you hired me."

"And Dumont?"

"When he is no longer needed..."

"I see. What of the American?"

"I will let Dumont take care of him. And then I will take care of Dumont."

"And all of this single-handed, while capturing the woman."

"Is not as difficult as you think. What is difficult is knowing where to look."

Frederick nodded. "I've run the numbers. Probability is only eighty-eight percent, but I think I can tell you where they are headed."

"And what of witnesses?"

"I'll make sure the site is cleared for you. Anthrax outbreak ought to do the trick. It'll keep the cops busy and the tourists at bay."

Vasily pursed his lips. "Let us hope you are right."

THIRTY-SIX

JON SAT IN the back seat of the rental car and tried not to fidget. They'd been parked in the same spot for better than an hour now, and his legs were beginning to cramp from all the walking he'd done earlier with Izzy.

Not that he minded the chance to explore the ruins. He hadn't been to Ephesus in ages, not since he'd come on a field trip following his junior year, shortly after Izzy left him—after she and her brother both quit the University for wherever it was they went. He'd spent time wandering the ancient wrecks, getting a feel for the land, mostly trying to come to terms with the ache in his heart. Seeing the remnants of so many lives lived so long ago, pondering their hopes and dreams, their fears and griefs, had given him a sense of perspective. "What is your life?" asked the brother of Jesus in his letter. "You are a mist that appears for a little while and then vanishes."

He'd made a choice then, born out of a sense of the smallness of his days, that he would remain content with his lot and be satisfied within his sphere. He abandoned all illusions of shaping history or being caught in world-shaking events. He wasn't even a chronicler of history, merely one who kept the records for others.

Of course, that was before Izzy swept back into his life, whisking him away into a whirlwind of danger, international intrigue, and ground-breaking discovery. He looked at her now, sitting in the front passenger seat, wearing her Ray-bans and wide-brimmed sunflower hat. She seemed frail and delicate—but there was a hardness to her, a stubborn streak that gave her an indomitable spirit which belied that delicacy.

She was firmly in command of this situation. Even a toughened mercenary like Sean MacNeil yielded to her authority.

And though he didn't want to admit it, he himself had likewise yielded, which explained why he was roasting in the back seat of a car parked outside the train station in Selçuk, Turkey, enduring both the heat and threats of disease—anthrax, no less—instead of sitting in his office back in Michigan, preparing for the fall semester.

"Shouldn't that train have arrived by now?" he asked. Izzy glanced in his direction, and Sean shifted in his seat, but neither of them said a word. He looked again at the train depot. Slender white columns supported a tiled porch. Beneath it, four portals, framed in white, marked the exits from the stone building. A series of wooden benches and small trees in planters sat along the walkway, providing little to no concealment should someone wish to hide.

They should have seen them by now.

Harry felt more than heard the train slow to a stop. He glanced outside the window, staring at the sign of the station as it swept into view, and swallowed nervously. The sign said "*Selçuk*," which he understood, but nothing else made any sense to him. He'd never studied Turkish. Why couldn't they have used a simpler language, like English, or Greek, for that matter? The days were long past when the world had a common tongue.

He turned back to the puzzle before him, staring at the words. He was no closer than he'd been hours ago. Soon the Schaumbergs would be hounding him for results: Evelyn asking him sweetly, and Schaumberg demanding answers, threatening harm if he didn't come through. The problem was, even if they holed up in a hotel room for a week, there were no guarantees he'd be any closer to resolving the mystery. It was almost like the darn thing was written in a different...

He stopped and stared at the letters as understanding dawned. Clenching the paper in his hand, he pumped his fist once. "Yes!"

The others looked up at him, anticipation seared in their eyes.

"Greek!" he exclaimed. "It's Greek! Look," he showed the paper to them, "the letters are almost identical to the Latin alphabet. It probably came from the Greek, originally, though you'd have to ask my colleague Dr. Munro about—"

"What does it say, doctor?" interrupted Schaumberg.

"Martin. I'm sure of it. See? The 'P' is really a capital *rho*. It's Martin."

They stared at him, confusion etched into their faces.

"From the Metaphrastes manuscript? No? It's one of the earliest accounts of the names of the Seven Sleepers of Ephesus. Gregory of Tours gives a totally different listing of names, and everyone just assumed his story would be more accurate, because it's older, but this, this lends support to Metaphrastes, most definitely!"

"What are the Seven Sleepers? " Evelyn asked.

"An ancient myth. Found in both Christian and Islamic sources. The seven sleepers were followers of Christ during the reign of Decius. Sentenced to death for their faith, they took refuge in a cave outside of Ephesus to pray. When the emperor learned where they were, rather than executing them, he chose to bury them alive. He ordered the entrance to the cave sealed. About two hundred years later, during the reign of Theodosius II, a shepherd opened the cave, seeking a suitable place for his flock. The sleepers awoke. Thinking only a single day had passed, they sent one of their number into the city to buy food. The man was stunned to see the city full of Christian crosses and other symbols, and the townspeople were equally surprised to see someone using such ancient coins. Thus, the story came out that the men had been asleep for nearly two hundred years, miraculously preserved and brought back by God as proof of the resurrection.

"The sleepers died shortly thereafter, praising God, and were buried in the same cave in which they'd slumbered for so very long. The same story is repeated, changed in minor details, in the Qur'an, which is why the location remained undisturbed despite nearly fourteen hundred years of Muslim occupation. It is still here, today, in Ephesus."

Schaumberg nodded. "The name must refer to the crypt." He turned to his daughter. "We've found it, Evie!"

Bryce's triumphant smile faded. He raised a cautionary finger. "There's just one thing. The site was excavated in 1927. A church had been built over the site of the cave, and several hundred graves were discovered. Also, during the Crusades, bones from the sepulchers were transported to Marseille in a large stone coffin, which remained a trophy of the church of Saint Victoire. Naturally, the bones were identified as the remains of the Seven Sleepers."

"That doesn't matter. We're not after bones."

"My point is: the site has seen a lot of traffic during the last eighty years. The thought that something would've remained hidden and undisturbed in all that time—it may just be wishful thinking."

The news seemed to have sucked the air out of the room, and a dread stillness took its place. Evelyn put her head in her hand. William picked his fingernail with his teeth. Finally, Schaumberg muttered, "Well. We've come too far to give up now. Thank you, doctor, for your assistance. Come, soon we will know for sure."

"You don't suppose they've given us the slip, do you?" Jon wondered aloud.

"Patience, doctor," Sean growled.

"They're inside," Izzy murmured. "No doubt arranging transportation. They'll want to move quickly, and they'll risk showing themselves as little as possible. They may not know they're being watched, but it's a safe bet they're expecting it anyway."

"How do you know?" Jon asked.

"Because it's what I would do. Here now," she said as a *dolmuşe* pulled up front, "this may be what we're looking for."

Sean raised a pair of binoculars to his eyes and studied the pale blue and white van that stopped before the depot. Jon wanted to ask for a look, but he waited, feeling a knot forming in his gut.

"I think we've got 'em," Sean said.

"Are you sure?" Jon asked. Sean passed him the glasses. He peered through the dancing ovals of the magnified view, studying the jostled image of the *dolmuşe*, wishing he could steady his hand.

But there! In the window for a moment only, he spotted Bryce's unmistakable jowls and mustache.

"Harry," he said aloud.

Sean started the engine, and Jon dropped the glasses to the seat. Seconds later, the *dolmuşe* pulled away from the station, heading south on Abuhayat Street, east on Şahabettin, and then south again on Atatürk. Sean followed them at a discreet distance. About a half kilometer later, they turned again, choosing a narrow, two-lane road that wound in a general, southeasterly direction past verdant orchards and slopes dotted with red poppies and Queen Anne's Lace. At the base of Panayirdag hill they turned north, blowing past a *Road Closed—Anthrax Alert!* sign that barred the path.

"Hey," he said. "What about the—"

"Saw it," Sean interrupted. "I just don't buy it."

"They're waiting for us?" Izzy questioned.

"Let's hope not," Sean replied. "But someone's waiting for someone, make no mistake."

Jon opened his mouth to object further, but thought better of it. Instead, he stared past the brace of coniferous green that loomed in front of them. On the other side of the mount sat the ruins of Ephesus. Directly in front of them lay the remains of *Yedi Uyuyanlar*, the cave of the Seven Sleepers.

They left the car and approached the ruins on foot, Sean in the lead, and Jon bringing up the rear. Ahead of them, a rusty, chain-link fence blocked off the ruins. Signs on the front of the fence warned that the site had been closed, but a large, gaping hole underneath the chain link provided easy access to the ruins. Sean led them up to the fence then raised his hand sharply. They stopped.

"What's wrong?" Izzy asked.

"Oh, it's a trap all right." Sean pointed out the motion sensors hidden in the trees, "and rather hastily constructed at that. Still think it's anthrax, professor?" He turned to

Jon, who was breathing through a handkerchief pressed to his face.

After a moment, Jon dropped the cloth. "Guess not. What do you want to do?"

"Och. Now we just got to find our way inside without being seen."

"How are you going to do that?"

"Give me a minute. I'm working on it."

THIRTY-SEVEN

NEWLY MINTED BROTHER Nicholas ran a hand over his tonsured scalp, feeling damp sweat glaze his fingertips. Tiny bristles of hair had begun to regrow in the artificial bald spot, turning his scalp into sand paper. His head itched and he longed to scratch it, though Father Joseph had told him to stop several times now. "You'll only make it worse," the Abbot had admonished.

So much had happened over the last few days, things he'd never be able to fully explain, much less understand. He shook his head and drew his hand away. Joe had warned him he wasn't really ready. "How hard can it be?" he'd asked in his naiveté. He should've known better.

Joseph had, but that didn't stop him from leading Nick through the vows anyway, and then taking the next two days to explain who Joe really was and where he came from, and what Brother Nicholas would be expected to do.

But Father Joseph was right. They were out of time.

Nicky stared across the gap in the hills at the team of three people huddled by the entrance to the grotto of the Seven Sleepers. Father Joseph said these were the people who had rescued him from his captors, pulling him out of a canal and even going so far as to give him the clothes off their backs. They were good people, he'd said, just misguided as to the truth. And prone to rash action as well, which was why they couldn't be trusted.

Beyond them, he knew, another group of people had already gone inside. These were the Schaumbergs—the ones that took Joe from the rescue mission and dragged him halfway around the world. With them went a professor they'd kidnapped. Evidently, he was now willingly assisting them.

That wasn't too big a surprise. Nicky had heard of Stockholm syndrome before: the tendency of kidnapped victims to choose the side of their abductors against those who were trying to set them free. It was a defense mechanism, the soul protecting itself by aligning with power. Still, it seemed strange to him.

The Schaumbergs, of course, were far beyond trust. Nicky was ready to take any action to oppose them, if only for what they'd done to Joe.

Father Joseph had counseled restraint, instead.

Nicky smiled, despite himself. He'd never been very good at self-restraint. He was more apt to fly off the handle than quietly reason his way through a problem. It's what got him into trouble with drugs in the first place—and why he'd had such trouble at school. It was also why he hadn't quite been ready for tonsure.

Then again, with all that had transpired, now was not the time for measured restraint, no matter what the Father said. Action was called for, and Nicky still possessed just the right sort of skills to pull that off.

"If we can find a way to distract them," he said to Father Joseph, "I bet I can get inside and out again before they know what hit them."

"Patience, Nicky," Joe replied. "We must let events play out as they may. God will make His way clear."

Nicky shook his head and turned his attention back to the entrance to the caves. The group of three was going in now. They looked like they knew about the trap that awaited them, the one the Schaumbergs either hadn't seen or cared to notice. Not that it would make much difference. The men who'd set the trap earlier that day were too many for them, outnumbering them by three to one.

The tall, white-haired Russian—a man Joseph had said was pursuing the Schaumbergs in Bruges—seemed to have eyes in the back of his head. He'd been the one to set the trap, installing motion detectors and laser tripwires throughout the entrance to the ruin. He'd also arranged to have the road shut down and the site declared an emergency health hazard which had frightened the tourists away right quick. Joseph assured him that's what had happened, anyway.

He kicked himself for not getting them there sooner. If only Joe hadn't insisted they strictly obey the speed limit signs, they might've made it before anyone else arrived. They could have been in and out before the others got there, and no one would be the wiser. Joe insisted that the Lord's timing was perfect, and that hurrying would only put them further behind. "Hurry is a temptation," he'd said. "You must ruthlessly eliminate it from your life."

So far, Nicky hadn't seen any evidence that taking their time was working out all that well.

Instead, they'd been watching the site all morning, arriving just after the Russian with his army of men and long before the local authorities evacuated the tourists due to the outbreak of disease. Up until about ten minutes ago, things had been quiet. Then the Schaumbergs arrived, their faces cloaked in white handkerchiefs. Evidently, they either bought the story about the anthrax and were taking minimal precautions, or they suspected it was a ruse, but weren't taking any chances anyway. They apparently didn't realize they were walking into a hastily laid ambush. A few minutes later, the other group came—much more cautious than the first.

Joseph tapped his shoulder. "I think it is time."

"You sure about this?"

"No, but the risk is too great now. I'd hoped we could just wait them out. They're unlikely to find anything without this," he pointed at the medallion Nicky still wore, "but I don't think we can take that chance. There are too many heads working together. 'This they begin to do: and now nothing will be restrained from them.'"

"That's from Genesis, isn't it? The story about the tower?"

"Very good, Nicholas. The tower of Babel. A testimony to man's near limitless potential, when he cooperates with others."

"Or as they used to say at school, 'Never underestimate the power of stupid people working in groups.'"

Joseph laughed. "Quite so. You think you can find your way to the entrance I told you about?"

"Does a rat have legs?"

"Then go. And be careful."

"I'll be back before you know it."

Sean took a laser pointer out of his pocket and aimed it at the nearest motion detector. "Ever try this before, doctor?"

Jon half-smiled, remembering how Demetri Antonescu, a former Romanian Securitate-turned-monk had taught him to do precisely the same thing when slipping past Sean's own safeguards at Izzy's house in Turkey. He'd been amazed then at how easy it had been. "Just once."

Sean eyed him carefully, as if weighing his veracity. Finally, he said, "Right then. On my go, you two hustle over to that rock. And keep yer heads down. I'll join you once you're in place."

He clicked on the beam. A red dot appeared on the surface of the motion sensor. Sean nodded, and Jon and Izzy stole across the path. Jon reached the boulder and turned around, crouched low to the ground. His heart pounded in his chest. He could feel heavy sweat running down the back of his shirt.

Slowly, keeping his eye on the motion sensor and his hand steady, Sean slipped across the sensor's path and joined them by the rock. "One down."

"How many more?" Izzy asked.

"Two or three at best. Worst, he's got the whole place wired. I'm thinking he didn't have much time, which explains why they're so bloody easy to find. Course, he might be a wee bit sneakier. Place two or three in plain sight, and a few more where you don't expect."

"Which do you think it is?" growled a deep voice. Sean stiffened, glancing apologetically at Izzy and Jon as someone pressed the muzzle of a gun to his cheek. Five other men swept around the rock, guns drawn. Izzy and Jon raised their hands.

"I'm thinking it was the latter. You'll be wanting this, yeah?" He held up his pistol with two fingers. The man took it from him and motioned him to his feet.

The man spoke into a microphone clipped to his shoulder. "We got 'em." He motioned for them to start walking.

"Out of curiosity," Sean said, "which one did I miss?"

After a moment, the guard said, "You missed the man down the street watching the road. We knew you were coming as soon as you passed the sign."

"So simple," he muttered. He whipped around abruptly, knocking the gun away and lashing into the man's throat with the ridge of his hand. The man gagged and fell as Sean reached for his weapon.

One of the men behind Jon grabbed him roughly and pressed a gun barrel into his neck. Jon's knees gave way. Beside him, Izzy met the same fate. Sean drew a bead on one of the men holding them, but it was no good.

Grimacing, he lowered the gun. The fourth man came around and relieved him of the weapon.

"I remember you," he said to Sean. "You're the one who blew up the house. You killed my best friend." With that, he smashed the butt of his gun into Sean's face. Blood spurted from Sean's nose. The man hit him again, sending him reeling into the dust.

"That's enough, Stefan." The man Sean had hit pushed himself back to his feet. "DuChamp wants them unharmed."

Stefan glared at his leader, and then kicked Sean disdainfully. "Get a move on."

†hiR†Y-EiGh†

ON!" IN SPITE of their circumstances, Bryce sounded delighted to see him. "It's so good to see you again!"

The man behind Jon shoved him into the cavernous room where Bryce, the Schaumbergs, and William waited. Around them, men stood with weapons at the ready. They were deep in the catacombs, near the back of the cave where the Seven reportedly took their long slumber. High walls of rock and limestone brick rose to a vaulted ceiling above. The floor beneath was dusty and marred by open holes revealing long, empty graves below. Behind them, sunlight poured through the open air where the church once had stood.

"Hiya, Harry." Jon stepped around the holes in the floor. "Came to rescue you. Looks like I got here just in time."

"Isn't this amazing? You won't believe what I've discovered—well, what we've discovered. It's most incredible."

"Sean MacNeil." A bald mercenary with the Schaumbergs helped Sean to his feet, steadying him by his shoulders. He studied Sean's broken nose and swollen eye from Stefan's beat down. "You're looking the same as ever."

"Hello, William."

"I had a mind to punch your lights out for ya. Looks like someone beat me to it. No great surprise there."

Sean straightened and grinned beneath his blood. "Well, you can always have a go, if you're feeling up to it."

"Aye, I still owe ya for Ankara."

"You wanting to collect then? Me wounded and all? Take your best shot, you limey bas—!"

"Enough!" bellowed Schaumberg. "We have more pressing matters."

"Sean," said Izzy, "are you okay?"

Sean turned away from William, wiping his blood from his face, and moved to stand beside her. "Just a scratch."

"And who might this be?" Schaumberg demanded.

"Her name is Isabel Kaufman."

DuChamp's voice rang into the cave where they were held. Faces turned as he entered the site. He strode in regally, coming to stand in front of them, a phalanx of armed men behind him. "She is a thief and a collector of rare antiquities, specializing in first-century manuscripts. She has been following you ever since you left the States. And this bloody mess beside her is Sean MacNeil, her personal bodyguard, a former IRA terrorist turned mercenary, still wanted by Interpol for—how many murders is it now?"

"Fifteen to a hundred, depending who you ask," Sean retorted. "I'm still counting, though."

Pierre smiled as if amused and moved on to stand in front of Jon. "Last, and, well, least, is Dr. Jonathan Munro, Director of Antiquities at the University of Michigan—the man who found and lost the manuscripts that made Ms.

Kaufman so wealthy. How curiously pathetic that you're here now."

"I came for Harry."

DuChamp sniffed. "Forgive me. I should have said, 'how pathetically noble.' And now over here we have Dr. Peter Schaumberg, a geneticist fanatically driven by the fate of his poor, dying son. Do you really believe you'll be able to save him with this quixotic quest?" Schaumberg clenched his fists and fumed. DuChamp clucked his tongue. "Next is Ms. Evelyn Schaumberg, a woman forever overshadowed by her grandfather's madness, and her younger uncle's disease.

"Then there's William Higgs—yet another overpriced thug. Finally, and certainly not least, we have Dr. Harry Bryce, professor of the Middle Ages, and the man we're all hoping has finally solved this great mystery. Doctor?"

Harry swallowed. "Well—"

"Silence," hissed Schaumberg.

"Wait," said Izzy. "We haven't finished our introductions yet. You haven't told them who you are, Pierre."

DuChamp clucked his tongue again, demurring with a shake of his head.

"Oh, allow me," Izzy insisted. "Lady and gentlemen, this is Mr. Pierre DuChamp. He is a rake and a thief, born into wealth long squandered by his profligate family, purveyor of things for which he has no use, except that they serve as accoutrements to prop up his frail ego. He is incapable of assessing true value or acquiring treasures on his own, so he relies on others to do the work for him, then sweeps in at the last minute and stakes his claim. He is a bit player in this drama, with no idea who he is working for, what side he is on, or what is at stake. In short, he is a fool, and the only reason he stands before you today is because he crawled out on the wrong side of the river I dropped him in."

DuChamp gave a polite bow. "At your service." He turned to Harry. "And now, doctor, if you would be so good as to tell us where we can find the Holy Grail?"

"Uh…" said Harry.

Izzy burst out with a laugh, followed by a chuckle from Dr. Schaumberg. Pierre looked nonplussed.

"Yes, Dr. Bryce," said Izzy. "Please tell us how to find the Holy Grail?"

"Well, uh, the Grail, that is to say, the legend of the Grail, is really about, um, the quest for enlightenment. It's not so much that it is out there, waiting to be found, as much as it is in here," he tapped his chest, "within." He cleared his throat.

"What?" asked Duchamp.

"You stupid, stupid man!" Izzy spat. "Do you really think we're after a drinking cup?"

"Well, more like a gravy boat," offered Harry.

"You really have no idea what you're up against, do you?" asked Schaumberg.

"Pierre," said Izzy. "For once in your life, do the smart thing. Take my advice. Leave while you still can. They'll kill you. They won't hesitate."

"She's right," Schaumberg added.

DuChamp's face clouded. Something dark like anger or fear filled his eyes. He nodded stiffly. "I know. But they'll kill you, too. They'll kill all of you if it suits them. One at a time, starting with the least useful," he glanced at the mercenaries and Jon, "until they get what they want. I'm not here as your enemy, Isabel. I'm here to save your life." He now looked at all of them. The arrogance in his tone had evaporated, replaced by something almost bleating. "You're correct; I don't know what this is all about, or what you hope to find in these tombs. All I know is that you must find it. And quickly. Please, I'm bartering for our lives."

Izzy shook her head. "No, Pierre. If we find it, then they'll have no more reason to keep us alive. They'll have everything. I'd rather die than see that happen."

"Oh, speak for yourself," muttered Harry. Heads flicked in his direction. "I don't know about you, but I have no intention of dying today. Not if there's a chance at surviving. I'll gladly give them what they want."

"Harry," said Jon, "I don't want to die, either, but I think we should think this through."

Izzy broke in, "If there's even a chance that the blood of Jesus is hidden away somewhere in this place, or that it would do what these people hope, we must ensure it does not fall into their hands."

"It is most certainly here," said Schaumberg. "And I have no doubt it holds the key to eternal life."

"The blood of Jesus?" asked Pierre.

"Of course it holds the key to eternal life," said Jon. "Just not in the way you people think. It was His sacrifice that saved us. Eternal life comes after death. In the resurrection."

"You can keep your resurrection," said Schaumberg. "And your faith. This is about science."

"Even if it's here, it won't do what you think it will."

"That remains to be seen."

"What are you talking about?" demanded Pierre.

"Will someone fill him in, please?" asked Sean.

"The blood of Christ!" both Izzy and Schaumberg shouted at the same time. They looked at each other, and then Izzy motioned for him to explain. "The blood of Christ was captured in a vessel by Joseph of Arimathea following the crucifixion. As he washed the body of Jesus and prepared Him for the tomb, Joseph preserved the blood in a pair of cruets. After the Church began, these cruets were used by Joseph and his successors to perform miracles of healing. Because of the value of this substance, and out of fear of the Romans, the Jews, and others who persecuted them, the cruets were entrusted to a secret society, birthed here in this cave: a monastic order dedicated to protecting the blood of the world's greatest healer for all generations to come. This is the origin of the myth of the Holy Grail, the Wandering Jew, and—" He pointed around the cavern, "the legend of the Seven Sleepers."

"Triprimacon," said Izzy, "is after this blood. They've been after it for hundreds of years now. In the Middle Ages, Paracelsus led his fellow alchemists on a quest for a substance they called the Elixir of Life. It could cure any disease, heal any injury—even make a man live forever. The elixir they sought is nothing more than the blood of

Jesus preserved in those cruets and hidden somewhere, we believe, in one of these tombs."

An expression torn between stunned bewilderment and hardened cynicism contorted DuChamp's face. "You're all either mad or brilliant. But if half of what you say is true, what makes you think I wouldn't want to find it myself? Can you estimate the value of such a prize?"

Izzy swore. "Pierre, think! These men are cold-blooded killers. You cannot give them the secret of life. It must remain hidden."

"Like hell it must," roared Schaumberg. "My son's life hangs in the balance. I know Triprimacon. They are everything you say and more. But I will not hazard his life just to sustain your sense of ethics."

"You cannot give it to them!"

"I have no intention of giving it to them. Why d'you think I quit? They wanted me to solve the puzzle for them, locate the cruets and develop the serum. They were using my son as bait. Initially I believed their promises. I was desperate. But soon it became clear to me that they had no intention of helping Collin. I had to take matters into my own hands. Yes, I kidnapped Dr. Bryce, for which I have already apologized. Extreme action was warranted. And for his part, he has agreed to assist me, which is more than I could have hoped for. Do you think I would surrender the blood now to you or anyone? We are at an impasse, but I swear to God, I will not blink first."

Izzy nodded, quieter now. "This changes things," she said.

"This changes nothing," sneered DuChamp. "You're forgetting that I have the guns."

"Pierre, these men are using you."

"And I, them."

"They won't hesitate to kill you."

He laughed. It sounded heartless. "That, my dear, is where you're wrong. Once again you've underestimated me, and flat-out misunderstood me. I believe I said, 'I have the guns.'"

THIRTY-NINE

VASILY CHAMBERED A round in his AK-103, prompting raised eyebrows from Alexandre's men. "We are betrayed," he explained, even as DuChamp's voice came over his headset, saying, "It's time we end this arrangement."

There was a brief exchange of gunfire within the cavern, covered by shouts and screams. Vasily grinned. It was time he became a god again. He slipped on his gloves. Logging in through a back door hack to a satellite he'd retasked, he brought onto his eye screen a real-time overlay of their position. He studied the heat signatures around the corner.

Two of their men were down. The remaining four were loyal to DuChamp.

Alexandre was swearing. "I should have known not to trust him!"

Idiot, Vasily thought, ignoring him. Sending DuChamp in alone with some of his men had been Alexandre's idea—a diplomatic ploy DuChamp had argued. "I can get them to talk," he'd said. Alexandre was a fool. He ought to have sent DuChamp in solo, or with their men alone. Never with his own guns.

Pushing past the men to brace himself against the wall,

he studied the satellite overlay and calculated the angle of his attack. Just on the other side, two of DuChamp's men were hustling the prisoners into an alcove even as the others retrieved the weapons from the dead soldiers. Vasily ducked around and fired a quick burst, dropping one and earning rapidly returned fire. He slipped back as the rounds exploded harmlessly against the far hillside.

Flash bombs pinged into view. The first one popped and fizzed, filling the area with acrid smoke. The second exploded, boxing his ears with a thunderous clap and his eyes with a brilliant glare. Dazed, he gasped and spun away from the cave.

More gunfire spat the ground beside him as he raced up the hillside. One of Alexandre's men cried out and fell, his leg blown off below the knee. Vasily dove into an arched alcove on the side of the hill, thrust his gun out and fired blindly down the embankment.

This was no way to treat a god! He checked his clip and looked again at the satellite overlay. Alexandre's men had scattered across the hillside, now engaged in a fruitless game of cat-and-mouse with DuChamp's hired guns. Two of them were attempting to flank Dumont by moving around the burial chamber on the far side. Farther away, creeping down the hillside, yet another figure moved. He zoomed in on him, watching the figure move stealthily closer to the cave.

The man was unarmed.

Vasily frowned. A tourist? The ruins ought to have been swept clean of them by the local police following

Frederick's lie about anthrax. It wouldn't do to have witnesses. Still, at this point at least, that was hardly his problem.

Alexandre cowered against a wall on the far side of the complex, tucked in an area known as the Abradas mausoleum. He'd sent two of his men around the burial place across from the catacombs, hoping to take DuChamp by surprise. Two others were drawing DuChamp's forces away toward the Apsidal hall, where Vasily had fled.

He cursed the white-haired Russian for his cowardice. Surely, this was all his fault! One of his men lay dying on the hillside, with no way to get to him in time. The others were dead where they'd been shot by DuChamp's men. Vasily had suggested mixing the teams. That's how this happened. It went against everything Alexandre knew. You keep your own men under your own command. That's what he'd been trained to do. But the Russian had insisted, saying they needed to keep an eye on DuChamp. It would have been better to keep DuChamp and his men separated entirely than let him have access to them to do the dirty work.

That Alexandre had trusted DuChamp enough to let him barter for the information they so desperately needed didn't matter at all. It was a calculated move. With the information on hand, he could use Vasily to eliminate the American and the rest of them with minimal struggle.

Once done, the only one remaining would be the Russian himself, significantly outnumbered and alone.

He didn't count on DuChamp's men neutralizing his own so efficiently. They were supposed to be nothing more than a private security firm—poorly trained and unused to combat. Glorified butlers with guns. At least, that was how DuChamp had described them when they showed up at the ruins. "I thought we might need more assistance," he'd said. "After all, the ruins are large and difficult to secure, especially when managing four stubborn prisoners."

The man was a fox. Crafty and clever, but now he'd trapped himself in his own pit, and he, Alexandre, would be sure he was buried in it.

DuChamp hefted the gun in his hand and scanned the ridge. He hadn't personally killed someone in quite a while, but not so long he forgot how. He put the weapon to his shoulder and squeezed off a round. The gun bucked in his hands, punching his shoulder. On the edge of the hillside, dirt sprayed outward as the round impacted the earth. *Not bad*, he thought. More or less where he meant to put it.

He studied the ridge line, searching for any telltale signs of movement. Behind him, a spatter of stones tumbled over to the ground below. Whipping about, he peered up, flexing his fingers on the gun. It was harder to see at this angle. A bead of sweat trickled down his temple, threatening to drop into his eye.

"Pierre?"

His eyes flicked in her direction. Izzy was poking her head around from the alcove where he'd stashed her. One of his men still stood there with his weapon raised, aiming at her and looking his way for guidance. The man was under strict orders not to harm her—a fact she seemed dimly aware of. He swore to himself. *Not now, Izzy. I don't have time for this!*

Alexandre squeezed off another round at the men around the corner. He wondered how many men DuChamp had. He might not have completely shown them his hand when the four men met them at the ruins. If he were smart, which he was, he'd have had at least that many and more hidden out of sight. Perhaps that's why he took so long before making his move—to give the rest of his forces a chance to get in position.

Vasily would know. His eye would give him access to the information, like a satellite relay. That's probably what he was using now. Alexandre slipped his Bluetooth into his ear and dialed the man's number.

"Vasily, how many are there?" he asked when the phone stopped ringing.

"Four. One more comes from the ruins, but he is unarmed."

Unarmed? That didn't make any sense.

"Are you sure?" he asked, then regretted it. Of course he was sure. He probably knew where each and every one of them was. "Where are they?"

"Go north ten meters. Very quietly. Two are around the corner."

"Pierre," Izzy called again. "You need to stop this."

"Can't talk now, dear. A tad busy at the moment." He wiped the sweat away and kept his eyes trained upward.

"At least two men are dead. How many more have to die before this madness ends?"

Why wouldn't she shut the hell up?

"There are eight of them, darling. That would make six more."

"And of us?"

He grinned wryly. "Depends on how well you cooperate, doesn't it? Not your strongest suit, in my experience."

She stepped out of the alcove. He gritted his teeth in frustration. *Couldn't she see he was trying to protect her?*

"They'll never stop hunting you. You won't be safe anywhere."

"All the more reason to kill them now."

"Not if we find a way to cooperate. We could all work together. Come to some arrangement."

"Sir?" asked his man, Stefan. Not the brightest in the bunch, but worth his pay, at least.

"Stefan, please escort Ms. Kaufman back to safety."

As Stefan reached out for her, William grabbed him from behind, lifting and snapping his neck before he knew what hit him. Swearing, DuChamp whirled about even as Sean retrieved Stefan's sidearm from his hip and pointed it in DuChamp's direction. William let go of Stefan's body and reached for the machine gun.

"Drop it!" Sean ordered.

DuChamp frowned, and then lowered the gun. William glanced from DuChamp to Sean, and aimed the machine gun at Sean.

Sean immediately shifted his aim to William. DuChamp raised his gun again.

"Well this is an interesting turn of events," he said. "A three-way stand-off."

Thrusting away from the safety of the wall, Alexandre scurried through the open, realizing Vasily could be setting him up even as he ran. Five meters, he slowed abruptly, creeping forward till he reached the corner. Taking a deep breath, he hurled himself around the corner, blasting death with his gun.

A spate of gunfire made DuChamp flinch and whirl, glancing back toward the rest of the ruins. His men were fighting out there. He turned around again. Neither Sean nor William had moved a muscle.

He swallowed. "So what do you propose we do about it?"

Jon stepped out of the alcove. "I have an idea."

DuChamp bit his lip. "All right then. Let's hear it."

FORTY

INSTINCTIVELY, NICKY DUCKED his head as yet another burst of gunshots echoed from the ruined walls. All his nerves were on fire now. Even growing up in the city and learning the drug trade, he'd never heard the sounds of a gun battle such as this. There were a few times when he'd been near a violent crime of one kind or another, and at least once when he'd been shot at. But usually the sound of gunfire in the city meant move away as fast as you can. Now here he was inching toward danger.

At the edge, he turned onto his stomach and eased himself down a narrow cliff face to a ledge below. The drop wasn't more than ten feet, but the last thing he needed was a twisted ankle. His fingers and sneakers sought purchase in the loose and craggy rocks. The prayers he'd been taught caught in his throat as he crept down, escaping the movement of his lips with no sound behind them but a ragged gasp. The sun beat hot on his back and made his hands slick with sweat, threatening his tenuous grasp on the rocks. He reached the bottom in once piece and scurried for cover. As he neared the corner, he saw a man peek around a wall only to fall spastically to the ground, his head bleeding. Yet another stray round bit the dirt to Nicky's left, whipping by his head with a vicious spit.

He ducked and moved forward. His stray hand reached into his pocket and drew out his rosary. He fingered the beads and prayed to God for protection. He crept ahead. The crucifix on the end swayed with each step, a tiny pendulum marking his progress. Every inch further was an act of faith, a movement made in obedience to the divine mandate he'd received, the sacred vows he'd willingly taken.

As he pushed his way up the rise, he peered into the cave straight ahead of him. He frowned. There were three men with guns in the cave, each pointing one at another. Four others remained hidden in the back of one of the tombs, out of sight of the gunmen. A fifth man looked like he was trying to negotiate a compromise of some sort.

A conviction grew in his mind. As significant as the relic was, as serious as the charge laid on him to secure and protect it, surely a human life weighed more in the eyes of God. He couldn't in good conscience save one without at least trying to save the other. He exchanged his rosary for Joe's old medallion, and held it up in the air. He steadied it with his hand, and then let it swing free. The compass needle wavered, moving alternately between north and a different direction. He was close. But not close enough.

After tucking it back in his shirt he scrambled around the hill, and inched closer to the cave's entrance.

He didn't see the man with the white hair, studying him from behind.

Vasily scrutinized the young man's moves, watching him navigate the cliff's face. It wasn't a far climb, but the man took his time. Either he wasn't in a hurry, or he lacked experience climbing. Vasily pursed his lips. He was no longer concerned with DuChamp's men. Alexandre was taking care of them. The Frenchman called him for updates, and Vasily obliged, leading him and his remaining foot soldiers where they needed to go to finish squashing the resistance.

But this young man captured Vasily's attention. Who was he? Why was he so eager to get to the cave? The young man reached the bottom and moved toward the entrance to the caves. He couldn't have been a tourist, as Vasily had initially thought. A tourist would have fled the scene by now. Neither was the man a cop. He carried no weapons, and had made no attempt to radio for backup. All he carried was a rosary and a strange medallion in his hand.

Whoever he was, Vasily meant to find out.

Joseph pressed his fist to his mouth, inadvertently biting into his knuckle. He should never have sent Nicholas in there! It was too dangerous. What was he thinking?

From the top of the hill, he watched as Nicholas moved closer to the goal Joseph had set for him. He'd deliberately put the boy in danger. How could he have done that to someone so young? Joseph should have gone himself. It was his responsibility, not his novitiate's. He shook his head. No, not a novitiate any longer. Nicholas had taken his vows, and the responsibility belonged to him as well. Nicholas had entrusted himself to God and dedicated his life to Divine service. He was in the Lord's hands now.

The white-haired Russian closed in on him, moving stealthily from rock to rock, like a lion stalking its prey. A scripture verse came to Joe's mind, from Saint Peter's first epistle. *Your adversary the devil, as a roaring lion, walketh about, seeking whom he may devour.*

In that moment, he realized what he needed to do. He closed his eyes a moment and prayed for the strength to carry it out.

The Lord may guide Nicholas's destiny, but that didn't mean Joseph wasn't meant to assist. He pushed away from the rock and scrambled down the hill, heedless of the noise he made. Perhaps Nicholas would hear and look back and realize the danger.

Vasily dropped into an empty grave and took several breaths to slow his racing heart. He hadn't been this stimulated by a pursuit in a long time. It was almost as if something unseen worked its will against him. Three times now, he'd almost given away his position. Stones scraped louder beneath his feet than he thought they should, echoing from the cavern walls, as if the ground itself were alarmed by his presence. He grimaced, pushing such thoughts from his mind.

Even though his progress was painstakingly slow, he'd steadily gained on his quarry. A stealthy approach precluded haste. If this sacred site wanted to reveal his presence, it would have to do so without his mistakes. He mustered all his skill to stalk silently. Now, the young man was only ten meters away. He'd have him in moments.

Another panicky burst of static came from his radio, and his hand strayed to his earpiece, as if reminding himself that no one else could hear the transmission. Alexandre was calling for an update again. He brought up the overlay on his eye again and studied the positions of the men. The satellite was almost out of range. Already, white noise obscured the image of the hillside, and the heat signatures were very faint. Soon it would go dark altogether.

"Move your man thirty meters to the west," he whispered.

"Then what?"

The screen flashed static and went out. He was mortal again. No other satellite would pass within range for at least an hour. And that was too long to wait.

Alexandre was growing impatient. "Vasily?"

"Then find your own way. I have other concerns."

He hung up and scurried closer to the youth who still advanced on the cave. The intruder had reached the edge now. Soon he would have to come out into the open, exposing himself to the guns.

Other concerns? Alexandre's eyes grew wide. What other concerns could the man possibly have at a time like this? He swore. He was down to a single man, and there were still two others out there, stalking him. Vasily was supposed to be helping them out!

Unless...

"*Mon Capitaine*?" His man awaited orders. Alexandre gave him Vasily's last instructions. Surely between the two of them, they could remove this final threat. And then?

Then he would deal with the Russian. Permanently.

Nicky swallowed hard, raised his hands, and crept around the edge. He only hoped they wouldn't shoot him. He froze when the cold barrel of a gun pressed the nape of his neck.

"Who are you?" said a voice in a thick accent. Russian or something.

Nicky shook his head. "No one."

"Hands behind your head."

Nicky complied. Rough hands pawed his sides, patting him down. "I'm unarmed," he said.

"Turn around."

He turned to see a white-haired man in black with an assault rifle pointed at Nicky's chest. There was something odd about the man's eye. "Do you think I will kill you?" the man asked.

"I sure as hell hope not."

"Then do not lie to me again. Who are you?"

"M-my name is Nick… Nicholas. I'm a monk."

"A man of the cloth. You come to pray for the dead?"

Nicky shook his head.

"Then why are you here?"

"I was sent to retrieve something."

"Indeed. And what would this be?"

Again, Nicky shook his head.

"Speak!"

"I cannot. I have made a sacred pledge."

The white-haired man smirked. "Then come with me. We will see about this pledge of yours."

Joseph drew up short and flattened himself behind a rock even as a spatter of stones skittered down the slope. He was too late. The white-haired man had Nicky at gunpoint, and if Joe drew his attention now, he'd lose all hope of rescuing his son in the faith. The man glanced at the hillside, but gave no indication he saw anything. Joe waited, praying desperately behind the rock before hazarding a glance back around.

When he looked again down the embankment, Nicky was gone.

FORTY-ONE

A SURRENDER? THAT'S YOUR idea?" asked
DuChamp.

"A cease-fire," Jon replied.

Sean and William exchanged a glance. DuChamp looked
exasperated. "And how will that change things?"

Jon took a breath and stepped between the gunmen.
Effectively, all three weapons were now trained on him.
He tried not to think about it. "Well, for starters, we could
actually find out whether or not there's anything worth
killing each other for. I mean, here we are in this ruin.
We're all after the same thing, more or less, but we don't
even know if it's here, right? Harry?"

Harry gave him a blank look.

"You wanna back me up on this, Harry?"

Harry nodded to DuChamp, not saying anything. Jon
decided it was the best he was going to get. He turned back
to DuChamp and tried to smile. "I mean, it's been fifteen
hundred years."

"Almost sixteen, actually," Bryce offered.

"Sixteen hundred years then." Jon wrinkled his nose.
"You see, that's a lot of time. A lot could have happened.

I mean, maybe there's a reason no one's ever found it till now."

DuChamp sucked his teeth. "So you propose we look for the relic first, and only then if we find it, do we commence with killing each other? Hmm?"

"Well, maybe not the last part, but that's the long and short of it, I guess."

He snorted. "How gentlemanly. Very well then, but have your men lower their weapons first. A show of good faith, you understand."

Jon swallowed and turned around. "Dr. Schaumberg? Izzy?"

After a moment, they each nodded in turn. Sean was the first, relaxing his hold so the pistol grip swung up on his finger. William lowered his submachine gun.

Smiling broadly, DuChamp looped the gun strap around his shoulder and swung it around his back. "Well then, we have an accord. Perhaps, doctor, you're not as useless as I first imagined."

"Thanks?" Jon lowered his arms.

DuChamp gestured at the tombs. "Now, if you could please point the way."

"Hold on a second," said William. "There's still that other team out there."

"Quite right." He lifted his radio to his lips and spoke quickly, "Alexandre, my dear man, would you be amenable to a cease-fire?"

A string of French epithets answered him.

"Yes, yes," he replied. "All in good time. But as it has

been pointed out to me, none of us know whether or not what we seek is actually here. What say we find it first, before any more blood is unnecessarily spilt?"

After a long pause, the voice on the radio said, "*D'accord.*" Moments later, Alexandre appeared around the bend, along with one of his gunmen. His weapon hung from a shoulder strap, and his hand lingered near the stock.

"Weapons down, *mon ami*," called DuChamp. The gunman looked doubtfully to Alexandre, who gave him a curt nod and passed him the rifle. Slinging his own gun off his shoulder, the gunman leaned them both against a rock and raised his arms to show he was empty-handed.

"Your sidearm as well."

Grimacing, the man turned around and pulled his sidearm from its holster, setting it on the ground beside the assault rifles.

"Where are the rest of your men?" DuChamp asked.

Alexandre's man shrugged. "We're all that's left."

"Tragic. Good call, Dr. Munro." He smiled and put his weapon down as well, and, directed by their employers, both Sean and William put the guns to one side. At last, smiling broadly, DuChamp called out to his men.

"Sullivan, Giraudoux, and whoever else may be left, would you be so kind as to remove these weapons from the prisoners?"

Alexandre swore even as his man dashed back to the rifles leaning against the wall, but he froze midway, putting his hands on top of his head as DuChamp's two remaining men appeared over the edge of the rise, their weapons trained on the rest in the group.

"A double-cross?" asked Izzy. "That's your idea of a cease-fire?"

DuChamp smiled broadly. "You yourself said I was a liar, my dear. I'm only playing the part I've been assigned." He motioned his men to come forward into the graveyard.

At that moment two shots rang out, and his men fell to the ground, dead. DuChamp pivoted abruptly, diving for his gun, but a final gunshot echoed from the rocks. DuChamp's body lifted off the ground and fell to one side, blood staining the earth from the hole in his skull.

Evelyn screamed and fell back against her grandfather, who put his arms around her protectively.

"Oh, Pierre," moaned Izzy. She turned and stared helplessly at Sean and Jon.

Vasily came into view, his white hair glistening brilliant in the mid-day sun. In front of him marched a young man in brown vestments and sneakers, a haggard look across his face. The Russian took a moment to study those who were left. Alexandre nodded to his man to get their weapons, but Vasily stopped him with a *"Nyet!"*

"Qu'est-ce que c'est?" Alexandre demanded, but Vasily cut him off with a glare.

"Now we do things my way," the Russian growled. He pointed to Jon and Harry. "You two. Start digging."

Jon felt sheer panic raking his insides. He closed his eyes briefly and forced it down, focusing all his energy on the task at hand. "Where?" He turned to Harry. "Where do we look? Any ideas?"

Harry didn't answer. His eyes were fixed on Vasily. Jon called his name and repeated the question. Harry stammered, "Dear God, he's going to kill us, isn't he?"

"Come on, Harry. Stay with me." Jon crouched down and kept his eyes off the Russian. He touched his friend's shoulder. "You need to help us out. Where do we look?"

"We n-need to look in Martin's t-tomb."

"Martin?"

"One of the seven—seven sleepers."

"Okay. That's good. You're doing great. Now, which one is Martin's tomb?"

Harry continued to stare at the assassin. "I don't know.

"Harry, please."

"I said I don't know! So many other saints and faithful men were buried here over the years."

Jon looked over the crypt, his mind working once again, studying the puzzle. "The graves in the walls would've been added later, as part of the church."

"So the floor?"

Jon met Harry's eyes. *The man is doing it*, he thought. The academic was rising within him, engaging the mystery. Solving the puzzle.

"Scripture says the church is built on the foundation of the apostles and prophets. The early Christians took that literally, burying relics of the saints in the floor of the church."

"Every altar has to have a relic in it," Harry offered.

"Exactly."

Evelyn stepped up next to Harry, surveying the floor graves. "Is there any way to know which one is his?" Harry glanced her way. She wore an expression of worried concern.

"They would have left a way for us to find out," Harry muttered.

Jon rose to his feet and looked over the graves. "What's the order of the names?"

"Metaphrastes. Metaphra—got it. Mary Jane, Mary Jane, don't eat any."

"What?" Jon frowned, wondering if his friend was losing it.

Harry worked his fingers. "It's a mnemonic. M. J. M. J. D. E. A. That's—ah—Maximillian, J-Jamblichos, Martin, John, Dionysios, Exakostodianos, An-Antoninus!"

"Harry, you're a genius."

"W-wait. It might be Martin, John, Maximillian, Jamblichos, Dio—"

"It's okay." Jon smiled and patted his shoulder. "So it's either the first grave, or the third."

"Wait. Is it right to left or left to right? Front to back or back to front?"

Jon shook his head, and ran a hand through his hair. "I don't know."

"Even if we start in the right grave, it could still be empty. I mean, the bones are long gone, taken to Marseille. For all we know, the cruets might have gone with them.

After nearly sixteen hundred years, it is highly unlikely we'll find anything here. Just as I warned you."

A report echoed in the ruin, and William gasped, sagging to the ground, a crimson stain welling on his chest. Sean caught him as he fell, lowering him to the ground. Heads spun between William and Vasily, whose lip curled in a snarl, his gun outstretched. Behind him, Alexandre motioned for his man to get his gun. Vasily kept his gun leveled at Sean.

Sean ignored him, pressing his palm against the wound in William's chest. "Bloody hell!" he exclaimed.

"Start digging." Vasily enunciated his words carefully, his tone dripping with menace. Jon leaped into the nearest grave and helped Bryce climb down. He glared up at the Russian.

"We don't know where to dig!"

Vasily turned his glare to the young man he'd marched in ahead of himself. "You. You know something. Don't you?"

The man shook his head. "I don't know nothing."

"You are lying."

"Even if I did, I wouldn't tell you."

Vasily loomed behind him, tracing the barrel of the gun against his neck. "I think you will."

The man dropped to his knees and ripped his rosary out of his pocket. He started muttering his prayers with his eyes clenched. Vasily growled and snatched the prayer beads out of his hand, clutching them in his fist.

"Leave him be!" Jon yelled.

Vasily leveled the gun at the young monk's head. "Perhaps you say your final prayers, now."

Sean held William's hand, and put pressure against the wound in his abdomen with the other, fruitlessly trying to staunch the flow of blood. William's breathing was rapid and shallow.

"Hang in there, mate," Sean said. He barely heard the drama unfolding by the graves.

A faint smile curled at William's mouth and he shook his head. "You still owe me one," he whispered.

Something like a shadow passed over Sean's face. He nodded once. Placing William's hand over the wound, he ordered Schaumberg, "Keep pressure on his wound." Schaumberg hesitated, but a glare from Sean drew him down to his wounded man.

Izzy said, "Sean, what are you doing?"

"I'm going to end this."

FORTY-TWO

S EAN—" IZZY WARNED, but he turned away from her, rising to his feet and moving toward Vasily. At that moment, Vasily caught sight of Alexandre's man reaching for the guns. He spun quickly, firing even as the man cried out and tossed the gun to Alexandre. The man fell. Sean charged. Vasily turned and shot Alexandre, who still juggled the gun his man had tossed him, dropping him as well. Vasily kept swinging his arm in a smooth motion, leveling his gun at Sean's head. His last shot punctured the air where Sean had been just a second before, but the mercenary dropped. He launched himself forward, drove his shoulder into Vasily's ribs, and took him down. The bullet pinged uselessly off the walls of the cavern.

Vasily and Sean tumbled to the ground. The gun skittered across the cavern floor. The men scrambled to their feet. Vasily came up first, launching a vicious snap kick at Sean's head. Sean barely blocked it, slipping back a step even as the Russian agent advanced with a furious combination of hand and leg attacks. Sean fought back, taking an elbow across his jaw. He saw stars. Instinct alone kept him on his feet. A quick jab caught Vasily's head, snapping it back and stopping his onslaught. Abruptly, Sean dropped low, wheeling a spinning sweep kick to Vasily's ankle. Vasily dodged the kick but lost his footing on the rocky ground and stumbled. Sean dodged in with a side kick, lashing into his ribs. Vasily absorbed the blow, grunting even as he caught Sean's ankle and twisted. Sean rolled out of the hold, coming up on the far side with his hands ready, favoring his ankle.

Vasily drew a knife from his belt, feinting at Sean's ribs. Sean raised his guard, leaving his stomach exposed. Vasily lunged, exactly as Sean wanted him to. He caught the Russian's hand just behind the wrist, twisting it into a lock and peeling the knife out of his fingers. Vasily responded with an elbow to Sean's forehead, driving him back and breaking the hold.

They charged in again with jabs and counter punches, each failing to land a decisive blow. Vasily caught Sean in an arm lock, twisting his shoulder against the socket, driving his forearm behind his back. Sean cried out, but his voice was drowned by a shot puncturing the air.

Both men stopped, panting and staring at the young man in the brown monk's robe and sneakers, holding Vasily's silver handgun aloft. Furious, Vasily released Sean, shoving him away.

"I'm thinking I got the gun now, maybe I should call the shots for a change."

Nicky motioned with the gun barrel, sending both Sean and Vasily over to stand with the others. "Hands up," he ordered. Sean massaged his shoulder. Harry and Jon put their hands on their heads, staring up at Nicky from the grave in the floor. "I don't know who you people are," he said. "Maybe you're the ones that took Joe. Maybe you're not, but I think you all should clear on outta here."

"You should put that toy down before you get hurt," said Vasily, his arms raised.

"You think I don't know how to use a gun? Don't let the monk robe fool you. I wasn't always this holy." As if to emphasize his point, he gripped the gun with both hands and fired a round into the air, and then pointed it back at them.

A sly grin creased Vasily's face. "Dah. You can shoot a gun. Good for you." He started moving closer, taking slow steps toward him.

"Get back," Nicky said.

"But shooting the air? Shooting a target?" Vasily continued his slow approach. "Is not the same as shooting a man."

"You'd better do it, son," Sean said.

"Are you prepared to do that?" Vasily continued. "What will happen if you kill me? Do you think I will go to heaven? Or will I burn in hell for all eternity?"

"Get back!"

"Bloody hell, shoot him!"

"My immortal soul hangs in the balance. Can you live with yourself? What will you say to God when He asks why you did not save me? When He asks you why you murdered me in cold blood?"

He'd almost reached him now. Nicky's hands were shaking on the gun, hot tears streaming down his face.

Sean bent down and picked up a rock in his good hand. Vasily put himself directly in front of the gun.

"Can you live with yourself? I think not."

Just as he grabbed hold of the gun slide, Sean struck him from behind with the rock, knocking him unconscious to the ground. Nicky stared at him for a moment over the prostrate form of the Russian. Then Sean bent forward, removed Vasily's laces from his boots, and secured his arms behind his back, grimacing as he used his mangled arm. When he stood, he held out his hand for the gun.

Nicky swallowed hard.

"It is all right, Nicky. Give him the gun."

Sean and Nicky both turned as Joseph shuffled into the ruin.

"That man was going to kill me," Nicky said.

"Aye," Sean answered, still holding out for the gun. "And he'd have slept soundly just the same. He's remorseless, that one is. I don't think God would've faulted you that."

"Give him the gun, Nicky." Joe nodded. He put his hand over the pistol and gently pried it out of Nicky's fingers, handing it to Sean. Sean checked the clip and slipped it into his belt behind his back.

Jon climbed out of the pit and bent over the prostrate form of Vasily, checking his pulse.

"He'll live," said Sean.

Jon nodded and moved to the other victims lying in the compound. After a moment, Sean turned to check on William, but it was too late. He straightened when

Jon returned after examining the rest of the men. Jon wore a harrowed, drawn expression. "They're all dead. DuChamp's men. These others." He shook his head.

At that moment, Schaumberg grabbed the gun from behind Sean's waist. Sean twisted about, but too late.

"Bloody hell! Haven't we had about enough of this?" Sean asked, his palms out.

"I'll say when it's enough," Schaumberg snapped.

Evelyn turned on him, her face taut. "Grandfather! Please!"

"Not now, Evie!"

"Do you think Collin would want this? How many more have to die so he can live?"

Schaumberg glared at her. "That," he snapped, "is up to him." He nodded at Joseph. "So glad you could join us, Mr. Lake. Now, if you please. Where are the cruets buried?"

"Don't tell him," Izzy said.

"Shut up!" he barked.

"Hey now," Sean growled.

"Mr. Lake?"

"Joe?" asked Nicky.

Joe put out his hand and patted Nicky's shoulder. "It's all right. Dr. Schaumberg, I cannot help you. What you seek isn't here. It hasn't been for a long time."

"Then where is it?"

"Gone."

"You're trying my patience, old man."

Joseph eased himself down into a sitting position against a rock. "It is true," he began, "the cruets were here. At one time. Long ago. My father told this story to me, and I will now tell it to you. It is all right, Nicky," he said as Nicky objected. "They've come so far and so many have died because of this. Perhaps it is time they heard the truth."

Turning back to the group he said, "Joseph of Arimathea, my ancestor, took the blood of Jesus from his body when he washed it, and saved it in a pair of cruets. This you know. This is the Holy Grail of which so much myth and legend has been written. He kept them with him, taking them to Glastonbury on his travels as a tin-merchant and then back again, performing miracles and spreading the Gospel of our Lord. But others arose—Druids he encountered in England among them—who sought the power of Christ for themselves. Just as Simon the Sorcerer tried to buy it from Peter, they tried to buy it, and failing that, to steal it for themselves."

Nicky came around and sat at Joseph's feet, listening to the tale.

"Fleeing persecution and fearing that others might steal the gift, Joseph entrusted the two vials to his seven disciples, who bound themselves with an oath not to sleep or rest unless the cruets were secure. The legacy was passed down from father to son, kept safe from persecution and strife until the sixth century, when in fear it was decided to divide the gift into seven parts and send them throughout the world in the hopes of protecting the gift. Should one be destroyed or compromised, the rest would remain in the possession of the Church. One went north to Germany. Another to the Vatican. John took his to India. A fourth went first to Spain, and thence to the new world. A fifth back to England. A sixth to Africa, and the seventh was kept here, in the tomb of my ancestor Martin."

Bryce sputtered from the grave in the floor. "Are you talking about the legends of Barbarossa? Prester John? The Fountain of Youth?"

Joseph gave him a wan smile. "Yes, Dr. Bryce. Everyone thought Ponce De Leon was looking for the Fountain of Youth. But that legend only became attached to the explorer after his death. In truth, a priest in De Leon's retinue carried some of the blood with him as a means to convert the native tribes. As for Prester John? He was the John mentioned in Metaphrastes' manuscript. And Dionysus, of course, became pope."

Bryce furrowed his brow. "Pope Dionysus reigned from A.D. 259 to 268. But the sleepers didn't emerge until Theodosius the Second, some two hundred years later."

Joseph smiled. "Dr. Bryce, you didn't seriously think these men slept for two hundred years, did you? Or that I am the Wandering Jew?"

"I suppose not." He blushed.

"The scriptures themselves tell us, *'His days shall be an hundred and twenty years.'* The Lord has put an expiration date on us all. The Hebrew writer warns us, *'It is appointed unto men once to die, but after this the judgment.'* And, *'We must all appear before the judgment seat of Christ; that every one may receive the things done in his body, according to that he hath done, whether it be good or bad.'*

"Nevertheless, I think you will find that all sleeper

myths and legends of eternal youth and life have their origins here, in this very spot. They all have a part of the truth, just as they all had a part of the blood. Life went out into all the world, and the Gospel went with it. Miracles were performed, and the legends grew out of that. We tried to keep it secret, but it was often put to use in times of great need, bringing healing to some and spreading the message of salvation. Word leaked out. Eventually, however, the blood was used up. The miracles passed out of thought and time, becoming only legends for scholars to speculate about. There is nothing left now but the memory."

"You lie!" Schaumberg snarled. He straightened the gun. "Tell me where it is!"

FORTY-THREE

I AM SORRY, DR. Schaumberg," Joseph said. "I do not have it. I sense nothing that I say will convince you. Your son's disease is tragic. But is this not more tragic, the man you've become in your quest to save him?"

"I've done what I *had* to do!" Tears streamed down Schaumberg's reddened face.

Joseph's voice was soft, pleading. "You've already lost your son. Must he also lose his father? You put your faith in the blood of Jesus to save your son. Trust that blood now to save your soul."

The gun shook in Schaumberg's hand. A grin tortured his face, and nothing came out of his mouth but a groan. Evelyn touched his shoulder.

"Let him go," she said softly.

He closed his eyes. "I can't."

"You've done everything you could do. Collin wouldn't want this."

"Collin—" he gasped, lowering the gun.

"We will pray for him," Joseph said.

Schaumberg opened his eyes, turning a baleful glare at Joseph. He raised the gun even as he screamed.

"No!" Nicky flung himself in front of Joseph as the gun

went off. Nicky's eyes widened in surprise. He turned to Joseph, grasping his shoulders even as he fell into the man's arms.

Sean caught Schaumberg's arm, raising it up and removing the gun. He ejected the clip and round from the chamber, and threw the gun away.

Nicky collapsed to the ground, and Joseph bent over him, holding his face. "Nicky," Joseph panted.

"Give me the blood," Schaumberg screamed.

Sean hit him, knocking him to the ground.

Joseph turned slowly toward the geneticist. "You vile wretch of a man," he growled. "If I had it, do you not think I'd use it now, to save my son's life? Here, here is your elixir!" He held up his palm, slick with Nicky's blood, offering it to Schaumberg. "Is this blood enough for you?"

Jon came over and bent down beside him. Joseph ignored him, cradling Nicky's head in his lap.

"Let me help you," Jon said.

"Leave us."

"Joe?" asked Bryce.

"All of you. His blood is on your hands. Leave us be." Pulling out his crucifix, Joseph made the sign of the cross over Nicky's head. "*In nomine Patri, et Fili, et Spiritu Sancti*," he began, his voice breaking.

Jon rose and helped Bryce out of the grave. He looked once at Izzy before turning and leading Harry out of the ruin. Sean picked Schaumberg up and gripped his shoulder. "Let's go," he said. Evelyn took his other side, and with Izzy following, they led the beleaguered doctor from the graves.

They shuffled out of the ruin, climbing over broken slabs of the ancient church and under the useless fence to where their vehicles waited on the other side. Jon tried to insist they check the wounded men to see if any still lived, but Sean grimly propelled him forward. "You can't save everybody, yeah?" he said.

On the outside, Schaumberg collapsed to the ground, covering his face in his hands as sobs wracked his body. Broken sighs and moans escaped his lips, but the only discernable words, which he kept repeating, were, "What have I done? What have I done?"

Jon shook his head, finding nothing with which to comfort the man. He turned to Bryce. "Come on. We've a plane chartered. It can get us home. I'm sure Sean can cook up something that will get us into the country without too many questions."

Harry licked his lips. "Do you think people can change?"

Jon looked at Schaumberg, and then at Sean and Izzy. He turned back to Harry. "Sometimes. But not enough to make a real difference."

Harry straightened. "I'd have thought you'd be more hopeful."

"I am, actually. Just not in our ability to change ourselves. I think change comes through Christ. My hope is in Him."

"I think I've changed. So much of what Joseph said has altered my view of the world. Of history. I've spent my life studying it, and now I feel like a rank amateur all over again."

"You've been through a lot."

"Yes. I'm not going with you, Jon. I'm not ready to go home. Not yet."

Jon frowned, wondering what had come over his friend. "Where will you go?"

"I don't know. Perhaps Marseilles." He turned and studied Evelyn and her grandfather.

Jon drew his attention back. "You think the blood is still out there? Even after everything Joseph said?"

Harry hazarded a glance at Izzy and Sean. "Let's just say I'm more open to the possibility now than ever. After all, Joseph also said the blood was divided into seven parts and sent throughout the world. It's made me think of the threads of truth running through so many of those Middle Age myths I'm so fond of. I'd like to follow up on some of those threads, see where they lead."

Jon pressed his lips into a thin line, realizing there was little left to say. Perhaps Harry didn't need rescuing after all. "Be careful." He joined Izzy and Sean, but then looked back to him. "You will be back for the fall semester."

"Count on it." Harry smiled.

Jon turned around and found Sean studying him. "So that's it, then?" Sean asked.

Jon shrugged. "We've rescued Bryce, saved the girl, and

kept Triprimacon from getting the blood. I think I'd like to call it a day."

Izzy folded her arms across her chest and raised an eyebrow. "Saved the girl?" Sean smirked.

Jon reached out and took her hand. "Just take me home. Oh, and there's that small matter of having your lawyer clear my name with the Turkish authorities."

She fell into step beside him as they walked away. "I don't remember saying that."

"And also something about returning a set of manuscripts."

"I definitely don't remember that."

"Izzy!"

Joseph continued praying until they were gone. Then he lifted the medallion from Nicky's neck and placed it over his own. Slipping down into the nearest grave, he held the medallion up, steadying it with his hand. It wavered briefly on its chain, and then turned, pointing steadily toward a part of the wall. He moved it closer until at last it swung away from his body and stuck fast to a piece of magnetite buried in the wall of the tomb.

Gripping the edges with his fingers, Joseph pried the boulder loose. *Hope is coming, Nicky,* he thought. *Help is on the way.* He shoved his hand into the darkness, probing the ancient shadows.

Frederick moved his last piece into position on the board. A risky gambit, but only if Casper didn't take the bait.

His mentor sneered and quickly captured the piece. A sly grin crept onto Frederick's face. There were only two moves left to him. One was desperate. If he took it, he had a fifty-fifty chance of winning or losing utterly. The other would end the game with no winner.

"How long do you think you'll survive?" Casper asked.

Frederick looked up, catching the old man watching him from across the board. His question had nothing to do with the chess game in front of them. After a moment, he smiled. "Without your precious elixir, one could ask you precisely the same thing."

His finger wavered on his piece.

An abrupt ring startled him. He took his hand off the chess piece and reached into his pocket. A second ring followed moments later, but this one from Casper's pocket.

Frowning, both men withdrew their phones, putting them to their ears and listening intently without speaking. After an equal moment, they both hung up and slipped their phones back into their pockets.

Frederick ran a hand over his mouth, and then moved his final piece.

Casper snorted. "Stalemate."

Frederick shrugged. "Up for another match?" he offered.

A wicked gleam crept into Casper's eye. "I'm not dead yet," he said. "Reset the board."

EPİLOGUE

THE HOSPITAL ROOM felt barren and cold. A single bed lay centered in the room, and its frail occupant lay buried beneath crisp, white sheets and an endless array of coiled wires and tubes. None of them were designed to prolong his life further, only mark its passing. The patient was thin and small, having never achieved his full size in life. Unnatural wrinkles in the patient's skin creased his drawn, haggard, face. His eyes, larger than they should have been, stared without focus at the ceiling, just waiting now for the end.

The heart monitor beside his bed continued to pulse, but the intervals between beats were getting longer.

A slender hand reached up, brushing a strand of thin, white hair out of the patient's eyes. The patient's breathing was slow, ragged. Soon, it would be gone.

Dr. Schaumberg pulled his hand back, and tried smiling for his dying son. It was too late to do anything else. A single tear ran down Schaumberg's cheek. Irritated, he swept it away. Despite everything, he still couldn't bring himself to pray.

So much had been lost. Evelyn had abandoned him and left for Europe, relic hunting with Dr. Bryce. Schaumberg's finances were used up. He was unemployed. And not even the faceless men at Triprimacon bothered to acknowledge his existence. In a way, that was worse than killing him. They no longer considered him a threat.

Interpol had questions, and charges of some kind or another were pending against him. The only bright spot was that Dr. Bryce had refused to testify.

But none of that mattered to the boy on the bed in front of him. And it didn't matter to the boy's father, either. Nothing mattered now.

He didn't see the hooded monks enter the room, but slowly he became aware that one of them stood by the foot of the bed, while another stood across from him. He looked up, but shadows veiled the monk's face.

The monks said nothing to him. The one across from him uncapped a vial of holy water, dabbed it onto his finger, and traced a cross over the forehead of the boy.

"*In nomine Patri, et Fili, et Spiritu Sancti. Amen.*" He clasped his hands and prayed silently.

Schaumberg stared, thinking he should say something. Do something. He was at a loss to know what that should be.

The monk made the sign of the cross over Schaumberg as well and said in English, "I forgive you, Peter Schaumberg." Then he bent quickly, putting his hand on the boy's chest, and above the boy's face, Schaumberg heard the monk mutter the words, "*Ṭlē qūm!*"

Collin coughed. The monitor registered this with a spike in its tones. The monk patted the child's cheek and then both swept silently out of the room. Schaumberg watched them go—staring at the younger one's sneakers and the familiar shuffle of the older one—then turned back to his son. The sign of the cross they'd drawn on the boy's forehead was red. He reached over and touched the sign, then stared at the liquid staining his fingertip. *This isn't holy water.*

Beneath him, Collin's skin grew taut and pink, and his breathing smoothed. He opened his eyes and smiled. "Daddy?" he asked.

Peter's heart broke, and he collapsed over his son in grateful sobs.

The End.